Hollywood Fire

(Book Two of The Winters Series)

L.A. Liechty

The Winters Series:

Winter Mountain (Book one)

Hollywood Fire (Book two)

ISBN: 978-0-578-71856-9

To Ron, Karolina & David,
Thank you for being my rock,
my family and my endless sources of support.

Chapter One
Gabriel Saxton

He was pissed. This morning was just not going well, and it seemed with each step, the list of things that were making this day even worse, were adding up. Just a cup of fucking Earl Gray…that's all he was looking for. Was that so much to ask?

Gabriel Saxton, tall, incredibly strong and always sharply dressed, was a man who, normally, had an even mix of good humor and dashingly handsome looks; but today, his muscular physique and well tailored dark blue suit were pretty much all he had going for him. His humor and good heart were being overshadowed by his ever expanding grumpy attitude.

"Rita?" he called out, though he wasn't even sure she was at her desk yet. He opened the lower cupboard doors under the bar section of his office hoping for a hidden back up stash, only to be disappointed by the empty box. *Damn it.*

He heard the sound of a purse being thrown on the chair in the hallway, and knew Rita had finally arrived. Surely she would point him to a back up stash of his much needed tea. Screw it that he was coming across like a drug addict desperate for his fix, he didn't care. On a particularly bad day, something as simple as his Earl Gray tea became the ray of light he so badly needed. He turned to see her walking through his office door; clearly surprised to find him there.

"Mr. Saxton. I didn't expect to see you this morning. Shouldn't you be on your way to the airport?" Rita seemed a bit flustered, unusual for her…and Gabe noticed it right away. She had been the head secretary for Saxton Security for years, and she never missed a beat; but Gabe saw the look in her eyes that told him she may have

1

missed it this time.

"My Earl Gray? Please tell me we have some here somewhere?" Gabe threw the empty box in the trash as Rita let out a breath.

"I'm so sorry Mr. Saxton. It is coming this afternoon. The shipment was late, but you weren't expected in this morning anyway, so I didn't think it would matter." She reached into the bag she was holding. "I have English Breakfast…" She offered him the box even though her body language gave away her full anticipation that he wouldn't want it.

Gabe let out a huff, and placed his cup back down on the counter.

"No. Thank you, Rita. I really wanted Earl Gray. *My* Earl Gray… the one from England." He knew it wasn't her fault that he was in a bad mood, and he was trying not to take it out on her. Rita had her shit together, and she ran this office better than anyone. The lapse didn't fall on her. He sat with a irritable thud in his big leather chair just as his brother Andy walked into the office.

Andy Saxton was a slightly smaller build than Gabe, but had the same strong, masculine features. They were clearly brothers, though Andy was a good twelve years his senior.

"Gabe!" Andy's voice was bright and disgustingly cheerful. Gabe cut him off sharply before he could finish his sentence.

"Don't say it. Don't even think it," Gabe said sharply.

"Come on. You know I have to." He sent a cocky smile Gabe's way and laughed as it seemed to aggravate him even more. Andy didn't seem surprised in the least to find Gabe in a foul mood, but it didn't stop him from wanting to mess with him a little. Pushing his buttons had always been somewhat of a personal indulgence for Andy.

"Andy, I swear to God, I will shove this stapler right up your nose."

"Come on, it's not that bad." Andy crossed over and sat on the edge of the big, black desk, as Gabe let out another cantankerous exhale. "You have to just get it out of your head." Andy looked back at Rita. "Was he this pissed off when you found him? Or did *you* say it?"

Rita had a shocked look on her face. "Heavens no, Mr. Saxton. I did not say it. Not this time. I know the…issues behind this one. I wouldn't dare. He didn't get his tea."

Andy laughed. "You and the damn Earl Gray. I think dad may have done you a disservice taking you back to England after mom died and raising you there. Sometimes I can't believe we are brothers. Embrace the American side of yourself; drink coffee!" He handed him his own cup of coffee which he knew Gabe would not take, but he enjoyed shoving it in his face anyway.

Gabe pushed the drink away, and looked to Rita in exasperation.

"Rita could you please get my other brother in here instead? This one is annoying me," Gabe pleaded.

Rita laughed. "I thought Nick was already with you on the way to the airport," she looked at her watch. "You know you better get a move on. LA traffic is not compatible with making it on time for a flight."

As Gabe was reading deeper into why Rita was antsy to get him out of the office, Nick walked in from behind her.

Nick, the middle brother, had the same dark hair and dark eyes as his brothers did, but was the larger of all three of them. All the Saxton's were tall, big and in great physical shape, and even though Nick was larger, Gabe's training and experience as an elite Marine Raider gave him the advantage over both his brothers. That did not, however, prevent them from messing with him whenever possible. Nick walked in the office with the same cocky smile Andy had plastered on his face and already seemed to be enjoying the conversation he had not been a part of, but understood completely.

"Please tell me the Earl Gray has put him in a slightly better mood? I can't handle a two and a half hour flight with what woke up this morning. He's like the swamp creature today," Nick said.

Andy laughed. "Yeah. It's worse than I thought."

Rita chimed in. "And he didn't get his Earl Gray either. All out till this afternoon," she looked to Nick with sympathy, "Good luck Mr. Saxton."

Nick took a deep breath. "Come on, Gabe. We'll see if we can find you some damn Earl Gray at the airport. The car is waiting downstairs. This pit stop at the office obviously didn't solve it."

Gabe was just about to stand up and resign himself to starting his day without his traditional EG tea, when his eyes caught the quick glance Rita threw to the pile on his desk.

"What's that look for, Rita?" he asked her. Gabe was gifted at reading people, and he noticed small things in mannerisms and behaviors that others could easily overlook. Rita was trying to cover for something; her face gave away an attempt to hide the fluster forming in her eyes. Gabe traced her glance without even taking his eyes off of her, and his hand landed hard on the top folder; *ahh*…he now had what she was hoping he wouldn't see. He lifted it up, "What's this?" he asked. Andy and Nick exchanged a helpless look, then Nick turned to Rita.

"Did you leave the file on his desk?" he asked in a slightly scolding tone.

Rita threw her hands in the air. "I didn't expect him in this morning! You were supposed to pick him up at his home and go straight to the airport."

"Damn it. I did not want to discuss this one today," Nick exclaimed.

Andy tried to take the file before Gabe could open it, but Gabe was faster and not only had it open, but was reading the file already. Andy looked to Nick as they both released a breath of defeat in their scheme to hide the unpleasant news from their brother.

Gabe's frown grew a few sizes. "What?" He looked up at his brothers. "When were you planning on telling me this?"

Nick took a breath. "Uhh…well…tomorrow. Didn't think you needed any more negativity today."

Gabe's eyes fell back on the unfortunate file in front of him.

Andy spoke up in his usual bright tone. "It's no big deal, Gabe. Clients come and go all the time. It's all good. Besides, Matthew Edson is a big time politician now. You hate those."

Gabe continued reading the file. "Yeah, but Matthew? I've known him for years. Hell, we just redid his entire security protocols…why would he unceremoniously dump us now? And without even telling me?"

"Sometimes politicians get too big for their britches," Andy replied. He wanted to ease Gabe out of the disappointment at losing one of their biggest clients. "Besides, losing one politician is still better than adding another 'damn Hollywood star,' right?" Andy did a pretty good imitation of Gabe's sarcastic voice.

Nick laughed. "Is he still bitching about Hollywood? Don't bite the hand that feeds you, Gabe. Our business grew to one of the biggest and best Security firms in the country because of those 'damn Hollywood stars' and their friends. Besides, not all entertainers are that bad. Jen & Diane are awesome." Nick smiled at Andy, enjoying his turn at pushing Gabe's buttons.

Gabe shot him an irritable look. "Are you seriously going to do this to me today?" he asked.

Nick feigned ignorance. "What?"

Andy laughed as Gabe's irritation grew. "You both officially suck," Gabe said.

Nick was still laughing as he spoke. "God, it's so much fun to have at least one thing over the Big Bad Raider." He high fived Andy as they enjoyed the joust.

Andy stood up. "Gabe, come on." When the scowl on his face expanded, Andy snapped the file away from him and continued. "Permission to speak freely?" he asked.

"No," Gabe's answer was quick and short, but didn't work.

Andy ignored him. "This timeline of yours is all in your head. Life doesn't work that way. It's a constant balance between the things you can control, and the things you can't."

Gabe scoured at his brother; he did not like conversations intending to point out his lack of control over anything. Being in control was Gabe's strength…but his greatest weakness when he fell short of it (which did not happen that often.) Andy continued, "Gabe, life is sometimes what happens to you when you're not looking. Maybe if you stop trying to force yourself into what you think is right for you, and just let go and allow life to flow through you instead…you might finally start to have the life you want."

Nick agreed with him. "Patience has never been your strong suit, Gabe."

"Are we done with this pep talk yet?" Gabe didn't want to hear any of it. Especially from his two brothers who had found their wives years ago. Jen & Diane were both great women, and Gabe loved them both like sisters, but it pinched at him every time there was a family get-together that he still was the only one without a significant other by his side. Especially given the family track record of amazing love stories. That was the one area of his life that Gabe felt little to no control over; and just happened to be the one that meant the most to him. It triggered him; and today…even worse. He needed to change the subject.

"OK, so we lost Edson as a client. Have we transferred everything over to his new security team yet?" Gabe asked.

Andy and Nick exchanged glances, seeming to agree that the change of subject might be a better course of action.

"For the most part. I will finish the final handover this afternoon after my meeting, and I will see you guys tonight," Andy said as he put the file under his arm. "I won't get there in time to hear your keynote address, but I will be there in time for the fabulous surf & turf dinner afterwards. Save me a lobster tail," He looked at his watch. "Nick, get him out of here or you guys are going to miss your flight."

Gabe let out a last huff and surrendered to the march towards his unwanted day.

Nick led the way out of his office, and just as Gabe was passing through the door, Andy called to him, "Gabe…"

Gabe turned to face his brother. "Yeah?"

"Happy birthday," Andy's smile grew.

"Fuck you," Gabe scowled.

Andy laughed at his brother. "Love you too, bro."

When Gabe made it to the car, Nick was standing next to the driver, Carl, with a grin on his face. *God, this was going to be a very long day.* He saw Nick nudge Carl, who looked uneasy, but followed his direction anyway.

"Happy Birthday Mr. Saxton!" Carl said in a loud, but unsettled voice.

Gabe was not amused. "You're fired, Carl," he said in a flat tone.

"Now now…you might want to see what he has for you before you jump to that extreme," Nick said with a little ray of glee in his voice.

Carl handed him a steaming to go cup. "Earl Gray, Mr. Saxton. Touch of honey and cream. Just how you like it."

The frown on Gabe's face shrunk as he reached for the cup in daring belief. "Are you serious? You got my Earl Gray?"

"I still had some from the box you brought me last time you came back from England." Carl smiled proudly.

Gabe took the cup and sipped the tea in delight. "Carl, you are the best. Totally not fired."

Nick was laughing as he looked to Carl. "I told you. Thanks for getting it Carl. We would have been in for the worst drive of our lives without it." Nick slapped him on the back in gratitude as Carl opened the door to the black sedan.

The traffic was heavy, but Carl was very good at navigating the backroads to the airport and avoiding the interstate all together. In LA the interstate was more of a parking lot than a road. The worst part was the inconsistency of it. At any time of day or night, getting stuck for hours on an LA interstate was to be expected.

Sitting in the car looking out the window as they drove, Gabe could feel Nick wanting to talk to him but unsure of what to say. "Nick, I'm fine. Just…grumpy. It will pass and I will be back to normal once this stupid day is over."

"It's not going to mess up your speech is it? This is a big security conference and our image is on the line." Nick smiled at Gabe's annoyance with him.

"Have I ever messed up a speech? No, it's fine. I'll be dashing as ever," he said sarcastically as he took the final sip of his tea.

Nick took a breath, deciding to dive into it. "It's just a birthday Gabe. Like every other one. Nothing has changed." Nick looked more closely at him. "I know you. You only get this upset when you feel like you've failed. That's nonsense." Nick's tone was a little more serious than before. Gabe didn't really know what to say. As much as he wanted to agree with him, he didn't. He couldn't help but feel that this birthday *was* different. He had been feeling like he was on the precipice of a grave shift in his life, but now…today, he felt like he missed the most important key to that mysterious change, and assumed he was now completely on the wrong side of it, with no understanding of how to correct his position. He felt…defeated…which is not a feeling Gabe was used to at all.

"Yeah," was all that escaped his mouth as he looked back out the window. He shook his head in bewilderment. "I can't believe I was wrong. I was so sure…I feel lost about this one Nick, I really do. It's not sitting well with me and I can't shake it." Gabe surprised himself that he was so honest about it. He had no secrets from Nick, or Andy, but the vulnerability behind this one was something Gabe wanted hidden, even from his brothers.

"Gabe you have to stop tripping yourself up. It's almost hysterical that you have no idea how lucky you are."

Gabe laughed. "Lucky? Me? Jesus, I feel anything but."

Nick softened his tone a little, but continued. "Listen, I know you got the short end of the stick as far as mom…you were a lot younger than us; it was harder on you. Losing your family like that…it's harder when your little. I get it, Andy & I both do."

"This has nothing to do with mom. I'm not pining after mom…or dad for that matter. I've made my peace with what happened," Gabe said.

"I know that. How could you not? You avenged the crap out of her! What you and your team did…Jesus, it was amazing. I've never seen anything like it. You earned your captain title in one swoop; without question." Nick was always in awe when he spoke about the mission that night…it was, after all, one of the most famous take downs the Raiders ever had, and started the path his team followed for years after that.

Nick laughed. "I mean, Andy and I are both pretty damn good

SEAL's, but we know full well if it came down to it, you could kick our ases. At the same time."

Gabe knew it was true, even though he never held that over his brothers. Gabe had physical skills in combat and tactical offense that could outplay even his brothers, though it would never be put to the test. Not with this family. The love and deep connection between these brothers ran strong, and being there for each other was always a spoken and unspoken truth.

Gabe laughed, "It wouldn't be easy to take you both down, but I think I could do it. Especially today." He smiled at his brother.

"Sure you could. That is, of course, why we have to bust your balls about any little thing we can." Nick's tone was humorous and yet serious at the same time. "Your life is exceptional; in all areas but one...the one, I dare say, that just happens to be the most important one to you." Nick paused, almost as if challenging Gabe to deny it; which he couldn't.

Career wise, Gabe had been exceptional. Remarkable, actually. Andy and Nick had both followed a family line of becoming Navy SEAL's, and they were both extremely good at it. But Gabe; he was phenomenal. Gabe had chosen the Marines, and very quickly found himself one of the best MARSOC Raiders the Special Operations Command had ever seen. His posts on the FAST Teams gave him incredible experience that even Andy and Nick never saw as SEAL's. He was the youngest Marine ever to be accepted in the elite MARSOC Raiders; not only the youngest, was one of the best ones ever; well before he retired from the Marines last year.

He wasn't lacking for anything from a career standpoint; it was his personal life that always seemed out of his reach; and his brothers never missed an opportunity to point it out. Not just because his brothers enjoyed poking some fun at Gabe's one weakness, but also because they knew it was important to him, and they felt a constant need to point out that Gabe's attempts at controlling that side of his life, were perhaps the very reason he hadn't found it yet.

Nick spoke again when Gabe had no response to what he had said. "Gabe, you can't control when you are going to meet the love of your life. We've been watching you struggle with this for years. It's the one thing I've never seen you beat; and you got yourself all caught up in this timeline you put in your head…what makes you believe that is even real?" he asked him.

Gabe was quiet for a moment, then shrugged his shoulders, "Obviously, today makes it clear that I was wrong." He got quiet again, hoping Nick couldn't pick up on the tremendous sadness that spilled out from him at saying those words. "It's just a…feeling I have never been able to shake. Believe me, I've tried."

"Is that why you've slept with so many beautiful women? Trying to escape this feeling that's been haunting you since you were a boy?" Nick laughed. "Nice problem to have!"

"It worked for a while. Kind of." Gabe faked a smile, hiding the depth of emotion that was swirling inside him. He didn't want to talk about the empty feeling he had been fighting ever since he could remember. Explaining it wasn't easy, even to himself. Gabe had a longing inside him. He had it well before his mothers death, so he knew it wasn't connected to that. It was something else…something deeper…he didn't really understand it, but the power of it always had his attention. Gabe always felt…behind schedule with his personal life.

It was ironic; of all the brothers, it had been Gabe that had idealized over the perfect wife and family since he was a little boy. He dreamed of it. Gabe was guided more by his emotions than his brothers were, and his ideals surrounding love and relationships were extreme. Nick was right that Gabe had been with many women, but never that deeply. Not yet. He was waiting…he knew she was there…he thought she would be there by now…*damn, today sucked.*

Somehow, as a child, he got it in his head that he would find her when he was forty. Why forty? He didn't really know, but it had been in his mind for as long as he could remember. He made the mistake one drunken night years ago of telling Andy (who promptly told Nick,) and they both had been poking fun at him ever since then about his 'fairy-tale timeline,' as they put it.

Maybe they were right…maybe he had made it up in his head as a boy, and somewhere along the line started to believe it.

His rational mind could explain it away…it could have come from all the stories he heard growing up about this remarkable family he was born into. The themes of love stories and heroics seemed to touch every generation in their line, starting with his grandfather. His mom's father was kind of the shining icon in the family, and he had met the woman of his dreams when he was forty. His mother's twin brother, Joseph, followed in the same steps as his grandfather, and found himself in love with the woman of his dreams when was forty. Even his mother, she met his dad when his father too, was forty. Perhaps, as a child, he got that in his head and somewhere along the line, he either believed it to be a passed on legacy, or, he had been using it as an excuse of why he hadn't found it yet. Either way, he felt today like he was the one who broke the tradition, and he felt like he was at fault for missing it.

Gabe wanted to shake it off, so he focused back out the window. They were pulling up to the airport, and Gabe saw that Carl followed his usual trick of letting them off at arrivals instead of departures. It was actually much faster this way. Gabe didn't wait for Carl to open the door; that was never his style. He stepped out of the car wincing as the sun shot into his eyes. He straightened up, tugged on his blazer and was closing the bottom button as his eyes wondered a little ways down to the far end near the taxi stand…and he saw her.

It was such a strange sensation. It was as if everything got quiet and still. He was sure his eyes must have been knocked out of whack by the sun, and he found himself trying to clear them to look again and double check his vision; but the sight in front of him…it sent a rush through him and he was thrown off by it.

She was beyond gorgeous, and Gabe had seen (and been with) many gorgeous women before, but this woman…it must be a trick of the light. She almost looked like she had a glow about her. Her long dark hair was blowing off her shoulders, and he found himself wishing she would take her black and gold sunglasses off so he could get a better look at her face, but he knew without knowing…this woman was incredible.

Gabe was so distracted by her that he forgot to cross to the back of the sedan to get his bag. He forgot about his flight; about Nick and Carl…he even forgot what the Hell he was doing there. Everything disappeared from his mind like an unexplainable magic trick. He was lost in the sight of her.

Nick crossed over, fidgeting with a zipper on his suitcase, as Carl placed Gabe's bag down next to him.

"You ok Mr. Saxton?" Carl asked as he followed the direction of Gabe's stare.

Gabe didn't answer. He hardly even heard him. It wasn't until Nick slapped him on the back and draped his arm around Gabe's shoulder that he snapped back to the moment…somewhat.

"Wow," Nick said as his eyes found the woman the two were staring at. "That is one Hell of a beautiful woman."

"You're not kidding," Gabe heard himself say.

He noticed details that others didn't…it was a talent he always had.

His eyes took in everything about her all at once. From the sparkling ankle bracelet gracefully wrapped on her left leg just above her open toed black heels, exposing her pink toe nail polish, to the soft white & pink leopard pattern purse she had slung over her bag. It was interesting to him…on the one hand, she had a very confident, strong energy; but he couldn't help but get a sense that there was a… hesitation about her….a concern behind her complete-package exterior.

Carl handed Nick and Gabe their tickets. "Gate 33. You better get a move on." When Gabe still couldn't break his eyes away, Nick tossed Gabe's bag on his feet. "Come on Romeo. We got to go."

Gabe found the strength to pull his gaze away from the woman and look at his brother. He felt dazed. "What the fuck just happened?" he asked bewildered.

Nick laughed. "I'd say the "boom," but I'm not sure that can happen without eye contact. So my guess is you have succumbed to your lunacy and have lost your mind." Nick took the tickets from Carl. "Thanks Carl. See you on Sunday when we come back."

Gabe picked up his bag, and couldn't help but look back to where the woman had been standing. He felt a bolt of disappointment…she wasn't there anymore. He followed the confused gaze of the taxi driver who was looking towards the airport, and caught a flash of the woman's white dress just as it cleared the doors heading back into the busy terminal. She was gone.

Chapter Two
Kayla Knight

Fuck this. She didn't want to be here; back in this city. She took a deep breath trying to quiet the rise of tension that was knotting up in her stomach. As the taxi pulled up to the curb where she was waiting, she debated her next move. It occurred to her that she had one…a move she could make.

The wind swept in and elegantly pulled her long dark hair up off her shoulders; gently dancing it in the air behind her, as the taxi driver opened his door and got out.

Kayla Knight, 28, was a 5'6 beauty with a quick wit and absolutely no desire to be back in Los Angeles. Though she looked every bit the Beverly Hills elite with her gorgeous face, high heels and perfectly polished demeanor, she felt herself to be anything but. Her black and gold sunglasses were doing a good job of keeping the rays of sunshine out of her eyes, but there was little she could do to keep the piercing heat off her arms. The only positive thought she could muster about being here was that she tanned pretty easily. She could at least get a nice golden sun kissed look to her before she was free to leave.

Leave…*hmm*…she looked at her watch; it was only Wednesday… she didn't technically have to be here till Friday night. If there was one thing Kayla Knight knew how to do better than anyone, it was leave.

The driver crossed over to her and reached for her bag to put it in the cab, but Kayla stopped him. He looked at her confused, but her decision had just been made. She smiled at the driver apologetically.

"Sorry. Changed my mind," she said as nicely as she could.

Kayla grabbed her suitcase, turned around, and walked right back into the airport. *Fuck this*.

Having just flown in from Switzerland, it would be logical to conclude that hopping back on another flight would be the last thing she would want. Turns out, there was one thing she wanted even less than that; being in Los Angeles. It was one of her least favorite places on Earth. There was only one other place she hated even more than LA…she brushed the thought of it off with the traditional promise to herself that she would never go back there again, so it didn't matter. It was a promise she made to herself a long time ago and intended to keep it.

As she walked through the terminal, she glanced to her right and saw the shelves of women's magazines with celebrities plastered on the covers behind captions disclosing intimate secrets of their pasts…some true, some not…but it didn't much matter. The herds of people that glanced at the covers as they walked by would believe what ever it said. Proof of innocence was a lot harder to establish than the thrill of scandal; she had learned that lesson far earlier than anyone should have to.

Scattered among the glamour magazines were some business and political ones as well, one of which caught her eye. She paused briefly as she looked at the man's face staring back at her. It took her a second, but she realized with an unwanted recollection that she knew that man. The memory from long ago flooded her. It's funny…so many years ago and yet it has been all around her everyday since then. Her eyes were still on the cover; Matthew Edson…Governor. *He is the Governor of California now?* Great…one more reason to get the Hell out of here. She picked up her pace and headed to the departure screens to see what her exit options were.

Any flight leaving within the hour…didn't have to be far, just…out of here. Her eyes found a flight leaving for Vail in forty-five minutes. Perfect. Vail was fancy, with high end resorts that were sure to have a room she could get at last minute. She could even squeeze in a spa treatment if she got lucky.

Kayla popped up to the counter to grab a ticket. After a brief conversation with the ticket agent, and a swipe of her credit card, she had it. There was one seat left; in the back. *Fine.* Last row of economy was still better than anywhere in LA. She dropped her bag for check in, and headed to the plane.

By the time she got through security and to the gate, they were well into boarding, and had just called the final boarding group. As she entered the aircraft, she could see to her left that business class was already filled with passengers accepting mimosas and coffee. Damn, she would give anything for a good cup of coffee; with the beans she loved. It was a daily habit, usually first thing, and it annoyed her to no end when she didn't get it. She made it worse for herself ever since she found the Kimbo beans from Italy. Now, no other coffee would do. She reminded herself how horrible airplane coffee was anyway, and convinced herself she didn't care. She turned to her right and made her way to the back of the plane. At least she got a window seat.

She plopped down, letting out a small breath of relief that she was on the plane and soon to be anywhere but here. She put on her earphones and played that song that always made her feel better for some reason. It was called "Somewhere You." She didn't even know who was singing it, but from the first moment she had heard it years ago, she fell in love with it. It made her feel…safe; a rare feeling for her so she cherished anything that could make her feel that way.

Lawrence had given it to her years ago. She had walked in on him listening to it and she asked him for a copy, which he gave to her. That night had been the scariest night of her life. Even at that young age, she was no stranger to fear, but that night had tested her past what any child should have to face. She shook it off, and focused back on

Lawrence and the song he gave her. Those were the first two good things in this world that she remembered, and both of them were still very much a part of her life.

Lawrence ran the biggest entertainment company in the world. He and his wife had been like family to her ever since she met them. She loved them both and would do anything for them; which is how she ended up back in LA. Lawrence asked her for a favor, and she accepted. She owed him. She would never have come back for anyone else, but Lawrence? Yeah, she would face Hell for him, but he didn't need her until Friday; *so hello Vail.*

She closed her eyes and ignored the world outside as she focused on the man singing to her through her AirPods. As it always did, it washed a sense of calm through her, quieting her mind and she drifted off to sleep.

Her eyes opened to the thud of the tires hitting the runway, and the announcement from the Flight Attendant welcoming them to Vail. She felt no sense of rush though…she was in the last row; it would be a while before she could get up and walk off the plane. She pulled out her phone and did a quick web search on resorts in Vail. The first one she found looked perfect. It was a Grand Hyatt. She loved those; they were consistent, had room service and good security. She wrote down the address and simply waited for her turn to get off the plane.

The thirty-five minute cab ride from the airport was enjoyable. The mountains and countryside were beautiful. She had never been here before, but it kind of reminded her of Switzerland. If she had to be stateside again, this place seemed to be more to her liking than anything else she could remember as a child.

Switzerland had become her home since she was a little girl, except for the year and a half she came back as a 12 year old. That was both an amazing time in her life and incredibly stressful. She grew tired of the constant worry that filled her while she was back in the states and jumped at the chance to return to Switzerland when the opportunity presented itself. Lawrence knew. She was pretty sure it was the strings he pulled that got her into the Interlochen Arts Academy at such a young age. She was the youngest one admitted to the four year high school program, and even had managed to enroll her in both the acting and singing programs. She supposed it wasn't that hard to pull off considering who he was and the achievements she had already made in that field by that time. How could they say no? They didn't, and she enjoyed every minute of her school years there singing, acting and hiding out in the mountains of Switzerland. But she always knew, at some point, facing the world again would be inevitable, though she did everything to convince herself she might be able to escape that fate. She had to laugh at her ignorance as she found herself just a few days away from having to go back to Los Angeles.

She brushed it off and concentrated on the beautiful resort hotel that was emerging in front of her. It was much more crowded than she thought it would be for this time of year. She didn't think March was high time in Vail, but the cab driver was saying something about a lot of conferences that happen out here at this time. It didn't dawn on her that she might have trouble getting a room at last minute.

The lobby was crowded as Kayla made her way up to the check in counter. The young man behind the desk smiled warmly at her.

"Hello, may I help you?" he asked her.

"Yes. I need a room for a few nights, if you have one." Kayla's tone was pleasant and warm, hiding any uncertainty she was feeling about being able to get a room at last minute.

The young man, whose name tag said Josh, was clicking several keys on the keyboard, as his smile started to fade a little.

After a few minutes he lifted his head. "Well, we are all booked out, but there may be one ray of light. I have a couple that is scheduled for a late check out this afternoon. The room might not be ready until after 6:00pm, but you are welcome to enjoy the spa, the lounges and the dining hall if you wish to wait."

Kayla was fine with that. "That's great. Thank you."

"Enjoy the facilities. The dining room is black tie tonight, but if you would prefer something more casual, we have a cafeteria that will also be open tonight on the far wing. I will have someone from the staff come find you when the room is ready."

"Thank you, Josh," Kayla said with a smile.

"My pleasure," Josh answered as he scribbled some notes to himself.

She only had to kill a few hours with no room, that shouldn't be hard. First step; coffee in the lounge. Then a nice long sit on the outside balcony looking at the beautiful mountains in the distance. She could read, she could write and enjoy being far from Los Angeles.

The black tie dinner was a question mark. She loved the idea of a really good meal and she saw the menu touting their surf & turf option (which she loved.) She did have that incredible black dress in her suitcase that she needed for Friday night. She could always pop into the bathroom and put that on. Maybe. If she had the strength to deal with the crowd she might just treat herself to the top notch dinner. If not, a cafeteria sandwich and soup would be fine with her too. Kayla could always enjoy the low end of things just as much as the fancy, ritzy titzy things.

By the time dinner rolled around, Kayla was having a hard time ignoring the allure of the steak and lobster dinner. As much as she didn't like the idea of being in a crowded, fancy restaurant, she had to admit, she was starving. *Fine*.

She slipped into the lobby bathroom and changed into her black dress. She touched up her make up and ran a brush through her hair, then stepped back to examine her reflection in the full length mirror. She was always incredibly hard on herself, but even she had to admit it; this dress was pretty great. It was low cut and fitted in all the right places, with a high slit on the left hand side, exposing her long leg and sparkling ankle bracelet. No need to change her shoes; the opened-toed black heels she had been wearing worked fine with this dress too. As she was silently criticizing herself on the less than perfect makeup job, a group of women walked into the bathroom. They all stopped and stared at her. Kayla hated this part; women were either incredibly nice or horribly jealous. She wasn't sure which category these women fell into. Sending a small prayer up for the former, she smiled at them.

One of the women spoke in a timid voice. "My God. You look amazing," she said to Kayla.

"You look like a movie star," the younger of the women said.

Kayla laughed kindly. "Oh, that's so sweet," she said, happy that they didn't recognize her.

Kayla grabbed her bags and headed out of the bathroom with a smile. "Have a good night," she said as the door closed behind her.

Ignoring the stares and the obvious attention was an ongoing battle for her. Sometimes it was easier, sometimes it really took a toll and left her wanting to run for isolation. The pull of the surf & turf was the only thing that kept her feet walking towards the fancy dining hall. It was really crowded, and she could feel the eyes of all the men around her. For some reason, it felt especially heavy tonight. Maybe this dress was not a good idea, but it was the only one she had with her. The closer she got to the dining hall, the more she regretted her decision.

She hesitated as the maitre d' approached her. His smile was bright, but not completely innocent.

"Are you meeting someone for dinner? Surely a woman as

beautiful as you is not dining alone…" he asked her.

A man's voice from behind her spoke. "She can dine with me, anytime," the man said laughing.

Kayla turned to see a much older man than she, standing amongst his colleagues; all of them grinning and challenging each other for her attention. She smiled politely at them, then turned back to the maitre d'.

"You know, I think I will wait for him outside. Thank you." With that, she did what she does best when uncomfortable; leave.

She turned down the hall and headed towards the far wing. *Soup and sandwich it is than.*

When she got to the entrance to the cafeteria, she was delighted to see it was completely empty, except for a lone employee sitting at the cash register reading her book. *Perfect.* It didn't matter to her that she was extraordinarily overdressed for a cafeteria…she didn't even care that her five-star surf and turf would now be a one star plate of whatever they had. She felt a sense of relief to have no eyes on her. It amazed her; even to this day, the fear of being recognized haunted her. Sometimes hiding in plain sight worked…other times it walked a dangerous line of revealing herself, and she had spent a lifetime practicing the art of not allowing that to happen.

After selecting a few things from the dinner options on the buffet line, and exchanging a bit of small talk with the cashier, Kayla took a seat at a nice, big table in the middle of the room. She pushed her bag just behind the chair next to her and sat down, still wishing she could have found something sweet and chocolate for dessert. They didn't have any, but she promised herself that once she got to her room, she could order up anything chocolate they had on the menu.

She thought the emptiness of the large room would make her feel better…it usually did, but she was disappointed to realize that the discomfort in her stomach about everything was still swirling. She missed the mountains of Switzerland. But as she looked out the window to the mountain range in front of her that was just as lovely, she realized it wasn't Switzerland she missed; it was the distance. The safety barrier of a huge ocean separating her from the country she was born in, and ran from. Being back in the States was unsettling. Knowing LA was just a few days away…she suddenly wished she had thought to get a bottle of wine. She wondered how she would really do with Friday night. She wasn't worried about putting up a facade of complete confidence and steller performance; she was a pro at hiding any feelings she didn't want shown. But she wondered how she would really be. She could feel the a anxiety kicking up in her about the things she desperately wanted to control, but was well aware she couldn't. All she could do, is what she had always done; pray for invisibility while standing in the spotlight. Shine so bright that they don't even realize they can't see anything past that. It worked before… for a while.

Kayla was so absorbed in her own thoughts that she didn't even notice the man who was standing beside her table, with a tray in his hand.

Chapter Three

Boom

He couldn't explain what it was that made him look up, but Gabe had never been more thankful for his spider senses than he was at that moment. The conversation with the millionaire standing across from him took an instant backseat, and his focus was now on the glimpse he caught of the woman at the far end of the room who had just turned to walk away from the dining hall. The sparkle of her ankle bracelet flashed out right before she disappeared behind the wall, and that same…strange feeling shot through him even from the split second sight of her. It was just like the one in front of the airport. Could it have been the same woman? How could that be possible? There was an increase in his pulse and an urgency running through him that he didn't understand, but one thing was clear to him; he had to find out who that woman was.

Nick and Andy crossed over to Gabe and the man he was talking with, which gave him the perfect opportunity to dump the potential client off on his brothers and follow the mystery woman that was pulling at him.

Nick handed Gabe a dessert plate with a big slice of chocolate cake. "Here is your birthday cake. Thought you should have the first piece," he said with a goading smile.

Gabe took the plate happily, which confused Nick completely. "Thank you," Gabe said as he quickly gestured to the man across from him. "Mr. Phillips, Andy is the expert on our ground based radar and access control services. This is the perfect opportunity for you to get your questions answered from him." Gabe saw that Nick was trying to ascertain the change in Gabe's demeanor, but he didn't have time to explain it to him. He had to get to that woman…who ever she was…he needed to find out. He looked to his brothers, who both now seemed thrown off by the smile Gabe could not hide. "Would you excuse me for a moment?" With that, Gabe walked towards the hall, cake in hand, to follow the lure of the mystery woman. He heard Andy whisper to Nick. "What's going on with him? Was he smiling?"

When Gabe turned down the hall, he could see a very quick glimpse of the woman in black disappearing into the cafeteria at the end of the wing. Why was it that every time this woman entered his field of vision, she was suddenly gone just as fast?

By the time he got to the cafeteria, she was sitting at a large table in the middle of the room. He was sure, even if the room had been filled with people, he would have seen her right away. He was drawn to her in a way that surprised him. He looked at the bag she had by her chair…the same white and pink leopard purse and those black and gold sunglasses resting just in the outside pocket of her bag. It was her. He was astounded. She is really here. He didn't want to waste time trying to figure out how that could be possible…about the miraculously slim chance he was just given that he would ever see her again. She was here, and he was not going to let her slip away again before he had a chance to meet her.

Gabe casually got a tray and placed his plate of chocolate cake on it, as well as a few random selections from the buffet. He didn't really care what he grabbed; it wasn't the food he was interested in. After clearing the cashier, he looked out into the completely empty seating area. He was determined to go sit by her, though he was at a loss of how to do it smoothly. He was surprised to find himself nervous. That was unusual for him. His confidence when approaching women was never an issue; but this woman…he didn't understand why, but he could feel she was…different.

She was absorbed in her own thoughts, and he was pretty sure she didn't even know he had come into the room. He surmised from the way she was poking around at the food on her plate and not eating it, that she was dealing with something that was heavy on her. He could tell from her body language and her energy that her contemplation was centered around something she didn't like. He wondered what could possibly be bothering a woman that beautiful. Her ankle bracelet caught the light as she crossed her leg, and a bright sparkle seemed to flow across the room, right to him. This woman always seemed to be surrounded by light, even though the sun was just setting outside, and the only light that seemed to be shining brightly in the room was coming, somehow, from her. It was amazing to him…how she pulled him in even though he hadn't really seen her face yet; hadn't seen her eyes. It was the eyes that always told Gabe what he needed to know about a woman; anyone for that matter. Gabe was incredibly intuitive and he was able to see more about a person through their eyes than most could. Most of the time, he found himself disappointed; at least as far as women were concerned. That's probably where his dislike for Hollywood stars came from. The fake, do-anything-for-attention women…it took a whole .3 seconds for him to see that, and it was always discouraging. He didn't get the sense that this woman was like that, but he wouldn't know until he looked in her eyes. Time to find out. He walked over to her table. Even just standing next to her he could feel an energy begin to course through him. He took a breath before he spoke.

"Excuse me," Gabe said in a smooth tone.

When she looked up, and his eyes locked on hers, he felt a shudder run through his very soul. Everything stopped. Boom. He didn't even think he was breathing. He felt as if an entire lifetime of emotion flashed through his heart in one second. He was instantly filled with that energy he could not explain, and did not understand. It was both confusing and yet familiar all at the same time. What a strange sensation…he was so blown away by his reaction to her that it took him a long moment to realize he wasn't reading her like he normally does. He felt completely stripped of all his advanced skills and tactics. It also occurred to him that he had forgotten to keep speaking. Never in his life had something like this happened to him. He found himself desperately trying to pull himself back into a coherent human being.

"Hi." God, it seemed like such a stupid thing to say, but it was the only word he could form out of the chaos that had erupted inside him when their eyes met.

She smiled at him. Her smile was…beautiful. Not just because she was beautiful…that smile…it felt like home.

"Hi," she said. Her voice was soft and strong at the same time. Feminine and soothing. Her voice was like music and it caused a rush of shivers on his skin. There was such a depth of emotion in her eyes, he could almost feel her through them.

"May I join you?" he asked her.

He saw the slight, but purposeful change in her gaze. It was subtle, but he saw it. Like she engaged a protective forcefield behind her eyes, attempting to shield herself from him. Curious. He was intrigued at the way she morphed into what was clearly a practiced maneuver. It wasn't fake, but was unquestionably a tactic; one that seemed to be second nature to her. Her smile turned into a charming laugh as she looked around at the completely empty cafeteria.

"Having trouble finding an open seat are you?" she asked.

Her laugh was enchanting. He couldn't help but laugh as well.

"I'm going for sympathy points. If I sit down at a table in here all by myself, I would just be pathetic," his charm floating effortlessly on his words.

Her laugh transformed into a challenging smirk. "I'm sitting here at a table all by myself. Are you suggesting that I'm pathetic?"

He chuckled. "Not at all. A beautiful woman can always get away with it, but a man…? Not so much. That's just sad. Especially today," he added.

"Why is that?" she asked him.

"It's my birthday," he admitted.

"Ahh, yes, that would be pathetic then wouldn't it?" She laughed again and took a moment to subtly scan his eyes. He knew she was making a deliberate evaluation of him…trying to decide how she felt about allowing him to sit down with her. It was a subtle assessment, but he picked up on it. It's what he does. He actually liked that she was keen enough with her awareness that she would do so. She took another few moments, and then she spoke. "Well if we are both going to be pathetic, then we might as well do it together," she gestured to the seat across from her.

Gabe felt his smile grow and knew he could do little to pull it back, but he didn't much care. He felt such a sense of joy as he sat down at her table.

She took a breath and leaned forward slightly. "Before this conversation goes any further, I have an extremely important question for you," she said.

Gabe tilted his head in curiosity. "Oh yeah? What's that?" he asked her.

"Where did you get that piece of chocolate cake? I couldn't find anything chocolate anywhere."

Gabe laughed. "My brothers' actually. They know I'm…unhappy about my birthday today, so they are taking every opportunity they can find to rub my face in it. They thought it would be hysterical to bring a huge chocolate birthday cake into the big dining room so everyone there would know." He couldn't believe how much it warmed his heart to see her smile. Her laugh was unlike any he had ever heard. There was such a warmth about this woman…and a realness he had never quite experienced before.

"Well, anyone who brings chocolate is good people in my book," she said.

He took note of that, as he was already doing with everything about this woman. He lifted the plate off his tray and handed it to her. "Here, would you like to have it?"

She looked him in the eye. "Don't tease about that. I don't know what kind of dainty, fancy women you might be used to, but I have no qualms about eating that entire piece of cake right in front of you."

Gabe didn't think his smile could brighten even more than it already had since he met her, but it did. The release of his laughter surprised him.

"Thank God," he said. "I can't stand the Hollywood types that want to give off a fake persona of perfection and pretend they don't want something as fabulous as a dessert like this." He loved that she was laughing with him. "Here," he said as he politely handed her the plate. He found himself stunned at the feeling that was flowing through him…what a contrast from the horrible day he had been having so far. In this moment, he couldn't even remember feeling anything negative before.

She took the cake with a smile that seemed to shoot through him. "Thank you. If you want some of it, you better get your fork and start, because I'm not going to be shy about enjoying this."

Gabe found himself picking up his fork and joining her in eating his birthday cake. He hadn't wanted any of it when his brothers handed it to him; but sharing it with this woman…that was irresistible, and to his surprise, chocolate cake had never tasted so good as it did in this moment.

"So, why are you upset about your birthday? I didn't think men cared that much about their age," she said as she dipped her fork into the cake.

"It's not the age. I just…it's hard to explain." He wasn't sure what to say.

"Try me." She said it in such an inviting tone that Gabe was moved to attempt to put it into words.

"Well, I had this idea of…things I wanted in my life when I was forty. Today, I'm forty one…and there are things I didn't find." He wasn't sure he was making sense, but he didn't think he could be any clearer than that. To his surprise, there was a look in her eyes that told him she might just understand what he was saying.

"I get it. Little things, or big things?" she asked.

"Both," he said after a slight pause.

"Well, what time were you born?" Her question was a little confusing to him. He didn't know why she was asking, but he answered her anyway.

"11:59pm. Pacific time. Why?"

She looked at her watch and smiled, "Well, technically, you are still forty. You have a few more hours. Don't know if that helps, but you still have time before your forty one."

Gabe leaned back in his chair somewhat dazed at the feeling that swept through him from her words. He felt…a release, like he had been holding his breath for years and finally was able to let it go. He didn't understand it, but the feeling was so comforting he didn't much care that it was coming from something he did not comprehend.

"Thank you. You are right," he said.

She smiled. "I'm hearing a slight British accent…are you English?" She took another bite of the chocolate cake.

"I'm both English and American. My mother was American and my father was from England," Gabe took another bite as well.

"Did you grow up in America?" she asked.

"Not completely. My mother died when I was a boy, and my dad decided to bring me back to England and raise me there." Gabe wasn't sure why he let that out. It was not common for him at all to be so open about his personal life, but for whatever reason, his mind was not filtering his responses to her questions.

"I'm sorry about your mom," she said. There was a very real sense of empathy in her voice and in her eyes. Gabe was struck by how the kindness in her tone seemed to wash over him. "Your dad sounds amazing. Raising you and your brothers after losing her? That's not easy. A lot of men wouldn't be able to do that." She lowered her eyes back down and played a little with her fork on a spot of chocolate frosting. He had a sense it was a purposeful change of focus but he wasn't sure why.

"It was really just me at that point. My brothers are older than me, and they had both enlisted in the Navy by that time. So they stayed here, to become Navy SEALs, and I went with my father."

"So what brought you back? Or do you still live in England?" she asked as she took another bite of the cake.

"No, I've been back for a long time now. I ended up joining the Marines. I had to one up my brothers'," he smirked.

She laughed, "Yeah? What out does a Navy SEAL?" she asked.

"A Marine Raider," he said with a humorous, slightly cocky smile.

Gabe saw a flicker in her eye, but it was so quick he wasn't sure what the meaning was.

"What is a Marine Raider?" she asked with an intrigued look.

"Marine Raiders are a special operations force of the Marine Corps. We are trained in tailored military skills and special operations

31

to conduct…sensitive, high level combat missions all over the world." There was clearly a lot more to it, but it was not common for a Raider to divulge more than necessary.

She seemed impressed with just a touch of skepticism.

"What is the motto of the Marine Raiders?" she asked.

Gabe chuckled…she was testing him, and in a way, he kind of liked that she didn't just take his word for it.

"Always faithful, always forward," he answered.

It intrigued him…there was a confirmation in her eyes when she heard his answer. He couldn't help but wonder how she would know that, but she spoke again before he could pry into his suspicion.

"Sounds like it would be a mistake for anyone to go up against you," she said.

Gabe smiled, "Well, Raiders can punch well above their weight class."

She laughed again. "No wonder your brothers enjoyed rubbing your face in your birthday. Seems like you brought that on yourself." She took another bite of the cake. "Are you still in the Marines?"

Gabe shook his head and reached for his next bite of cake. "No. I retired last year. I decided I needed to be in one place. Being a Raider had me flying all over the world and I thought…well, I didn't want to miss the next stage of my life because I was always on the move."

She looked at him curiously. "What's the next stage of your life?" she asked him.

He smiled. "I'm not sure yet. Think that's why today bothered me so much."

She took a breath and spoke in a very sympathetic tone. "Yeah. Not knowing what your next move should be can be difficult." She put down her fork and leaned forward. "So what brought you here to Vail?" she asked him as she lifted her glass to take a sip.

Gabe sat back. "My brothers started a security firm many years ago, and when I retired last year, they asked me to join them. So I did, and we came here to give the keynote address at the security conference this afternoon."

She put down her drink. "And how did it go?" she asked.

"Fine," Gabe answered.

She tilted her head. "You don't seem very thrilled about it…"

Gabe let out a breath, deciding to continue allowing this strange side of himself to reveal things he normally wouldn't.

"I'm not, really." He shifted in his chair. "I guess I got too used to the challenges of being a Raider…and this world of private security for businessmen and Hollywood elites is proving to be…disappointing."

She chuckled as she reached for her fork again. "That sounds horrible. Especially the Hollywood part. Los Angeles in general. Well, all of California actually." She laughed again as she pulled her eyes back to the cake.

Gabe grinned at her. "Not a fan of California, huh?" he asked.

"No." She didn't say it with emphasis, but he sensed she wanted to change the subject away from that. "So, where do you live?" she asked.

Gabe's grin was colored with a humorous irony as he answered her. "Los Angeles," he admitted.

She laughed and a sarcastic look of pity swept across her face. "My condolences," she said.

"Oh, it gets worse," he added, "My home is in Beverly Hills." They both laughed at that.

She let her fork drop to the plate with a slight thud. "That is dreadful. How do you survive it?"

He laughed as he pressed his fork into the cake for another bite. "That's a good question. I'll let you know when I figure it out."

Gabe had become very aware that this woman was extremely good at keeping the conversation on him, and he was pretty sure that was an intentional navigation on her part. She was incredibly good at it. What he found fascinating was the equal mix of tactic and sincerity. This woman was not fake, and the questions she asked seemed to be rooted in a very honest curiosity. But her honesty was being used like a cloaking device and it was his sense she had rehearsed exactly how to do that for most of her life. The ease with which she manipulated it was skillful. He wondered what her story was, but before he could get to asking his own questions of her, they were interrupted by someone from the kitchen staff.

The young man who approached them held out a cup of coffee to the woman across from him. Gabe had to smile at the shaking hands of the twenty something man who was desperately trying to come across strong, but clearly was unsure how to handle his attraction to the beautiful woman.

"Here is your coffee. I'm sorry it took so long, but we wanted to make a fresh one for you." He smiled at her.

"Thank you. Were you able to find out what kind of beans they are?" she asked him sweetly.

A look of embarrassment came over his face. "I'm so sorry, I forgot to ask."

Her eyes were soft on him in an attempt to make sure he knew she was not upset. "No problem. Just curious. Thank you again."

The young man walked away as she added cream to her cup.

Gabe couldn't help but smile...it reminded him of his pickiness about his tea. "What kind of beans were you hoping for?" he asked her.

"Well, it would be wishful thinking for them to have my favorite beans, but I was at least hoping for anything Italian." She took a sip and very quickly put her cup back down in disappointment. "These are not Italian. Yuck. That's hardly even coffee."

Gabe laughed again and readjusted in his seat and casually leaned forward on the table.

"So what brought you to Vail?" he asked her before she could direct the conversation again.

He saw her mind filtering her answer as she looked out the window. "Well, I like mountains…I love Grand Hyatts, and I've never been here before. Sounded good." She took another bite of the cake and seemed much happier with that than the coffee she was no longer touching.

"That's vague," Gabe said intrigued with the lack of information she provided him with her answer. "Do you normally just hop on a plane and fly off to a new place at last minute?"

She tilted her head at him. "What makes you think I did this at last minute?"

Gabe was fascinated by her…she was unlike any woman he had ever known, and whatever it was that pulled him to her was tugging at him even more.

"I saw you outside of arrivals at LAX this morning." He could see an unease behind her eyes, but he continued. "Our driver always drops us off at arrivals, and when we got out, I saw you. Then I saw you turn around and go right back in the airport…obviously to catch a flight to here. I'm curious…" he leaned back in his seat, captivated at the wheels he now saw turning behind her gaze about how she should respond to him. "What makes a beautiful woman fly into Los Angeles, and then turn around and leave as soon as she gets there?"

She swallowed her bite of cake, and hid behind her smile. "How do you know it was me you saw? LA is filled with a million women with long dark hair. Could have been anyone." She was masterfully balancing sarcastic humor with the distraction of suggestion, and Gabe was unquestionably intrigued now at what the real story was behind this woman.

"It does not take a Marine Raider whose entire career has been focused on intelligence and observation skills to remember a woman like you," Gabe said.

She looked down at her plate and started to poke around at her food again. Gabe hit a nerve with that, he knew it, but he was unsure why. He could see her shrinking back into herself a little bit while at the same time lifting her head and projecting an air of absolute confidence. *Fascinating.*

"Well, if you saw me at the airport, why didn't you come up and say hi?" she challenged him.

It was an interesting way to redirect the conversation, but Gabe went with it anyway. "I should have. I guess I got nervous."

She laughed. "I highly doubt that. You're practically James Bond with your accent, fabulous suit and Marine Raider skills. I think it would take a lot more than a woman in heels to make you nervous."

Gabe laughed. "Not necessarily," he took a breath. "The truth is, you always seem to disappear so quickly, you hardly give a guy a chance."

She looked up at him with a smirk. "Well, a woman has to have her own skills too, right?" she laughed.

Before Gabe had the opportunity to respond, he caught a glimpse of his brothers by the entrance of the cafeteria. It surprised him that he hadn't seen them, and he wondered how long they had been standing there. He could tell that they were captivated by what they were seeing.

A member from the hotel staff came into view and started to approach their table. The young man walked up with a timid smile, and a look that seemed to suggest an apprehension. He nodded to Gabe, but turned his focus to her.

"Please excuse the interruption. I'm so sorry ma'am, but we ran into a problem regarding the room you were waiting for. There was a miscommunication…when my shift started, I did not see the note Josh left about the room you requested, and I had already extended the stay of the couple who originally booked that room, so it is not available."

Gabe saw her trying to appear ok with it, but he could see she was a bit rattled by the unfolding situation.

"Is there another room I could have?" she asked.

"I'm so sorry. We are completely booked out, and I've even spent the last thirty minutes trying to find you a room at another hotel…I can't find you one."

She let out a breath and smiled through her unease. "Ok. Thank you for trying. I guess I will just head back to the airport and see if I can catch a flight back then."

Gabe was instantly filled with a visceral resistance at the thought of her leaving.

"Don't do that. You just got here." Gabe turned to the manager, "There must be something you can do?"

The manager shook his head. "I'm sorry, I don't know what else can be done if all the rooms are booked out."

Gabe was determined not to let this woman slip away again so fast. He was just getting to know her and really wanted to keep talking with her. He had an idea. He looked to the manager again.

"Well, I am in the executive suite…am I correct, that that suite is connected to two additional rooms that are otherwise separated? Couldn't we just disconnect one of those rooms and give it to her?"

The manager spoke up. "Yes, that could be done very easily. If that is alright with you sir. It would change your three room suite into a two room, but you would still have the kitchen connected to yours. You would just lose one of the extra bedrooms."

They both looked to her as she shook her head politely. She looked at Gabe with a kind smile.

"You do not have to do that. That is so nice, but I don't want to compromise your suite like that."

Gabe was about ready to beg her to accept it. "Please take it. I do not need two bedrooms. I would love for you to have it. Besides, your alternative is to fly back to Los Angeles tonight…you really want to do that?" A look of dread came over her face and he took advantage of her dislike of it to drive his point home. "It's LA. Hollywood. It's horrible. Why would you want to do that to yourself…" She smirked at his tactic. "It's really ok with me. I don't need the extra room. Please take it. No strings attached, I swear. I will even let you have the chocolate covered strawberries they left for me in the kitchen," he smiled at her.

She laughed. "Oh, you do know your audience, don't you?"

"I learn very quickly," he said confidently. Gabe looked back at the manager, who nodded his head.

"All you have to do is close both doors in the room. They lock automatically, and tomorrow morning Ma'am, you can come to the front desk for a key to your room. It will be ready first thing."

She smiled after looking at Gabe for a few moments longer, then turned to the manager. "Thank you."

She looked back at him after the manager walked away. "Are you sure this is ok with you?"

Gabe had never been more certain of anything in his life. "Absolutely sure."

Chapter Four
Impulsive Need

Kayla was a bit perplexed at finding herself so comfortable with this man. Everything about this entire encounter was so unique. If any other man had approached her at the table, she would have had a thousand ways to get out of it and walk away, but when she looked up and saw him…every perfectly memorized excuse she had written for herself just vanished from her repertoire, and she went blank. She did her best to convince herself that he did not see how much he had taken her breath away, and she was thankful to her conversation skills that she had been able to guide the discussion away from herself.

The elevator ride was filled with a light hearted chit chat between them and a mother and daughter who were riding up to their floor with them. The little girl was really cute and couldn't stop smiling at Kayla.

The girl looked up to Kayla. "I really like your ankle bracelet. It's so pretty," she said to her.

"Thank you so much. I'm really glad you like it. You just made my day sweet heart."

The shy smile on the girl's face increased as she blushed at the compliment from her.

"You know something?" she said to the little girl. "I have a feeling that you are amazing and can do anything you want to with your life." She smiled at Kayla, seeming to take her words into her impressionable self confidence; good. Kayla always liked to empower children whenever she could.

The doors opened and they got out. The girl and her mother went to the right down the hall, and Kayla followed him to the left. As he opened the door to the executive suite, she found it curious that she felt no fear about walking into this man's room. This was way out of the norm for her, but something about him…his smile…his eyes…his accent? She was sure that his being a Marine Raider was part of her trust that he would not hurt her. She knew what Raiders did; the kind of men who were selected for those fast teams were honorable. But there was something more that had moved her to take him up on his offer and spend a little more time with him. She was not clear on why, but there was a feeling she had running through her ever since he said hi, and she was having trouble ignoring it. Was it his voice, his kindness, his gorgeous looks? Jesus, she didn't know, but whatever it was, she did not feel any concern about being here with him.

The room was gorgeous. Huge open living room with a kitchen off to the left. The windows infront of them had a magnificent view of the pool lights below and the stars in the night sky above. The room was softly lit with a glowing light in the corner and the light from the pre-lit fireplace.

"Wow, this room is beautiful. You have good taste." She turned to him as he walked into the living room area after closing the main door. He smiled warmly and put his key down on the dining table. He pointed to the connected room off to the left.

"That room has the same view. It's all yours. I'm glad you decided to stay," he said.

He moved closer to her, but was purposefully allowing enough distance to keep her from feeling uncomfortable. She felt herself smiling as she looked into his eyes. They were so…captivating. She was having a hard time understanding why it felt so nice to be in this moment with him, but she couldn't deny it, and she wasn't even sure she wanted to; another feeling that, normally, would have her questioning herself to no end, but in this moment…for whatever reason, she felt better than she had in a very long time.

He reached behind him to the kitchen counter and brought over a silver tray of chocolate covered strawberries and handed it to her. "As promised."

"These look amazing." She looked at him bewildered, as he set them down in front of her on the dining table. "You are seriously going to just give me these and let me take them away, into that room and close the door? Never to be seen from again?"

He laughed. "Yes. No strings attached, as stated. Although, I would like to offer an invitation to breakfast tomorrow morning, if you would like. I will even try to arrange some Italian coffee beans for you if that bribe might get you to join me."

There was something so warm and comforting about him. He was not crossing lines or pushing himself on her in any way, which was kind of an unusual experience for her. She knew he was attracted to her, she wasn't naive about that, but she was impressed at his self control and willingness to let her go. Not many men had that kind of strength. It made an impression on her that she was not used to at all, and she found herself being pulled in; like a magnetic draw that she was becoming more and more aware of, and she suddenly felt herself not wanting to escape to her room. What a strange realization for her, she wasn't exactly sure how to respond to it.

Neither of them spoke. Neither of them moved. They both seemed locked in each others eyes unsure of what was happening, but the energy in the air between them was swirling into an inescapable temptation. She was instantaneously overcome with a need to wrap herself inside the energy coming from this man. The power of the pull to him outweighed anything else in her mind...and she could feel her conscious self stepping away and freeing her from the restraints she normally places on herself.

There was no explanation for it and no way to put into words what happened, but in that moment, they both succumbed to a power neither of them could control. She felt herself moving into him as he moved into her…and he kissed her.

When their lips met, a bolt of emotion coursed through her like nothing she had ever experienced. She was overtaken with a need that was so foreign to her and yet so very familiar at the same time. She felt herself moving closer into him, and as she did so, his arms welcomed her and pulled her in further. He gently moved his body into hers as well and she found herself submersed in his embrace; lost in a kiss that, somehow, was infiltrating her very soul, exposing an entire layer of herself that was a part of her she didn't know was there. She felt like she was dreaming, and yet it felt more real than anything she had ever experienced. But one thing was crystal clear; in this moment, she needed this man…and was so overcome with it that she couldn't even question it or filter what was happening.

He pulled her tightly into him…and if felt amazing to be in his embrace. She could practically feel him surround her with an unexplainable forcefield that she was gladly submersing herself in. There was no part of her that wanted to stop this, and no part of her even wanted to question that decision. Her arms found their way around him and pulled him into her with a need she was powerless over.

With his lips still locked onto hers, he lifted her easily in his arms and carried her to his bedroom. She wasn't even sure how their clothes came off, but she didn't spend much time caring. When he placed her in his bed, she found herself bewildered at how sheltered she felt underneath him, and it occurred to her in that moment, that she had spent her life desperate for what she was feeling right now. That was enough for her. She turned off her mind, pulled him onto her and relished in a safety like she had never known.

* * *

Gabe could hear his inner voice, but just barely. That part of him that was always in control, always tactical and always strong…the part that was trying to tell him he was going way too fast with her, but it seemed so completely removed from him, and that made it impossible to pay attention to. That part of him that should be holding himself back seemed to have been separated from his body and sent immeasurably far away. He could not stop touching her. He could not pull his lips off her, nor his body from hers. It had absolutely not been his intention to find himself naked above this woman tonight when he offered her the room. He did not plan this, and part of him still couldn't really believe it was happening. But it was, and he was powerless over the extraordinary magnetic pull he felt to her.

He wasn't even sure how the first kiss happened, but when it did, even the Raider in him couldn't stop it. And now…the touch of her naked body beneath him…so perfectly integrated under his large frame…like the puzzle piece he had been waiting for his whole life.

It wasn't just the physical feel of her; though that far exceeded the feel of any woman who had been in this place before her. He felt her needing him; he felt it in how she touched him, in how her body responded to him. What was happening to them both as his hands explored her skin, his lips caressed her lips and his body pressed down onto hers…it was more than just physical. It was as if there was an intense conversation taking place between their souls. He couldn't hear it, but he more than felt it, and he could not pull himself away from it. He couldn't. Every fiber in his being needed her just as much as she needed him, and he had no rationale for understanding it. But he didn't care. He shut his mind off as he clasped his hand on hers and entered her.

He didn't even make a conscious decision to do it; his body just took over, and suddenly he found himself feeling her all around him and almost unable to withstand the pleasure of it. She felt amazing. His entire body was on fire as he moved in and out of her. His lips were still locked on hers and the kiss that had flared up between them seemed to be locking their very souls together under the strangely familiar seal of the searing passion building up in them both.

Time was inconceivable and he honestly could not judge how long he had been making love to her. The bliss in the feel of her was extraordinary and the build up so intense he was sure he was on the brink of insanity. He moved in and out of her faster and faster as the scorching pleasure reached a breaking point that even he wasn't sure he could handle. He held onto her with all he had as the explosion burst out of him and shot deep into her.

He could feel her body pulling him in as he pulsed inside of her. His lips never parted from hers, and he found himself still unwilling to pull away. Feeling her settle under him from the mind blowing moment was an incredible sensation and he did not want to let go of it.

When the tremors of his climax finally started to subside, and his breathing came back down, he rolled slightly off of her, but found himself unwilling to release her from his arms. He moved to the side and pulled her into him and he felt her fold in as if she was born to fit perfectly in his embrace. He felt dazed, in a way. It took everything out of him, and he knew she had felt the same, because he could hear her breathing start to change; she was falling asleep. She seemed to push herself even further into his grip as she did so, and within minutes, he knew she had fallen into a very deep sleep.

It was probably the most serene moment of his life. There was a peace in this moment like nothing he had ever known, and for the first time in his life, he felt…calm. Absolutely calm.

His eyes were heavy and he felt like the weight of the world that he had been carrying since time began was lifted off of him, and he could breathe in a way he never quite had before.

His eye caught the digital clock as it changed. He couldn't help but smile just as his eyes started to close and the clock switched to 11:59pm.

She wasn't sure what it was that woke her, but her eyes opened. As she waited for the obscure numbers from the clock on the nightstand to come into focus, she felt the weightlessness of the absolute comfort she found herself in…and then her mind began to wake up. The numbers came into focus; 4:15am…it was a strange mixture of sensations. Her body felt more relaxed than she ever remembered, but her mind was starting to kick into gear faster than her ability to keep up with it.

She was still snuggled in his arms. His breathing was deep and strong, and his arm and body wrapped protectively around her. The immeasurable feeling of comfort and safety was unlike anything she had ever known, and she so badly wanted to stay wrapped inside it forever; but the part of her that had stepped away last night and freed her from her normal responsibility of maintaining emotional distance was back, and was not pleased. She felt a wave of fear rush through her mind…how did this happen? How did she let herself go like that? It was unexplainable and she felt a sense of vulnerability coursing through her veins that she desperately wanted to be free of. So many things were running through her mind at once, but the one overriding thought louder than anything else was that she needed to leave.

She wondered if she would be able to free herself from his embrace without waking him up; God, she did not want to have to look in his eyes. How could she face this man after her behavior last night? She needed to run from him before there was any confirmation from his look that she was nothing more than any other easy woman. She could not believe she had done this. The shock of the reality of it was still cascading through her mind, and she wanted to sweep this under the rug as quickly, and as quietly as she could.

He was snoring slightly in his sleep, so maybe he was out deep enough that she could squirm her way out of his grip without him noticing. She managed, a little at a time, to free herself and slip out of the bed. She moved as quietly as she could. There was just enough light in the room from the fireplace that was still burning for her to find her dress, her underwear and her shoes. She gathered her clothing and slipped into the main room. He rolled over in the bed, but was still sleeping.

Kayla had never gotten dressed so fast. In one swoop the dress was on and her underwear pulled up underneath it. She didn't even take the time to put her shoes on, she just scooped them and headed to the door. Her bag was still sitting there right by the kitchen counter. She grabbed her bag and opened the door as quietly as she could.

No one was in the hall (thank God,) so she slipped out and ever so slowly closed the door. When it was soundly shut, she made a beeline for the elevator. Her heart was pounding at the thought that he might come out and see her running from him, but he didn't. The elevator doors opened, she got in and frantically pressed the close button until the doors shut tightly.

She let out a breath of relief. She still could not believe what she had let herself do…and with him. She really liked him…there was a feeling with him that she was still wrapping around herself. But now that she had just jumped into bed with him, he would never think of her as anything more than a cheap, easy lay, and that was so embarrassing. Heartbreaking actually, because she wasn't like that…but now he would never know that.

She began convincing herself that maybe this was for the best.

Maybe it was the perfect way to keep him away. He might not be the man she felt like he was anyway, and she certainly wasn't the woman he thought she was. This was the best solution. Now she wouldn't have to face the discomfort of anything serious that could wind up ultimately hurting her…or him.

Leaving was always the best choice.

She put her shoes on as the elevator beeped it's way to the lobby. When the doors opened, the lobby was relatively empty, except for the manager on duty behind the front desk.

Kayla lifted her head and gathered her confidence and strength, expertly separating her outward appearance from any sign of the internal war she had begun with herself since her eyes opened this morning.

The manager looked up as she crossed towards the front door. It was the same young man who had approached her last night about the room, and it was very apparent that he remembered her.

"Good morning. I have your room key ready for you," he said as he handed her the key.

Kayla smiled at him as warmly as she could. "I appreciate that so much, but you know what? Something has come up and it turns out I have to go this morning anyway, so I won't need it."

"That's a shame, I'm sorry to hear that. Will you be coming back?" he asked her.

"I'm afraid not, but thank you so much," Kayla said.

"Do you need a taxi to the airport?" he asked her as he moved out from behind the counter.

"Yes, as a matter of fact I do," Kayla answered him.

"Right this way. I'll make sure there is one for you." He led her out to the front entrance and waved a taxi over from across the street. The taxi pulled up, and with another thank you, Kayla got in the cab and made her exit.

When they made it to the main road, and Kayla was sure her exit had succeeded, she let out a breath. She felt a sense of relief…but was very aware she felt an equal amount of sadness; a feeling Kayla hated to experience, so she allowed herself to quickly fill again with the anger she felt at herself that she had let herself go like that. Her internal lecture was interrupted when her phone rang. It was Devin.

Devin Wilkons had been Kayla's best friend for years. She had met him at Interlochen on the first day she had arrived. Devin had also come to the school from America, Detroit actually, and neither had any idea what to expect on that first day. Somehow, they had found each other immediately upon entering the building for the first time, and magically bonded as life long friends do. His humor was an ever welcoming ray of sunshine for Kayla, and he always reminded Kayla of the good in this world; something she really needed right now.

Kayla answered her phone. "Devin…" she wasn't even sure where to begin.

Devin knew Kayla as well as she let anyone, and he picked up on the tone in her voice right away.

"Damn, has LA messed you up that much already? You sound horrible." His voice was melodic and cheerful, but had a tone of care in it for his friend. "What's going on?" he asked her.

"You are not going to believe what I just did. I can't even believe it," she answered him, unsure of if she even wanted to let him know.

"Did you leave already?" he kidded with her.

"Yeah, yesterday right when I landed, but that's not what I mean."

Devin started laughing, "I made a bet with myself that you would do that. Where are you now?" Kayla could hear him lifting his mug off his counter and taking a sip of what was most likely coffee.

"I'm in Vail, heading to the airport to fly back to Hell."

"Ok. A spa trip to Vail before dealing with LA, I get it. Nothing wrong with that. So what's the problem? Spa didn't relax you?" he asked her.

She took a moment, almost choosing to not even tell him, but she needed to let it out…maybe to punish herself. She wasn't sure, but whatever force had taken over her higher reasoning skills last night, it needed to be destroyed, and maybe letting Devin know might give her the reinforcements she needed to not ever do this again.

"Devin…I did something last night I have never done in my life…I can't believe myself…"

She could hear Devin placing his mug back down on the counter a bit harder than necessary.

"I know you are not about to tell me you slept with someone…" he said in disbelief. When the dead silence fell on the phone she could hear Devin inhaling a deep breath. "Oh dear Lord. Kayla Knight! You secret slut." He was laughing. "Oh girl, the fuckening has come! I bet you are already lambasting yourself like nobody's business." He was still laughing and then his voice came back through the line in a coherent tone. "Tell me everything." His voice had no blame or ridicule. In fact, he almost seemed to be happy with her terrible mistake.

"Devin…what the fuck did I just do? I never do this kind of thing. I have no idea what came over me…"

Devin cleared the laughter from his voice and she could feel him centering his tone into a pin point focus.

"Kayla, you never sleep with anybody! The last guy you slept with, that I know of, was years ago. Damn, it's about time you let yourself back into the game. Stop beating yourself up. Just breathe and tell me what happened."

"That's just it. I don't know what happened. I mean, I know, but I can't explain it. I should never have let him sit down at my table. That was my mistake. I should have walked away."

"Yeah, like you always do. OK, I'm going to stop you right here for a moment." He gathered his breath and his tone got more serious. "Kayla, every once in a while, you got to let someone catch you. I know you don't want to hear that, and I've spent our entire friendship watching you hold yourself up and push away anyone who tries to get too close to you. I don't pretend I understand why; and I don't need to, but I can tell you this, you're human…and sometimes humans need to be loved. Even you. Whether that's physically, emotionally or both. Sometimes that connection is necessary. Even for you."

Kayla stayed quiet. She didn't like the vulnerable feeling that iced through her at hearing things like that and she wasn't sure how to deflect her reaction from it. Devin took a breath and continued.

"How did he react when you left him. Did you crush the poor guy or were you at least civil," he asked her. When Kayla was silent Devin jumped back in. "Kayla Knight you did not just sneak out while he was sleeping…" she didn't answer him again. "You ran out?"

Kayla's defenses kicked in, "Well what was I supposed to do? I panicked. I didn't want him to think that's the kind of woman I am."

"Well now he's gonna!" he answered her. "OK, step back…tell me how you met. Who was this guy…start with his name." When Kayla fell quiet again, Devin couldn't hold back his surprise. "Oh dear God in Heaven…Kayla, are you telling me you didn't even know his name?" He took a shocked breath and then continued, "Oh, no…this is not…I can't even…no, Lord help me...you better start talking right now and tell me about this man, because either he is the most incredible man on the planet, or I need to get my ass on a plane to you right now because you have lost your mind."

Kayla took a breath…how could she explain it? *She* didn't even understand it. She did her best to brush it off and begin convincing herself what ever it was was over now, so best to move on. "It doesn't even matter anymore, does it? I'm about to fly back to LA, I don't know his name, he doesn't know mine…I will never see him again, so whatever this was…it's over."

"Don't be so sure about that. If I have learned anything in this life my dear it's that God works in mysterious ways. And the other thing I know is that this kind of thing is not normal for you; which tells me being back in LA is fucking with you." Kayla heard him take a beat, finish his coffee and speak again. "I'm getting on a plane. There are some good auditions happening in LA right now anyway. I'm coming out there and we are going to drink several bottles of wine in the crappiest city on earth together. I'm not letting you deal with this LA thing by yourself."

Kayla let out a breath, "You don't have to do that…but it would be so great if you did."

"I'd cross the world for you, you know that. You're my best friend. Besides, LA had some very cute men the last time I was there, I wouldn't mind if some tall, handsome stranger swept *me* off *my* feet too. You can't be the only one getting lucky."

"How do you know he was tall and handsome?" Kayla asked.

Devin laughed. "My dear, have you looked in the mirror lately? What other kind of man is going to have the balls to come up to you. I know this man was fine," he said without question.

Kayla laughed. "I can't argue there." She found herself taking in an involuntary breath as she remembered his eyes…his smile…the feel of him…damn, she couldn't deny the incredible sadness that filled her at the thought she would never see him again.

Just before his eyes opened, he felt himself reaching for her. Even in his half asleep state, it was an unusual realization for him; that the feel of this woman was already ingrained in him. But his hands found an empty spot on the crisp bedsheets where the feel of her silky skin should have been. His eyes opened in a quick and instantly alert second. She was not in bed with him. The clock on the nightstand read 6:20am. He sat up and quickly realized she wasn't in the bathroom either. He was shocked that she had been able to get out of the bed without him waking. His training and career had practically prevented him from sleeping through any movement, noise or change in surroundings; but he had fallen into such an incredibly deep sleep after making love to her, that the drain of his energy had overridden his normal light sleeping habits. He looked around, her clothes were gone. He quickly got up from the bed, crossing into the kitchen and livingroom area. He noticed immediately that the additional bedroom was still open with an untouched bed still perfectly made and no sign of her anywhere. Her suitcase and bag were gone. Panic shifted through him; *shit, did she leave? Why would she do that? How long ago did she leave?* He couldn't believe that she had been able to slip out without him waking up. It occurred to him she might still be in the lobby, maybe he could catch her before she disappeared from him again.

Gabe threw his pants and shoes on and grabbed his shirt; he was still putting his shirt on as he ran out the door and headed to the elevator. When he got to the lobby, a quick scan left him without the release he was hoping for…he didn't see her. There were a few people scattered just inside the front entrance, and the manager from last night working at the computers. Gabe crossed over to him. He looked up when Gabe reached the counter and instantly recognized him.

"Good morning sir," he said after lifting his head up from his computer screen.

"Hi. Have you seen…" It suddenly occurred to Gabe that he didn't know her name. He was amazed that that small but important piece of information had been so easily absent from his mind and he was livid with himself that he had allowed that to slip past him. To his relief, the manager spoke before he had to admit it out loud.

"The beautiful lady from last night?" his question came with an unmistakeable curiosity and Gabe was pretty sure the manager was piecing together the obvious night of passion that had just taken place. The quick glance at Gabe's untucked shirt and the uneven line of spastically closed buttons was enough evidence to any man with half a brain about what the situation was.

"Yes, sir. She left a few hours ago. Do you still want the key for the extra bedroom, or would you prefer that we reattach the room to your suite now that the young lady will not be needing it?"

Gabe felt a heaviness in his heart at hearing that.

"Did she say she wouldn't be needing it?" he asked him.

"Yes, sir. She said she got called out and was on her way to the airport almost immediately." There was a sympathy in the man's voice; Gabe was pretty sure he wasn't hiding his incredible disappointment at hearing that.

As embarrassing as it was to allow anyone to know about his failure at getting her name, he needed it. If he was going to be able to find her again, it was the one thing that was essential. He hated what he was about to ask, but he swallowed his pride anyway.

"Do you by any chance know what her name was?' he asked.

The young man had an unmistakable look of pity behind his grinning, and judgmental eyes, as he spoke. "No sir. We never officially booked her in so we do not have that information."

Gabe ignored the anger he was feeling at himself that he so stupidly overlooked such an important detail, and nodded his thanks anyway. He felt lost. Gabe wanted more information, but he was certain this man did not have the answers he was looking for. She was gone and he had missed his window to stop her.

"Ok," Gabe acknowledged. "Thank you."

As Gabe turned away from the counter, Andy and Nick were crossing the lobby towards him. Gabe tried to mask the emotions swirling inside him, but knew his brothers had already seen his forlorn expression.

"You look like shit," Nick said in a surprised tone when they reached him.

Gabe was not sure what to say or how to explain any of what had transpired.

"Gabe; this is not what I was expecting to see from the luckiest guy in the entire resort." Nick almost laughed.

"Where is the guy who took that beautiful woman back to his room last night?" Andy couldn't help but smile at him. "We saw you two. It was like watching a movie. I've never seen you like that."

"It was amazing actually. We saw the look on your face when she looked up at you." Nick was laughing in dismay. "If that wasn't 'the boom', as great uncle Joe cleverly named it, then I don't know what is," Nick added. "Where is she?"

Gabe had no idea what to say. The emotional rollercoaster he had just been on was taking it's toll on him and he found himself having trouble getting his feet on the ground. His brothers figured it out pretty quickly, and their energy changed. As much as they enjoyed the hell out of poking at him when the opportunity presented itself, they loved him dearly, and Gabe could feel they both got a sudden understanding that he was actually upset.

"Gabe…what happened?" Andy asked.

Gabe looked up. "I couldn't explain it if I tried," he said.

"Where is she?" Nick asked.

"She left. Manager said she got in a cab for the airport a few hours ago," Gabe answered.

"You're obviously upset about it…call her, Gabe. Get her back," Nick said.

Gabe shook his head and shrugged his shoulders, "I…uhh…didn't get her phone number."

Nick and Andy exchanged looks, clearly surprised at the lapse.

"OK, well that's easy enough." Nick pulled out his phone. "What's her name, we will pull it up."

When Gabe fell silent, Nick and Andy could not hide their look of dismay at that.

"You don't even know her name? Even for you that's absurd." Andy's voice was slightly stunned.

"What the Hell happened?" Nick asked.

Gabe shrugged his shoulders helplessly and answered, "…the boom…"

Chapter Five
Mysterious Ways

Gabe opened his fridge and stared into it blankly, as if somehow something in it would have magically changed in the last twenty minutes. He felt so unsettled and restless. All of the usual distractions were just not working.

He was glad to be back in his home. His brothers came back early with him; more out of brotherly support for him rather than any real desire to be home early. It worked out well; Andy got a call about a possible new client anyway, so coming back early became justifiable for more reasons than just Gabe's heavy mood change.

The invasively distracting weight of his regret over how he handled things with the mystery beauty was weighing so hard on him, he was running out of ways to fight it off. Failing at anything was such a foreign feeling for him, and it just about pierced him in half that the one time he fumbled so disastrously was with her. He slammed the fridge closed in frustration and just stepped back in his marble kitchen and leaned against the counter. He looked out across his open livingroom through the huge picture window to the city below, just behind his pool.

He reached his hand inside his pants pocket and clasped onto the only thing he had left of her; her ankle bracelet. It had fallen off her leg in his bed, and he saw it resting on top of the bedsheets when he came back to his hotel room. He found himself constantly running his fingers over it as if to make sure the memory that had been haunting him had actually been real.

His mind was combing through his conversation with her looking for any clues as to how he might be able to find her, but she left him with nothing. The only clue he had was her love for a certain brand of Italian coffee beans, but he didn't even know the name of that either. He cursed at himself again for being so taken with her that he didn't even remember basic things like getting her name.

He tried to shake it off and focus on something else. Work was always the first choice when his mind held onto something he wanted to be free of. Andy had arranged a meeting tonight about the potential new client. It was unusual for Andy to set up meetings like that in the evening, and on a Friday night no less, but Gabe didn't care. He was glad for the chance to fill his head with any thoughts other than her. He didn't even ask who the meeting was with. Gabe could feel himself floating through it. At some point he was going to have to have a serious talk with himself about this career choice. He felt extremely unfulfilled at the security firm. It was a great company, and his brothers ran it superbly, but his restlessness about it had been there since he started…and now, even more so. And once again, he found his thoughts focusing back on the woman he had let slip away. *Damn.* He missed her…and he couldn't even fathom the thought that he might never see her again. He just couldn't accept that. It was his guess that she was in LA somewhere…maybe…but the truth was, he didn't know. He cursed himself again that he didn't ask for her name. How could he have forgotten that?

He shook his head again in bewilderment about everything. How could he have found this woman and lost her just as fast? He was still unclear why he was so affected by her, but his pull to her was so intense, there was very little need to spend time trying to understand it. What he had to figure out was how to find her again, then he would start processing why she ran from him in the first place.

His phone rang, and pulled his focus back from the nagging thoughts swirling in his mind. He was glad for the distraction.

"Hello?" he said.

"Darling, it's me. I'm so glad your home. I saw your car in your driveway across the street. Sweetheart, I am in desperate need for cream. Do you by any chance have any I could have?" It was his next door neighbor. Well, they actually lived across the street, but in this Beverly Hills gated community, someone across the street was actually closer than the house next door. Betty was a much older woman, and one of the kindest souls Gabe knew. She and her husband had been in Gabe's life since as long as he could remember. Anyone who thinks rich, famous Beverly Hills people are all terrible has never met these two. They were intimidating to most; considering who they are and how far their reach into the power of Hollywood goes, and even Gabe was on his best behavior with them when in their company, but Betty was such a warm, kind hearted woman, that Gabe was always moved to help her out with anything she might need.

"Betty. How are you my dear?" he said in a light hearted tone. He opened his fridge to look for the cream as she answered him.

"I'm wonderful. It's beautiful outside and I am about to have my morning cup of coffee...but I need cream. A person of taste never has coffee without cream!" She was laughing.

Gabe found an unopened container of cream in his fridge. He hadn't needed it when he woke the other morning and discovered he had no Earl Gray...it was a horrible way to start any day; but that day had ended as one of the best in his life...then the worst again...and of course, that brought him back to the thoughts of the woman who had slipped away from him but was still very much running through his mind.

"Yes, I have a container. I'll bring it right over to you," he said with hope in his mind that the diversion might be helpful to ease the discomfort that had been circulating through him since yesterday.

"Thank you. That's wonderful. The front door is open, just come on in the kitchen." That was common for her. When she was expecting someone, she always unlocked the front door so that she could go about her business while waiting for them and not have to waste time walking through her extremely large Beverly Hills mansion when the door rang.

Gabe grabbed the cream and headed over. He noticed the rental car in their driveway just behind the four cars that they owned. It wasn't out of the norm for them to have someone over for a meeting or social visit. When he got to her front door, he saw it slightly cracked open. He had warned her so many times about not doing that, but she always refused to listen to him.

He opened the door and walked into the large, marble front hallway. "Betty," he called as he closed the front door behind him. "How many times have I told you not to leave your door cracked open like that."

"In the kitchen Gabe. Come on in." Her voice was cheerful as always, and he shook his head knowing he would never get her to change her habits. He could hear her chatting with someone but couldn't quite understand what the conversation was. He continued around the corner into the kitchen, noticing the new rug gracing the hallway floor.

"I like the new carpet, Betty." He turned into the kitchen. "Here is your cream." He had more to say, but when he entered the kitchen and looked up, his voice completely escaped him. He couldn't believe it, and the shock that raced through him almost knocked him off his feet. His eyes locked on hers...the woman who had slipped away. She was here. Standing in the middle of the kitchen, looking back at him with the same shock racing behind her eyes as well. He was stunned.

"Hi," Gabe said trying to cover his flood of emotion.

As quickly as the shock hit him, a wave of joy and relief seeped into every pore of his skin. She was here, right in front of him. He wasn't sure he was breathing.

He saw in her eyes that she was just as stunned to see him, if not more, but he also saw, buried deep behind that forcefield of hers, that she was glad to see him; at least before her mind started to talk her out of it.

Betty crossed over as nonchalantly as anyone, and reached for the cream Gabe had in his hand.

"Oh Darling, thank you so much. You saved the day. I am apparently about to try the best Italian coffee beans there are, and I had no cream." She was laughing as she turned back towards the woman he could not take his eyes off of. "Gabe, this is Kayla Knight. Kayla, this is Gabriel Saxton." She crossed back to the espresso machine to pour the cream into two cups of coffee.

*Kayla Knight…Kayla…*he repeated it in his mind as if it was the answer to the million dollar question that had escaped him since Wednesday; which it was.

Gabe saw in her energy that she was nervous; probably for more than one reason, but he guessed she was uneasy about allowing Betty to know they had already…met. He was very aware that Betty had turned around and was watching them so he reached out his hand to shake hers and help her with the cover she was looking for. Considering what transpired between them, he was not surprised she might want to keep that private, so he made every effort to help her know he would not divulge that information.

"It's very nice to meet you Kayla," he said as his eyes continued to scan her. When Gabe clasped his hand around hers, that familiar, unexplainable bolt of energy shot through him into his chest. The memory of clasping her hand while she was underneath him in his bed overtook his mind and he was filled with the images of that night. That amazing night. He relished in the recollection. Just the feel of her hand…he didn't want to let go of it.

"It's nice to meet you too…Gabe," she answered as she tried to divert her eyes, but he saw that she couldn't quite do it.

Gabe was pretty sure Betty picked up on the extra long moment between them, but she played it off as if she didn't. He reluctantly let go of Kayla's hand…slowly, but his eyes could not pull away from hers. He had so much he needed to say to her…to ask her, but he knew now was not the time. Betty crossed over to Kayla with a grin and broke him free of his thoughts.

"Lawrence and I have known Gabe for years." She handed Kayla her cup of coffee. "He is a wonderful man, so every time I hear you say everyone in Los Angeles is fake and horrible, I'm going to remind you about Gabe." Betty smiled her warm, loving smile and took a sip of the coffee she had for herself. Her eyes sparkled as she looked to Kayla. "Oh my goodness, you are absolutely right! This coffee is amazing. Thank you for bringing me some, dear." She took another sip, then turned her attention to him. "It's too bad you don't drink coffee Gabe, I would ask you to join us." She took another sip. "Oh, this *is* outstanding."

Gabe was not going to turn down this opportunity; no way…he would drink a glass of motor oil if he had to. Leaving now was not an option, and he spoke before he could even think. "I would actually love to try some, Betty."

Betty looked at him in confusion. "Gabriel Saxton…are you actually going to drink a cup of coffee?" She laughed and looked to Kayla, "This one is all about the Earl Gray Tea. He is just as picky about his tea as you are about your coffee!" She was still laughing as she turned to pour another cup.

"Well...I've been told Italian beans are...unforgettable," Gabe said as he looked in Kayla's eyes. He saw her smile even though she was trying not to. The incredible feeling that was bursting inside of him from seeing her standing here in this kitchen was making it's way to his face, and he knew he couldn't stop it.

Betty crossed back and handed him his cup. She waited in disbelief that he would drink it.

Gabe took a sip and found himself enjoying the warm sensation running through him. Maybe it was because Kayla was standing here, right across from him. Maybe it was because these were her favorite Italian beans; whatever the reason, Gabe had never enjoyed an Earl Gray tea as much as he was enjoying the coffee he was drinking in this moment.

He smiled. "This is fantastic coffee." His eyes fell into Kayla's again, and that familiar sense of calm he had when she was wrapped tightly in his arms, was settling all around him again. Memories of her being in his bed flooded his mind and a rush of heat raced through him.

Betty turned to Kayla. "You work miracles my dear. If you can get Gabriel Saxton to drink coffee, and enjoy it, than there is nothing you can't do." She was laughing again as Lawrence walked into the room with a folder in his hand.

Lawrence Rodgers might be a seventy-eight year old man, but he was anything but feeble. He carried with him the energy of a powerful man who had been at the head of the most impressive entertainment company in the world, and the confidence that came with that was never separated from his demeanor. He was not arrogant, or unkind, but one was always on their best behavior with him anyway. It's not that Gabe was intimidated by him, not at all. But Gabe always had a very professional respect for him and the influence he wielded.

Lawrence looked up at Gabe with pleasant surprise. "Gabe. I didn't expect to see you." He stretched his hand out to shake his and continued. "What brings you over this morning?" He pulled back and was standing next to Kayla.

"Betty called with a cream emergency." Gabe smiled and took another sip of the coffee baffled at why he was enjoying it so much.

Lawrence looked questioningly at his wife, "Betty, the second fridge in the pantry has plenty of cream in it." Gabe saw a twinkle in Betty's eyes.

"Really? I had no idea." Betty answered, though Gabe was pretty sure that was an absolute lie. He instantly understood that Betty had purposefully called him over…Betty had a bit of a match maker side to her and perhaps it had been her gut instinct that Gabe should meet Kayla. Perfect…he was grateful for the meddling and had never loved Betty more than in this moment.

Kayla finally found her voice, and it was Gabe's feeling that she spoke first to, once again, guide the conversation to the safe topic of her choosing.

"So how do you guys know Gabe?" she asked with a practiced voice that showed no sign of the nerves Gabe sensed were flowing through her. He found himself smiling again as she raised the cup to her lips and drank her favorite coffee. God, it was so good to see her again…

Lawrence spoke up in his strong, but friendly tone. "We've known Gabe since he was born." Lawrence smiled and looked to Kayla, "Gabe is the son of Joline Winters."

Gabe saw the recognition beam across Kayla's face. It was the standard reaction when people discovered who his mother was. She was, after all, an extremely famous singer. His mother had been a top artist on Lawrence's label and the families had been close for years.

Kayla looked to Gabe with a layered smile. "I know her music well. She died before I was born, but I grew up listening to her. She was wonderful."

Gabe could feel an emotion under her words and surmised it was her way of offering him deeper condolences on the loss of his mother at such a young age.

"Yes, she was, thank you. I'm glad you liked her music," he said to her.

Lawrence gave it a moment and then lightened the mood. He turned to Kayla.

"I tried hard to get him to follow in her footsteps, but Gabe decided the Marines was the path he wanted instead." He looked back to Gabe, "I still say you would have been fantastic."

Betty jumped in. "Of course he would have, Lawrence. But I think we can all agree that what he achieved in the path he chose was more than any of us could have hoped for." She looked at Kayla. "Gabe was an exceptional Marine." She smiled and sipped her coffee again.

"Yes he was." Lawrence said with a smile that Gabe understood completely. There was no question Lawrence had a vision for him in the music world, but the results of his time as a Raider had an even deeper appreciation for Lawrence, and he knew the admiration Lawrence had for what he had done.

Lawrence changed the energy and turned to Kayla, handing her the folder he had under his arm.

"Here you go Kayla. Everything you need for tonight. The version you asked for is on the top. Two copies. You all set?" he asked her.

"Yes. I'm heading over now to double check everything, but I'm sure it's fine," she answered him taking the folder.

"Did you find someone to go with?" he asked her.

Kayla laughed as she looked through the papers that were in the folder. "Ha. In this town? No. I already told you, I'm fine doing this alone."

Gabe was intrigued at the interaction between them. Lawrence clearly had an affection for her, but he was at a loss as to who she was to him. He knew that Lawrence and Betty never had kids, and he didn't remember any nieces or nephews being in the picture in all the time he knew them. But Lawrence had a watchful concern for her and he wondered why that was.

"Kayla, I can count off a hundred men who would love to take you to this tonight. Surely you can't tell me all of them are unacceptable to you. It doesn't have to be a date, just have someone there with you. It looks better," Lawrence argued.

Kayla clearly had no intimidation, fear or need to appease him in any way, and Gabe was fascinated by it. Very few people argued with Lawrence Rodgers, and even fewer of them ever found themselves in his presence again when they did. But there was a very strong, deep connection here that prevented either of them from worrying about saying what they really thought. *Who was this woman?*

Betty jumped in with an almost grandmotherly tone. "Kayla, he worries about you, that's all. Of course you can do this little thing on your own tonight. But wouldn't it be more fun if someone went with you?"

"Betty, I'm fine. Besides, it's too late to ask someone now, so let it go you guys. I can handle it."

"We know that. That's not the point." Lawrence was going to argue with her but Gabe couldn't ignore the incredible opportunity that was forming infront of him - and he had a sinking suspicion this was exactly why Betty had called with the fake cream emergency, so he knew he would have her as a back up.

"I'll go," Gabe said innocently.

All of them looked at him with three very different expressions.

Kayla, of course, looked terrified. Lawrence looked surprised, and Betty, as he suspected, had a smile on her face.

"That's a wonderful idea," Betty said.

Lawrence looked at him in an attempt to understand exactly what his motivation for that suggestion was. Gabe almost felt like he was being stared down by an overbearing father, but he didn't care.

"Do you even know what it is?" Lawrence asked him.

"No. I have no idea. But I have nothing to do tonight anyway, and...I'm happy to help Betty prove to Kayla that not everyone in Los Angeles is horrible." He smiled at Kayla as he watched her searching her mind for an excuse she could pull off without raising suspicions in Lawrence and Betty as to why she would object to him.

Lawrence looked a little deeper into Gabe's eyes. "Don't you have a meeting tonight with your brothers'? I thought Andy mentioned something about that."

Gabe took a quick breath but nothing was going to prevent him from the chance to take her out anywhere so he could have some time alone with her to find out why she ran out on him.

"No. Andy and Nick have the meeting tonight, not me. I have absolutely nothing to do and was going stir crazy in my house anyway." Gabe turned to Kayla. "I would be very happy to go with you tonight."

He could see a tremendous amount of fear behind her eyes just before she put on that perfected facade of composure.

"Gabe, that is very sweet of you, but don't let these two bully you into this. It's not a big deal and I am absolutely fine doing this on my own. In fact, instead of worrying about this, I think you should take this opportunity to get even with Betty for tricking you into bringing over cream she apparently didn't need, and insist that she give you her old espresso machine, and some of the Italian beans I brought, as an apology. Now that you've discovered what great tasting coffee really is, you should have the means to keep enjoying it."

Lawrence looked puzzled. "Gabe drank coffee,…and liked it? When did this happen?"

Gabe was not going to let her win this misdirection; not when it could cost him his chance to be with her tonight.

"I can always buy my own espresso machine. In fact, if I go with you tonight you can explain to me which one I should get and how to use it. I would love that," Gabe said.

He caught the smile that was creeping on Lawrence's face as he looked to Kayla with a laugh.

"Well, you walked right into that one." He looked back to Gabe and the thoughts going through his mind were not easy to read, but Gabe felt like, for whatever reason, Lawrence was now in favor of the idea. "I think it would be great if you went with her actually."

"Lawrence…" Kayla said. She looked to Gabe trying one last attempt at protecting herself from having to face him later. "Don't let him intimidate you. You do not have to do this."

Gabe smiled at her. "I know I don't have to, and I am not intimidated by Lawrence. I would really like to go with you tonight."

He knew she had no way of arguing without exposing the secret he knew she wanted kept from them. He saw her give in.

"Fine. It's at 8:00pm." Kayla said.

Gabe was thrilled with everything about this. He didn't know what it was they were going to and he didn't care. He just wanted to be with her.

"What time should I pick you up?" Gabe asked her.

Kayla shook her head. "You don't need to pick me up. I will meet you there."

Gabe was going to protest but he saw Lawrence grin. "I wouldn't even try to argue with her Gabe. This one is as stubborn and independent as they come. Take what you can get."

"Ok. Where am I meeting you?" Gabe knew how to pick his battles.

"The Pantages. It's downtown. You know where it is?" Kayla asked.

Gabe smiled. "I know exactly where it is."

"We can meet out front around 7:30," she said.

"I will be there," Gabe answered with a joy in his voice he could not hide. Gabe reached for his phone. "What is your phone number…in case we have trouble finding each other."

Kayla pulled her cell phone out. "Give me your number Gabe." He gave it to her and she typed it in her phone. Then she looked up. "Ok, I have your number. I'll text you when I get there." He was not happy about not getting hers, but he knew, now that he had her name, he could easily find her number; one of the benefits of knowing everything there is to know about security.

Gabe looked at her with a smile, "You are not going to stand me up, right?"

She smiled. "No. I promised Lawrence I would go, and after all the trouble Betty went to to rope you into this, she would lecture me to no end if I did. I will text you."

Fate had been extremely good to him so far regarding this woman, and had just brought her back into his life again. He took a breath; trusting this next step to fate again.

"Ok. I'll be waiting," Gabe said to her. She smiled at him and he was clear on one fact; he would not lose this woman again.

Chapter Six
The Pantages

It was hours later and Kayla still could not believe what had happened this morning in Betty's kitchen. Of all the people who could have walked into that room to join them, how in the world was it him? She felt her heart stop when she turned and saw him…and then she felt her heartbeat racing through her entire body. Even now. It was an extremely abnormal mix of emotions; one part of her was terrified, embarrassed and ashamed…the other part was thrilled, relieved and ecstatic. Balancing the uneven turmoil inside her was getting very difficult. With everything she had to deal with tonight, this was either too much to add to the mix, or an incredibly welcome distraction. She wasn't sure which it was.

She looked in the mirror again critically judging her make up job, as she always did. The image of herself in that black dress again brought back a myriad of memories from her night with Gabe when she last had it on…and off. She felt herself shiver at the memory of his hands on her. Though she did not want to admit it to herself, there was no way to deny how amazing his touch felt. She had been struggling with herself since then to find ways to shake it off and forget it, but she knew that was impossible…especially after he so miraculously walked right back into her life again this morning.

She was grateful for the lunch date Lawrence and Betty had to get ready for that put an end to the coffee time this morning. The thought of leaving and having Lawrence and Betty divulge any information about her to Gabe was unsettling. She wasn't sure how to keep herself low key tonight…but there was not a lot she could do about it now, was there? She looked at her watch, it was 7:25pm, which meant he was probably already there; waiting out front wondering what the Hell he had gotten himself into. Maybe he didn't show up. It would make hiding from him so much easier, but she had a very strong feeling he was not about to let that happen. She thought briefly about not texting him…she could claim she wrote the number down incorrectly…but she knew that would not only be an unbelievable excuse, it would also be rude, and she didn't want to behave like that. Maybe this entire evening would prove too much for him anyway and he would walk away on his own afterwards. She admitted that would hurt her… deeply, but better now than later, right? She looked at her watch again…she waited as long as she could, now she had to do it.

She picked up her phone and texted him.

Hi. Have you run for the hills yet or are you here? She hit send. Almost immediately she saw that he was texting her back. Then the message came in.

I don't run. Ever. Yes, I'm out front. Where are you?

She took a deep breath. OK, time to put on her best performance. She texted him again.

Go around the block to the left; stage door. Ask for Leon, he will let you in and bring you to the VIP room; open bar. I'll meet you there. Think we will both need a drink to get through this crap! :)

She was trying to be funny, to lighten the weight that was about to crash down on her. She knew, by now he had figured out that they were attending a music awards ceremony. The huge lit sign on the front of the theater would be hard to miss. She gathered from her conversation with him in the cafeteria that he was just as repulsed by the typical Hollywood crowd as she was, which made her question how he would respond to the rest of the surprises about to come out tonight.

On my way. See you soon, he texted back.

She took her time walking through the crowd towards the VIP bar room. If she was lucky, she would get to him with only a few minutes until the lights would flash signaling for everyone to take their seats. How deep of a conversation could they get to in such a short amount of time?

When she got to the entrance, she took a deep breath, and then walked in. She saw him right away. Somehow her eyes knew exactly where to look, and apparently so did his. She had no time to filter her reaction, and she felt her breath escape her lungs just as it had the very first time she saw him.

He was standing across the room, by the bar. He looked amazing dressed in a dark black suit, silvery blue tie and those stunning eyes looking right at her. His smile was a smoldering combination of ease and confidence.

She lifted her head and walked over to him, using every ounce of performance skills to cover the anxiety swirling in her at having to be face to face with this man that somehow got right into her very being.

"Hi," Kayla said when she reached him.

"Hi." His tone was so soothing and the smile that flashed on his beautiful face was the sexiest one she had ever seen. Keeping herself distant from him was not going to be easy, that much was certain.

He looked at her with a humorous smirk. "So…a big Hollywood Awards show, huh?" he asked. "That's ironic."

She laughed. "Yes. See, I told you not to let Lawrence and Betty bully you into this. Little did you know what you were getting yourself into."

The smile on his face warmed even more right before he spoke. "That is the understatement of the year." His voice had a deep layer of emotion which made it very clear to her that he was not just talking about tonight. The look in his eyes was both heartfelt and earnest. She felt herself take in an involuntary breath and had absolutely no idea how to respond to him. The distraction of the bar tender was a welcome relief.

"Can I get you two something to drink?" he asked them.

Kayla looked at the man behind the counter and smiled, "Yes. Gin and Tonic please; extra lime."

She felt Gabe's eyes still on her and was very aware he was reading past what she wanted him to see. She felt a wave of fear rush through her and became, for the first time, thankful for the chance to disappear in the lights of this evening.

Gabe pulled his eyes from her. "I'll have the same." He looked back at Kayla. "My mother always drank that too."

Kayla smiled back at him, reaching into all her tricks to come across completely in control and relaxed.

"Yes. I'm not surprised. Most singers drink this. The mix of gin with the quinine is really good for the throat."

Gabe looked at her curiously. "Are you a singer?" he asked her.

Before she had to answer that question, a very pretty woman with long blond hair came over to them, smiling a very familiar smile at Gabe.

Gabe!" she said as she reached them.

"Diane," he answered her as she hugged him sweetly. "What are you doing here?" He asked her as they broke the hug.

"Working. Seat filler. Not as great as being on stage, but you take what you can get in this town," she answered him. "The real question is what are *you* doing here? You hate these things! In fact, wasn't it you just a few weeks ago who said if you ever have to deal with another Hollywood star you would consider digging yourself a grave and jumping in it?" Diane found that hysterical and was laughing as she turned to see Kayla standing there. Then her laugh subsided almost instantly and her smile was a mix of embarrassment and awe. *Damn…*

Kayla had an instinct that she recognized her. She jumped in before that could be put to the test, and reached out her hand.

"Hello. It's nice to meet you," Kayla said warmly.

"Diane, this is Kayla. Kayla, this is my sister-in-law Diane. She is married to my brother Nick," Gabe said.

Diane seemed to lose her voice for a second and then spoke rather shyly.

"Oh my goodness. I can't believe I said that out loud. I was just kidding anyway." She gathered herself and shook Kayla's hand. "It's so nice to meet you Kayla." She seemed flustered, and Kayla was hoping since her back had been turned to Gabe, he might have missed the look in Diane's eyes when she saw her.

Diane turned to Gabe. "Are you her date tonight?" she asked him in astonishment.

For the first time since she met him, Gabe looked unsure how to answer the question just put to him. His eyes found Kayla's as he was thinking through what he should say, and he held her gaze for a moment before he spoke.

"Well, I suppose the answer to that question would be completely up to Kayla," he said with that warm smile of his.

Diane turned back to Kayla, and she had absolutely no idea how to respond. The bar tender gave her the perfect distraction as he handed them their drinks. Kayla took hers with a thank you, and looked back to Diane.

"Would you like a drink? Bryce makes a great gin & tonic." The bar tender smiled at her compliment, as Kayla took a big sip of hers. She saw Gabe's smile grow as he was reading into her deflection of the question. She wondered how long it would be before he flat out asked her why she ran from him. She had her work cut out for her tonight if she was going to succeed in dodging that conversation.

Before Diane could answer the lights started to blink, signaling for people to take their seats. Diane directed her attention away from the bar tender back to them.

"Oh, I have to go." She looked at Kayla. "I hope I get to see you again Kayla. It was so nice meeting you." Diane turned to Gabe with a quick hug. "I'll talk to you soon. Enjoy the show." With that, she picked up her pace and headed out to the back of the theater.

Kayla smiled at Gabe, wanting to direct the conversation again.

"So, you hate Hollywood, and yet your sister-in-law is an actress?" She laughed as she took another sip of her gin & tonic.

Gabe smiled. "She only does bit parts here and there, so I don't think that counts." He laughed as he brought his drink to his lips.

A theater employee crossed over to them; headset on and clip board in hand. She smiled at Kayla.

"Ms. Knight, are you and your guest ready to take your seats?" she asked her.

Kayla turned to her and politely answered her. "Yes." She took another quick gulp of the gin and tonic, and then glanced up at Gabe. "You ready for this?"

He had a suspicious look in his eye; clearly he was trying to piece together what was going on here, but there was no hesitation in this man whatsoever. He didn't even need a swig of his drink before he smiled and answered her.

"Absolutely," he said.

When they reached their seats, the lights had just gone dark and the opening began. Gabe was only half paying attention to what was occurring on stage; his main focus was on the woman sitting next to him. Who was this woman? He knew she was beautiful and that she pulled eyes in her direction, but the way people were looking at her tonight…he knew it was more than just her gorgeous looks that was drawing the attention. He suddenly wished he had taken the time this afternoon to do some research into her, but he had chosen instead to spend what little time he had today in preparation for tonight with the precious few things that he did know about her.

Throughout the show, Gabe's attention was a swirling mix of the overlapping questions about Kayla that he was trying to answer for himself, as well as his awareness of the incredible heat he could feel sparking between them, even here in this crowded theater. His hand was resting on his knee which placed it very close to where her hand was on her leg. The slit in her dress made it impossible for him not to glance at her skin…and the images of having his hands gliding on her body went through his mind again like a flame. It took a great deal of strength to keep from lifting his hand and placing it on hers. He so badly wanted to feel her again.

He would give anything to be alone with her; to talk with her. Really talk. He wanted to know everything about her. He wanted to talk about that night. He wanted to have that night again; minus the running away from him part. That would have to be topic number one; why did she run out on him after that? He knew there was no way she didn't feel what he felt…and it was his guess that, perhaps, the power of the feeling between them was exactly why she ran…but he needed to know.

His thoughts were interrupted when the same employee with the headset came over quietly and leaned over to Kayla with a whisper. He saw Kayla nod and turn to him.

"Would you hold this for a minute? I'll be right back," she said as she handed him her purse and got up. As she walked down the aisle, Diane swept in and took Kayla's seat. Gabe was confused.

"What's going on?" he asked Diane.

Diane looked at him with a laugh. "What do you mean? She is up next." She must have seen the complete confusion on his face, and she continued. "Gabe, do you not know who she is?" Gabe shook his head, and Diane's face brightened in that way it does when she knows something the Saxton brothers don't. "Oh dear brother-in-law…that's Kayla Knight. Lawrence's best kept secret. She is the voice behind all the amazing soundtracks he has been having. That song is going to win best song tonight, I'm sure of it."

The act that was on was just finishing up, and she turned her face forward back to the stage, joining in the applause. Gabe was still confused as she spoke over the quieting crowd.

"It's amazing that she is here. She has been MIA for so long. Hold onto your seat Gabe, you are in for a surprise."

Then the spotlight came on the stage and Kayla appeared. When she did, the audience fell so quiet a pin could drop and everyone in this 3,000 seat theater would hear it. Gabe felt a wave of multiple emotions course through him at seeing her in the spotlight. She looked incredible. Of course she did, he knew she did…but standing up there on stage…that light she always seemed to be grounded in was beaming out. The music started, she raised the microphone to her lips…and then she sang.

He understood now why shivers ran over his skin when he first heard her speak to him. He did know that voice; and the shivers that washed over him now were overtaking his entire body. To say he was blown away by her would be an understatement. The emotion in her voice…it grabbed a hold and seemed to wrap itself around his very soul. It was extraordinary how in one breath she seemed so vulnerable, and in the next, the strength behind her belted out notes were mesmerizing. He knew Diane was watching him, reading his reaction to Kayla, but he couldn't pull his eyes away from the stage to acknowledge it.

When Kayla got to the last note of the song, Gabe could almost feel the eruption from the crowd before it started. She held the note longer than he thought was even possible and the crowd was on their feet applauding and cheering before she even finished. Never in his life had he experienced a performance like this. He took back everything he had ever said about his feelings towards Hollywood stars; and understood, without question, that this particular star was the one he was unwilling to let go of. Whatever that meant, he knew, with absolute certainty, that he needed her in his life.

With the performance completed and the award accepted, Kayla had done what she promised Lawrence she would. This had been important to him, even if she didn't really know why this one in particular was, it didn't matter. It was done. She loved it; the being on stage part. She was good at it, she knew that. If it could be the only part of her required for this career, she would gladly have made her presence here in this town as loud as anyone else…it was the off stage, behind the scenes mess she wanted no part of. Had it not been for landing smack dab in the middle of it as a child, she might not have known about the dark side of some of this. It was that part of her that needed to remain hidden; safely tucked away and out of the world's memory. It wasn't just the people in this room, it was more the press outside the stage doors. It was the press that dug into things, asked questions and plastered stories that gave the writers their desired fame at the destruction of peoples lives. The danger they would put her in was of no concern to them, and she knew it. Maybe after all this time, it would not be in the forefront, and she could escape into the spotlight of performance to steer clear of the hidden past she did not want brought out into the light again.

The stage manager was ready to bring her back to her seat. Her duties were done, and she could watch the final number from the crowd. If Gabe hadn't been there, she would have snuck out the back door and left. But he was here, waiting for her and she knew she couldn't run out on him again. Facing him now was going to be even harder. She was pretty sure he wasn't going to let this evening go without bringing up the night in Vail…and also this side of herself that now was so blatantly obvious it could not be overlooked. Maybe it was the perfect cover for not having to talk about that night…keep him distracted with career talk…maybe he would forget to ask her about anything else. Either way, another drink or two was definitely in order.

The stage manager led the way and reached her seat before Kayla, so that Diane could get up and return to the back. She took a breath, wondering how nonchalantly she could slip into her seat without having to look at Gabe. She was more nervous thinking about his reaction to her now, than for any performance she ever gave in her life. She felt exposed with him…most likely because he was already deeper inside her than she had ever let anyone. She didn't want it that way, but she felt for him and was losing the battle with herself about reversing that.

As she sat down, she immediately felt Gabe's eyes on her. Finally she turned to look at him. There was that smile again, even deeper than before. He handed her her purse as his look conveyed the myriad of questions swirling in his mind, and then he spoke.

"You have some explaining to do," he said with a deep and very curious grin.

Kayla put on her best puzzled expression. "Do I?" She found herself smiling as Gabe laughed.

"Yes, you do," he said.

* * *

When the lights came up and the crowd stood, Kayla found herself bombarded with handshakes and compliments. She was fine with that; it was part of this side of the business and these people were easy to deal with. She was sure to make sure Gabe did not get lost in the flood of activity and was impressed to see how well he carried himself in this situation. He was such a strong personality and it was the first time in her life that she didn't feel like she had to hold up the man standing with her. He made it so easy. He held his own, joined in the conversations and even knew several of the people coming up to her. Soon, she found herself comforted by the realization that she was standing next to a man that was as strong as she was…if not stronger… and to her surprise, she began to enjoy the quick interactions with the various greeters as they made their way towards the lobby.

She felt Gabe's hand on her back and it sent shivers down her skin. His touch was extraordinary…comforting and calming. She found herself moving her body a little closer to him as they made their way.

"Kayla!" The call came from a little ways in front of them, and Kayla knew the voice right away. Suddenly Devin appeared. Devin was taller than Kayla, with dark skin, a gray suit and that smile that Kayla had loved since she was a girl. She smiled and hugged him when he cleared the people in-between them

"Devin. You made it," she said.

"Of course I did. Last minute flight made me late, but I did get here in time to catch your number. Had to stand in the back like a damn sardine in a can, but I saw it. You were amazing as always."

Kayla looked to Gabe, "Devin, this is Gabe Saxton. Gabe, this is Devin Wilkons. Devin has been my best friend since high school. Funniest guy you will ever meet, and one hell of a singer."

Gabe smiled warmly and shook Devin's hand. "It's nice to meet you, Devin. Why the last minute flight?"

Devin laughed and spoke without a thought, "I know how much this one hates LA, and apparently even her spontaneous trip to Vail got her all messed up. I knew when she told me about that that I needed to bring her some reinforcements."

Gabe immediately had his eyes on Kayla, and she felt the myriad of questions about that remark burning into her. She needed to end his speech; quickly. "Devin…" she was pretty sure Devin got the message, but unfortunately so did Gabe. To her relief, Diane came up to them as well. Distractions were always welcome.

"Kayla! You were amazing." She looked to Gabe, "Didn't I tell you?"

Gabe brought his eyes back to Kayla and she found herself wishing there was another spotlight she could hide herself in; but there was none, at the moment, so she lifted her eyes up to face him. It amazed her…every time she looked in his eyes, she could actually *feel* him; like a blanket of serenity encapsulating her. His voice was filled with emotions she had never heard in another man's voice.

"Yes, she is extraordinary," he said.

Kayla broke the gaze and attempted to hide behind social pleasantries by introducing Devin to Diane. Diane recognized him right away; this one knew everyone. "Oh my goodness, you're Devin Wilkons. You were the one that sang on that show "America's Best," right?"

Devin smiled; he was very good at this part. "Yes. I'm the one who ended up getting kicked off right before the end, but I sang the hell out of it up to that point, right?" He was laughing and his warm energy made Diane laugh as well.

"You were robbed! I voted for you myself. You should have won," she said.

Devin put his arm around her sweetly and looked to Kayla. "You have such good taste in friends!"

Diane was instantly comfortable with Devin, as is usually the case with him, and she could see her enjoying his humor.

"I'm actually Gabe's sister-in-law, and I've only just met Kayla tonight. I had no idea Gabe would even be here. Last I heard he and his brothers were supposed to be in Vail for a conference, but they came back early because Gabe was upset about something." Kayla felt a wave of nerves run through her again as she caught the smile that flushed on Devin's face. He was connecting the dots that Kayla was hoping he wouldn't. Diane turned to Devin.

"Usually when that happens, the last thing he would do to feel better would be to go to anything Hollywood related." She laughed.

"Oh? Gabe was just in Vail?' he said as he looked at Kayla.

Kayla went for a drastic misdirection. "How about a drink? I could definitely use one." She felt Gabe's energy change, as he politely took the reins of the conversation.

"Actually, I would very much like to be selfish and steal her all to myself, if that is alright with you both." Gabe looked at Kayla. "We have a conversation that we started a while ago that I would like to continue." He smiled at her as she lost her breath. Devin had clearly pieced it together, and was, without question, on Gabe's side.

"Of course. That's perfect. I would much rather continue talking with Diane anyway, about how fabulous she thinks I am, so you guys go on, while we talk about me." Devin looked to Diane who seemed to have put it together as well, and was looking to Devin as the source of the gossip she was yearning for. "Drink Diane?" Devin asked her.

Her answer could not have been any quicker. "Yes. Great idea. VIP bar is this way." They scurried away, and Kayla suddenly found herself face to face with Gabe, stripped of the buffer she was hoping she could hide behind for the rest of the evening.

"Any possibility that you are done with all this, and just want to say goodnight to me and go home now?" she asked him with humor.

He laughed. "Not a chance, but that much was already clear to me, even before tonight."

There was such a great depth behind his eyes, and Kayla felt a wave of nerves fill her as she realized this man was already able to see past the light she thought she could use to hide herself. Fate had, somehow, thrown her into the grip of the one man she could not protect herself from. Thank God he was a man with Marine Raider skills because if she could not keep herself from him, and her worst fears ever came true, he was going to need it.

Chapter Seven
The Road Less Traveled

He knew this evening was going to be a delicate balancing act between the questions he wanted to ask, and the ones he knew she would answer. He was still trying to ascertain what the real reason was behind the fear that seemed to wrap itself around her. It was unclear and distant, yet strong and constant. He was grateful that the keen, tactical side of himself had found it's way back to him regarding her. He felt like he was finally getting his head on straight, even though he was very aware there was a big part of him that was still completely blown away by this woman; but emerging from that, was a part of him that, somehow, felt a very strong and familiar hold to her. He still couldn't explain any of it to himself, but in this moment, all he cared about was getting her out of this theater to a private place where he could begin the slow and deliberate walk of getting to know her, and making sure she got to know him. It was important to him.

"Come on," he said as he reached for her hand.

She paused...her hesitation was clouded in that trepidation of hers she hid so well; except that he was very good now at seeing it.

"Where are we going?" she asked him, without taking his hand.

Her uncertainty with him was precious...almost endearing in a way. He smiled at her, curious to see how much that fear would flare with his next words.

"Trust me," he said; and flare it did. He saw the extra flash of fear at the word he understood now was a problem for her. "That's not... comfortable for you is it?" he asked her.

"What isn't?" she asked doing her best to convince him she didn't know exactly what he was saying.

"Trust," he answered as he watched her eyes for the information he knew she would not be allowing to be revealed with her words. As he suspected, she didn't know how to answer him and she shifted her eyes away looking for anything she could to deflect his question. He kept his eyes on her as he spoke. "I think the problem isn't that you don't trust me. I think the problem is you know you already do."

This time he could almost feel the panic course through her. He knew he was right. It occurred to him in this moment that a great deal of the needed information he wanted about this woman was going to be coming from the things she didn't say, rather than the things she did. That was fine with him; he was an expert in that area and he was confident he could, not only learn what he needed to know about this woman from her silence, her eyes and her demeanor, but he would also be able to find ways to make sure she learned who *he* was. Slowly. That was the key. He had to move slowly with her; and that was just fine with him.

"OK, what if I promise you that, for the rest of this evening, I will not ask any questions about Vail, or why you ran from me," he said to her. He was hoping the hurt didn't come out in his voice; he still felt it when he thought about that first moment he reached for her, and she wasn't there. There was such a feeling of loss in that…he wanted so badly to assure himself that would never happen again.

She brought her eyes back to him. "Really? I have a pass to avoid that conversation?"

He smiled. "For this evening, yes." He saw a relief in her. It was a good move on his part. He needed to keep finding ways to get her to stop running from him, then he could find ways to encourage her to move closer. All he needed was time. He reached for her hand again, hoping this time she would take it. "Come on. I have a little something for you I think you are going to like."

She tilted her head with skepticism, but she did, finally, take his hand.

Kayla clasped his hand, trying to ignore how incredible the feel of it was. His hand held hers with a perfect mix of strength and comfort; that safety…why was it that every time he touched her she was overcome with a desire to simply curl up underneath him and stay there forever?

He led her across the street and around the side of a popular, and very busy restaurant. Almost immediately, a big Italian man in a fine suit opened the door with a wide smile.

"Gabriel!" the man said as he reached out to shake his hand.

"Antonio. Nice to see you," Gabe said as he shook his hand.

"I wait for you. You take a long time, but now you are here." Antonio turned to Kayla and his smile brightened even more. "And with such a beautiful woman. Why you make her wait so long before you bring her here to my fabulous establishment?" He laughed and shook Kayla's hand. "Come in, come in. I have a beautiful, private table ready for you in the back room. Come."

"Sorry we're a little later than I had said. The show ran a bit longer than I thought," Gabe said as he placed his hand on Kayla's back to guide her through the door. Even such a simple thing…touching her back…she loved the way he felt.

Antonio spoke over his shoulder, in his strong Italian accent, as he led them to the private room down the hall.

"I know, I know. We have TV in back. The show was good, yes?" he opened the door and turned to Kayla. "Ahh, my dear you were fantasimo. I love your voice. You make me cry. Me! A big Italian guy. You were wonderful. Bellisimo!" He gestured into the private area, "Please."

The booth was beautiful, and she loved the privacy of it. Enough room for wait staff to come and go, but the added touch of a door that kept the rest of the busy crowd separated…it was exactly the kind of dining experience Kayla loved.

She sat down, and Gabe shook Antonio's hand before he sat down as well right across from her.

"Thank you again Antonio," he said.

"Of course, of course. But when you call, and I hear you ask me about Kimbo coffee beans! I fall off chair! Of course I have Kimbo, but Gabriel knows this? How is that possible? Mr. Tea!" Antonio was laughing and looked at Kayla. "The beautiful woman has taught the big, tough Marine something, uh?" His laugh bellied out, as one of his waiters came in to pour champagne in the two glasses that were on the table.

Kayla grinned at Gabe, "You called ahead and asked if he had Kimbo beans?" she asked.

Gabe smiled that warm, confident smile of his. "Yes, I did. Not just Kimbo, but the Kimbo Extra Cream beans. Did I get that right?" he asked her, though she could tell he didn't need to confirm that.

She found herself a bit stunned. "That is exactly right. I'm amazed…" she was still trying to figure out how he remembered that from what could only have been a glance at the bag that had been sitting on Betty's counter when he joined them this morning.

"I told you. I learn very quickly," he smiled at her.

Antonio spoke up again after the waiter had filled the glasses and moved away. "I have already instructed our master baker on your request for the fresh made chocolate soufflé's. They take thirty minutes to prepare."

Kayla looked back at Gabe. "You also arranged for chocolate souffles?"

"Well, this place is famous for them, and I have a very fond memory of how much you like chocolate," he answered.

Her eyes got lost in his when she saw the warmth of the memory that flooded him as he said that. This man had a magic about him, and she could feel herself getting swept up in it with very little chance of catching herself.

"I kept the kitchen open for you. What can I have the chef make you? I have beautiful scallops in a lemon butter wine sauce, very delicious," Antonio added.

Kayla pulled her eyes from Gabe and smiled at Antonio. "That sounds amazing. I would love that."

"For me as well. Thank you Antonio," Gabe said.

"Ci. My pleasure." Antonio smiled and closed the door, leaving them in privacy.

When she looked back at Gabe, he raised his glass. "To just having a really nice evening. No pressure…just two people talking about anything good and enjoyable."

She raised her glass, "Perfect,"

They cheered.

Gabe was struck by the amount of joy that radiated all around them as they talked, laughed and discussed light topics and various subjects. He lost track of time as they enjoyed the meal. She had been at ease with him, and he felt a sense of relief for that. That was the most important achievement for tonight, and had been his number one goal. If he could get her to a place where her self protective tactics were relaxed, then he knew he could begin getting her to trust him, to open up to him and feel good about doing so.

Gabe had moments when he had to remind himself that he was on a bit of a reconnaissance mission here, trying to learn all he could about her in these precious moments when her guard was down; but even he found himself enjoying this evening so much that he forgot; from time to time. There was a part of him that felt like he already knew her; as if he had known this woman his whole life. It was a curious sensation.

He had learned a few things about her; one being that she had lived in Switzerland since high school. When she talked about it, he noticed her centering on her home in the mountains. The privacy of it led him to believe she lived alone. She never mentioned family, which he found intriguing since her move to Switzerland was during her high school years…usually parents, and/or siblings, would fall somewhere into a conversation covering that time period, but she mentioned none of that. That signaled to him that there was a story there. Anything she avoided talking about was a shining clue to him of the importance of it.

In fact, the only other people she really talked about were Lawrence and Devin. She was mentioning that Devin came back to the States eventually a few years after they both had graduated from Interlochen, but that she stayed. She was very vague about why, or what she had been doing there, besides recording her vocals on the myriad of soundtracks for Lawrence's movies. It was time for him to poke, just a little.

He dipped his spoon into the already half eaten chocolate soufflé, as he casually asked his first probing question of this evening.

"Your parents must have been really proud of you, huh? Getting into such an elite arts highschool and going on to become a top singer on platinum soundtracks?" He had his eyes on her as nonchalantly as possible, but he felt the shift in her energy immediately upon his question. She hid it well, and anyone else would have missed it, but he knew. There was something behind this.

She just shrugged her shoulders and moved her eyes back to the soufflé. "Not everyone cares that much about the arts." She was trying to throw it away, but he didn't want to let it go that quickly.

"Really? Even for people who don't understand or care about the arts, getting into that school at thirteen is a big deal; and not cheap either. Not to mention, it involved you moving to another country. How could your parents not have had an opinion on that?"

He saw her shift in her chair and that forcefield of hers was making it's presence known again.

"I paid for the school myself." She took a sip of her coffee.

Gabe was confused. "Care to elaborate on that?" he asked her. "How does a thirteen year old pay for an arts school?"

She smiled shyly, and leaned back in her chair. "Do you remember the movie "Chancing Tomorrow"?" she asked him.

"I certainly remember the name. I never saw it, but it's one of the more famous movies. In fact, Lawerence had wanted me to come to the premier of that in LA, but I was on a mission and couldn't go. For some reason, I never saw that one. But even when I got back, that movie was still the talk of the town. Won a lot of Oscars as I remember." Gabe's mind began to click and he started to put it together. He leaned back in his chair. "The biggest talking point about that movie, as I recall, was the performance of a twelve year old girl who was, apparently, phenomenal. In fact, I believe that little girl was the youngest actress ever to win an Oscar for best actress." Gabe smiled proudly at her. "That was you, wasn't it?"

"Yes, it was," she said humbly. She leaned forward and took another sip of her coffee, then continued. "Lawrence made sure my contract was top notch, and in so doing, he secured my financial future."

Gabe was intrigued. He had known Lawrence his whole life, and did not remember him ever getting involved on behalf of anyone contract wise. He wondered why he did with Kayla.

"That was very generous of him. He doesn't do that with everyone," Gabe said.

"He is a good man," Kayla said simply as she picked up her spoon for another dip into the soufflé.

Gabe put down his coffee cup, wondering how he could keep prying into this without seeing those defenses going off in her eyes again.

"So, that's how you met Lawrence?" He took note of the distinct pause she took before she answered his question with that deflecting humor of hers.

"Well, it would be hard to be in one of his movies without him noticing," She laughed, and moved on, as is what she does when she wishes to avoid something. Gabe found that interesting. "Anyway, after the movie came out, Lawrence pulled some strings and I got into Interlochen. So I went back to Switzerland."

Gabe caught that. "Back? You were there before that time?"

She looked a little flustered, and that definitely had his attention. "Yes, I moved there when I was little." She reached for her champagne. Gabe could feel a pulse under that…there was something of importance here that she didn't want known. He had to walk a line…the last thing he wanted to do was allow her defenses up again.

He lightened the tone and reached for another bite. "So are your parents still in Switzerland?"

Kayla paused again and he could feel her misdirection before she even began. "I've been talking far too much. I would much rather hear about your parents," she said with a smile.

He took note of her boundaries around knowledge regarding her parents, and let it lie; for now. Perhaps following that line of questioning with Lawrence might be a better idea. He smiled and followed her lead.

"My parents were great, actually. They were very loving; to each other as well as to us," he said.

"Your father passed as well?" she asked.

Gabe nodded his head. "Yes. My mother, when I was a boy as you know, and my father when I was seventeen."

She had a very sincere look of empathy in her eyes. "I'm sorry Gabe. That's hard." He saw something deeper behind that. He didn't know what, but he trusted what he felt.

"Yes it is." He leaned forward. "The hardest thing about it is to resist the temptation to close off and retreat into yourself as a result." He looked into her eyes. "It's easy, when you…hurt as a child, to convince yourself you have to hold yourself up, and not allow anyone else in." He saw her lower her gaze in an attempt to shield herself from allowing him to see the emotion he just pinched in her. "It's important to give yourself permission to learn there is another way."

He knew she heard him, and he felt her trying to block his words; but he was pretty sure they landed anyway. He was piecing it together now. He didn't know the details, but he knew now that the key to understanding this woman was not her life after she met Lawrence and started her career…it's what happened before that. He would figure it out, he just needed time.

It wasn't until Antonio came back in the private room, offering them their third cup of coffee, that Gabe realized how late it was…or early. It was almost 4:45am. Niether of them could believe so much time had gone by. Antonio was amazing about it, downplaying his need to stay their so late in order not to interrupt them. He claimed he had book keeping to catch up on anyway, though Gabe was pretty sure Antonio simply did not want to kick them out. He was a good man, and Gabe was grateful.

As Gabe walked her back to the parking garage where her car was parked, he couldn't help but keep his body close to her, though he resisted his very deep desire to hold her hand. She was relaxed with him and he didn't want to make any move that might have her questioning him, or her feelings for him. He knew she had them, and he knew she was still trying to fight them.

The streets were empty and quiet, and their conversation, as well as the clicking of her heels on the sidewalk, were the only sounds that could be heard as they walked together. It was peaceful. Everything about being with her was…amazing to him.

They made their way to the parking garage, and up ahead of them, he could see her rental car coming into view. He knew they were close to the end of the walk and his time with her tonight. There was so much he still wanted to say, about Vail, about his feelings for her, about his desire to see her again…but how to bring it up with her was always a question mark. But he needed to. He looked at his watch.

"You know, (as someone wise once tought me), the details are important; technically, it is not this evening anymore," he said with a slight smile.

She smirked at him. "Damn…You're using that against me?"

He laughed, "No, not *against* you. But there are a few things that I think need to be talked about." He thought for a moment about how best to say it. "I need you to know; it was not my intention…when I offered you the room; I did not mean for that to happen...and I feel badly that I wasn't strong enough to stop it. I hate to think that… maybe you ran from me the next morning because you thought that I… planned that."

She shook her head. "No, Gabe. I know that. I didn't feel under any pressure from you, and I certainly did not see that as the price for the room you offered. I never would have followed you up there if I had thought that in any way. I knew you were not like that."

He was relieved to hear her say that out loud, though he already knew it to be true. Still, he felt like it was the best way to get the conversation started. He took a breath.

"So…why did you run?" he asked softly. She stayed quiet for the last few steps, then they stopped in front of her car. He faced her, waiting for her response. He could feel her struggle with it.

"Kayla, just talk to me, please. I would really like to know what happened with you," he said.

She looked up at him, still very uneasy with how to answer him. "It doesn't matter. You wouldn't believe me anyway, so let's just…let it be."

He was not going to do that. "It does matter. And what makes you think I wouldn't believe you? If there is one thing I have learned about you, it's that you are incredibly honest. I know your tactics by now." He smiled at her surprise. "If there is something you don't want me to know, you just avoid it…skillfully, or, you go quiet…but you don't lie. Please tell me."

She released a breath and spoke in a tone that almost seemed to be challenging rather than revealing. "I just…I don't do things like that. I've never done something like that."

It seemed so obvious to him, "I know that," he said.

She looked at him in complete surprise. "What do you mean you know that?" she asked him bewildered.

Gabe couldn't help but smile at her confusion, and he searched for a way to explain it to her.

"Kayla, I have been with many women. I have had my share of one night stands and meaningless flings; that night in Vail was neither." He took a breath. "I can't explain what that night was…but it was… powerful, and amazing…and…important to me…and I think you know that." He saw her breath escape her and her heart rate increase. "My only regret is that my…inability to stop myself that night may have given you the perfect excuse to convince yourself that what happened between us was not…significant. It was." He saw a thin opening in the defenses behind her eyes…a longing…for him. "You are important to me. So, before you get in your car and drive away, you need to know… I would like to see you again. I would like to see you stop running from me. I would very much like to have the chance to gain your trust and get to know you better. I would also like you to know, that a really big part of me desperately wants to kiss you before you drive away tonight…but I am not going to, because I want you to know that I meant what I said; and also, because I know from experience that it's really, *really* hard to stop kissing you once I start." He smiled at her and took a small step backwards.

She couldn't help but smile. "You know, your willingness to let me go has a big pull on me."

"I'm *not* willing to let you go. Just willing to wait as long as it takes for you to trust me. Or at least, for you to admit that you trust me." He saw the smile she tried to hide. He lightened his tone. "I'm taking a big chance here. History has proven that you have a tendency to be a flight risk."

She laughed as Gabe stepped back a little further to let her go.

There was a big part of him that did not want to see her drive away. He did not want her sleeping in any bed tonight that wasn't his. He knew it was critical to let her go, but he desperately didn't want to. Before she stepped in her car, he spoke.

"Kayla," she looked up at him and he took a moment, holding her gaze, before he spoke. "Take a chance on me," he said.

Chapter Eight
And So It Begins

By the time he pulled up into his driveway, the sun was already shining brightly in the sky. The birds were chirping and the soft California breeze whispered over the top of his hair as he got out of his car. He closed the car door and casually leaned back against it, while taking in the panorama of Los Angeles below him. For a man who disliked LA, he found it funny that the smile on his face and the gratitude in his heart could be, in any way, connected to that city…but they were.

He held his phone in his hand, debating about texting her. He wanted to, no question. He had wanted to ever since she drove away from the parking garage, but he was trying to restrain himself. If there was a way to convince himself it was simply the protective side of him wanting to make sure she got to her hotel safely, maybe he could justify it; but he knew it was more than that. He missed her…again. Her presence within him was so resounding, and so deeply vibrant, it was impossible not to feel empty when she wasn't by his side. His longing to connect with her one more time before his head hit the pillow overroad his self established test of strength, so he texted her.

Thank you again for last night. Betty was right you know…you do work miracles. I had three cups of coffee, and I actually enjoyed a Hollywood celebration, very much…

He hit send. Several seconds later, he saw she was texting back, and was astounded at how good it felt to see those little dots moving on his phone. She took a while to respond and Gabe was pretty sure she was censoring what she should say. He couldn't help but smile at her never ending attempts to control her interactions with him.

Her message came in.

Thank you as well. And don't worry about the 'enjoying Hollywood' part…I'm sure it's just the caffeine messing with your brain…I have no doubt you will snap out of it.

He laughed. It was clever…but the more she tried to buffer herself from him, the more he could see through it. He couldn't resist it and he texted back.

No snapping out of this one. I'm all in now.

She took several moments this time before she texted back, but he saw the little dots finally start to blink, and found himself curious how she would deflect this one.

Well, good coffee will do that to you.

He laughed again, but he couldn't let that lie either.

I'm not talking about the coffee…

He was well aware she knew that, but it was important to him to remind her of it anyway. She didn't respond, and he knew he had sparked that fear in her again, so he texted one more time to help ease her back.

Sleep well.

After a moment, her message came in.

You too Gabe.

He smiled and lowered his phone, looking back out over the city, breathing in the feeling of peace that was all around him. He couldn't have been standing there more than two minutes when his phone rang. When he saw no caller ID, he had a sinking suspicion it might be Betty. He always instructed everyone he's done security with to remove the caller ID when calling from their landlines, and who else would be calling this early? Only someone who knew he was awake… who had a view of his driveway, and who might have a vested interest in how last night went. He answered.

"Hello?"

"Just getting home Gabe?" Lawrence's voice came over the line, and Gabe had to admit, it caught him a little off guard. He instinctively straightened up, which a very distant part of himself found comical.

"Lawrence; is this a coincidence, or have you been waiting up all night to see when I got back?" Gabe asked with a flare of humor.

He could hear a chuckle on the line. "It is actually a coincidence. Betty and I are sitting here on the upper front balcony having our morning coffee, and we couldn't help but notice your bright red car pulling in the driveway; and also that you seem to be wearing the same suit you had on last night. Betty suggested the phone call. Personally, I thought it might be a better idea to just grab my rifle and fire a couple warning shots instead, but Betty frowned on that idea." Lawrence chuckled again.

"Well, considering your piss poor aim, I'm glad Betty won that argument," Gabe said humorously.

He knew Lawrence had been kidding, but he was very aware that, for whatever reason, Kayla was…personal for him. She was personal for Gabe as well, and he wanted to make sure Lawrence understood that.

"Since you're up, Lawrence, can I come over and talk to you for a minute?" Gabe asked.

He could hear Lawrence getting up as he answered. "Yes. Door's open."

When Gabe entered the front hallway, he could hear Betty rustling around in the kitchen.

"Hi Betty, it's me," he said as he closed their front door.

"Come on in Gabe," Betty called to him.

When he walked in the kitchen, Betty turned from the dishes she was putting in the dishwasher and faced him with a smile.

"Hello darling. How did you enjoy the show?" she asked as she dried her hands with a dish towel.

Gabe smiled. "It was amazing," he answered.

Betty's face beamed with joy. "Kayla is fantastic, isn't she?" she asked.

Gabe knew he couldn't hide his feelings from Betty. He was pretty sure she already knew anyway. "In more ways than one, Betty."

She smiled at him. "You have no idea," she said.

Gabe found that curious. "What do you mean?"

She took a breath and seemed to get a bit more serious than she normally does. "Gabe, I'm a hard woman to impress." She crossed over to him with a very real, and humble energy. "I'm well aware that Lawrence and I have a bit of a birds eye view of the world, and our position in this life has given us a unique perspective. I've seen a lot of good in this world….and a lot of bad. But Kayla? She is something special."

"I know that," Gabe said. Betty looked in his eyes as if searching for something in them. When she found it, she smiled and her energy returned to that normal cheerful demeanor of hers.

"Lawrence is in his back office. He said to send you right in," she said as she went back to her dishes.

Gabe found that intriguing. Meeting with Lawrence in his back office was usually reserved for those very rare occasions when a secure discussion could not take place at Saxton Security. It was not the normal room for them to meet in unless the discussion was of the upmost importance and Lawrence wanted to ensure the privacy of it.

Betty called over her shoulder as she placed the last of the dishes on the rack. "Lower level, behind the back living room."

Gabe knew that. He remembered it well. Because of the incredibly sensitive work he had engaged in with Lawrence over the years, they had taken a great deal of care in creating that hidden back office so that the information in that room was profoundly protected. Much of the critical evidence that they had collected (and used) over the years was stored in that secure room; as well as back up copies of everything in each of the Saxton homes. It was a team effort between Gabe, his brothers and Lawrence, in the mission they had started so many years ago.

The door was open, and Gabe knocked as he walked in.

Lawrence was standing behind his desk, organizing some papers in one of the many folders in front of him.

"Come on in Gabe," he said.

Gabe closed the door behind him and walked in. There was a little bit of tension in the air, he could feel it right away, but he was unsure if it was coming from Lawrence or his own unease. He had never felt this with Lawrence before, but then again, the subject matter between them had never been Kayla. Now it was.

He took a breath. "Lawrence," he began, but Lawrence raised his hand softly and cut him off.

"Let me stop you, Gabe." Lawrence looked up at him and held his gaze for a moment, then continued. "I'm not her father, and even if I was, she is a grown woman, and you are a grown man. It shouldn't be any of my business."

Gabe spoke, "…and yet it is."

Lawrence acknowledged the truth in that. "…and yet it is," he said.

Gabe stepped forward. "Lawrence, she is important to me. I need you to know that." Even Gabe was unprepared for the wave of emotion that accompanied his statement, but it was there none-the-less.

Lawrence sat down in his big chair behind the desk and gestured for Gabe to sit in the seat across from him, which he did.

"I gathered that. Your brothers told me about Vail," he added. When he saw Gabe shift uncomfortably in his seat, he continued. "They didn't mean to. When they saw her picture it came out before they knew…my position in this. Then I forced out the rest of the story from them." Lawrence still had his eyes on Gabe, scanning him, but Gabe did not hesitate.

"I apologize that you didn't hear it from me," he said. The look on Lawrence's face lighten a bit.

"It's ok, like I said, it shouldn't be any of my business, and…you did come right over this morning, which I assume was to broach the subject."

Gabe wanted to make sure Lawrence was hearing him. "I really feel for her. I mean it."

"I know. Not only from your brothers, who went out of their way to drive that point home once they saw my reaction, but also Betty. I trust my wife. She told me she saw something in how you looked at Kayla, that had her convinced you truly care for her."

Gabe did not want to hide that fact from Lawrence in any way. He wanted him to know it. "I more than care for her."

Gabe saw a profound smile behind Lawrence's gaze, before he shifted in his chair and changed his tone.

"Good," he said.

"Lawrence...who is she to you?" Gabe asked.

Lawrence took a breath, still seaming to scan him with his eyes.

"Tell me what she told you, Gabe," he asked him.

Gabe let out a breath and shook his head. "Not much. She is very tightlipped about herself. I'm sensing there is a story there about her parents, but that one was hard to crack. Do you know?"

There was a depth in Lawrence's eyes, but reading him was difficult.

"Yes I do," he answered simply.

"I would like to know. It's important to me to understand her," Gabe said.

Lawrence took a moment and leaned forward. "Gabe, there are precious few people in this world that Kayla trusts; I am one of them. I can not betray that trust; and I won't, not even to you. As much as I am important to her, that one will walk away from anyone who has wronged her, and if I shared things about her with you that she did not want me to, she would walk away from me too. I cannot. What I can do, is encourage her to trust you." Lawrence leaned back in his chair again. "Besides, I have no doubt, with your...intuition and observation skills, you will be able to piece together what you need to know."

Gabe had a mixed reaction to that; on the one hand, it was frustrating as hell to be sitting across from the man who had the answers he so badly wanted, but on the other, he admired greatly Lawrence's steadfast resolve to protect her.

"Ok. I respect that. It makes it harder, but when something is important to me, like this is, I will figure it out. All I need is time," Gabe answered.

Lawrence changed the energy slightly. "Good, because time is exactly what I need your help with."

Gabe looked at him questioningly. "What do you mean?"

Lawrence got very serious, and Gabe had an instant recognition that this discussion was now about to be significantly consequential.

"I don't want her going back to Switzerland. I need her here; and I can't tell her why," Lawrence said.

Gabe leaned back trying to ascertain the reason behind the tone with which he said that.

"Why?" Gabe asked, knowing the answer was not going to be because he missed her.

Lawrence finally spoke. "There is chatter Gabe, and I'm seeing some quiet chess pieces being moved into positions that have me… concerned. I think the remnants of the snake we have been chopping up for so long are gathering to bite back."

Gabe knew exactly what he was saying, and he could feel his body ice with the understanding of it.

"Who?" he asked.

"That's just it. I'm not exactly sure. When we made the decision to start this and break up that ring, we took down a lot of people; politicians, commissioners, generals, entertainers, and billionaires; all people of tremendous power. We knew what we were doing when we started this, and what we have done has been extraordinary; but power hungry people like this…they don't forget, and they always try to strike back."

"What has your nerves up, Lawrence?" Gabe asked.

"Matthew Edson."

That was not the name Gabe was expecting to hear. "What? Matthew? Why?" Gabe asked.

Lawrence took a beat. "I heard from Andy that Matthew separated from your security company recently, is that correct?"

That hadn't sat well with Gabe either. "Yes, he did. Without so much as a word to me. That caught my attention too, but I'm not understanding why it caught yours?" Gabe looked closer at Lawrence. There was a penitent look in his eye, and it stirred up only one unnerving thought in Gabe's mind.

Gabe leaned forward in complete disbelief that he found himself having to ask his next question. "Does Matthew know about the Livy Ann missions?"

Lawrence took a long moment to answer the question, and Gabe could not quite figure out what was going on in his mind. Lawrence took a breath before he spoke.

"Yes, he does. Not in detail, and none of the missions past the first one. But he did know about that one, and it is my fault that he does," he admitted.

Gabe was totally surprised to hear it. It was more than unusual for Gabe to be in the dark about anything regarding those missions; after all, it had pretty much been his entire careers work.

"Why?" Gabe asked.

Lawrence leaned back in his chair, and took a long moment to begin his explanation.

"Gabe, when your mother stumbled onto this entire mess, I felt responsible for it. I was the one who introduced her to Jacob Sykes. I had no idea the monster that man was. I didn't think he was anything more than a billionaire who wanted to invest in her tour and hobnob with A-list entertainers." Gabe could see the overbearing discomfort swirl up in Lawrence as he recalled the memory of it. Lawrence let out a strained breath as he continued with the recollection that still haunted him to this day. "I will never forget what I heard in your mother's voice when she called me that night to tell me what she had seen in his home. The only phone call worse than that one, was when I was told they found her car in the ocean at the bottom of the cliff." Lawrence's voice cracked with emotion, and Gabe felt the wave of pain that always filled his heart when recalling that dreadful night. Lawrence gathered himself somewhat and continued. "I knew Jacob had done it; even before the police investigation started raising all the unanswered questions about the car accident…I knew it was Jacob who killed her, and I knew why."

Gabe let the stillness sit for a moment before he spoke. "Lawrence, her death was not your fault," Gabe said.

"Whether it was, or it wasn't, doesn't change the fact that it *felt* like it was." Gabe had only seen tears in Lawrence's eyes when this topic was being discussed. It just about killed him and Gabe knew that. Lawrence cleared the emotion and continued. "That feeling…the guilt I carried about that…I could not carry that again."

Gabe knew what he was saying. "Livy Ann," Gabe said. Lawrence nodded, but did not speak, so Gabe did. "Lawrence, her death was not your fault either. Any one of us would have given our lives for her if we could have. We tried. All of us. After we took down Jacob, both teams focused like a laser beam on trying to save her. It couldn't be done. You and I both know it. These men were never going to let her live, not after what she did to them." Gabe always spoke with honor and gratitude when he mentioned the girl that was lost that night. Little Livy Ann, the six year old that escaped Jacob Sykes and, somehow, had the wisdom to bring with her a small bag of evidence from his home…that small bag was the key they needed to bring down the son of a bitch. Without her, they never would have been able to get him, and they always honored her memory with every additional take down from that point forward.

Gabe shook his head in awe as he spoke. "How she knew to grab those video tapes before she jumped out of the window…" Gabe was at a loss for words. "Her sacrifice saved all the women and under aged girls in that house…not to mention was the beginning to taking down the entire trafficking ring. With every mission we did and every arrest we made after that, we honored her. You do not need to carry any guilt for Livy Ann."

Lawrence spoke again. "I wanted to do more than make plans to honor her memory…that is why I called Matthew that night. I brought Matthew in thinking he could use his resources at the FBI to find Livy Ann. I had to try." Lawrence looked at Gabe who was listening intently. "I should have told you he knew. I guess, once it was clear Livy Ann could not be saved, I overlooked the detail of Matthew's knowledge on the subject, and I never informed you that Mathew knew it was us behind the take down of Jacob Sykes."

Gabe stayed quiet for a moment longer. He couldn't blame Lawrence for trying. Gabe nodded his head to offer his understanding of Lawrence's explanation.

"OK. Are you thinking that Matthew is somehow getting involved with the scattered traffickers who are trying to regain their footing and start up the ring again?" Gabe asked.

"Whether voluntary or involuntary…I have to admit, I'm having some concerns about him." Lawrence answered.

"Can you be more specific as to why you are concerned?" Gabe asked.

Lawrence leaned forward on his desk. "As soon as his campaign was over, his communication with me dropped off the map. Even returned phone calls began coming in from his secretary, not him. Just before he got sworn in as Governor, I learned from a very good friend at JPMorgen that he moved all of his accounts and ended his banking association with them. He has now ended his long time working relationship with Saxton Security, and transferred all of his security details to an unknown security firm; of which there are very few records of existence except for an incorporation just before he signed with them. I'm assuming his communication with you has dropped out just as much, since you were surprised at his departure from your security team?"

Lawrence was right…these things were not painting a good picture.

"Yes. He has not reached out at all…since winning the election," Gabe answered, and then got up to allow the unease flowing through him to have a release. He crossed behind the chair he had been sitting in, leaning on it as he allowed the various thoughts to spin through his mind.

Lawrence spoke again. "There's one more piece."

Gabe looked at him. "What is it?" he asked.

Lawrence let out a breath. "I don't know if it's true, but I am catching wind that Jacob Sykes is being considered for a prison transfer."

Gabe straightened up at that.

Lawrence continued. "The request hasn't been made official yet, but if it does, and it gets granted…"

Gabe finished the sentence. "Then it is the perfect opportunity for an organized escape."

"If he does, he is coming after us. No question," Lawrence added.

"Getting to you, or us, would be extremely difficult for him," Gabe said.

"I know. That is why I am concerned about Kayla," Lawrence said. "You know how these men work. If they can't get to me, they will get to someone close to me. It's no secret in this town that I have watched over Kayla's career in a way much more prevalent than any of my other artists. It wouldn't take them long to realize she could be used to get to me. They wouldn't think twice about it."

Gabe felt a piercing cold ice through him at the thought of Kayla being swept up in any of this. He could never allow that to happen.

"If she is in Switzerland without protection, they could grab her easily," Gabe said. "That is not going to happen. I will not allow that to happen."

Lawrence looked at Gabe and leaned back in his chair. "The meeting you were supposed to have with your brothers' last night was with me. I want Saxton Security on her, but now…I'm in a bit of a bind here…your involvement with her makes this a little…tricky. I know her, Gabe…she would not be ok with knowing I am having discussions with you behind her back about her security, and she most certainly would…question your true reasons for being with her if she found out I hired you to protect her."

Gabe took a breath then looked at Lawrence. "Then don't. Take Saxton Security off of her and let me do it on my own, by my choice. Put Andy and Nick on Matthew instead…on anyone who pops up on the radar as far as the Livy Ann Missions and any payback resulting from those. I'll watch Kayla, you guys watch everyone else. If anything looks like it's going to intersect, we discuss it, and then take out the threat before Kayla is in any danger."

Lawrence looked at him. "Kayla tends to be unpredictable when her…defenses are up. There are a number of reasons why she would admittedly object to being watched over…this is not something she would be comfortable with."

"I know." Gabe let out a breath and placed his hands on the back of the chair in front of him as he thought. "First of all, let's make one thing very clear; this is not a job for me. Her protection is now my responsibility by my choice. I am not a hired gun."

Lawrence nodded his head. "Agreed."

Gabe spoke after a moment. "The first hurdle we need to get over is getting her to stay here. Any thoughts?"

Lawrence leaned forward again on his desk. "The only thing I can think of, that has a chance of working, is to give her another title song to record…and try to find excuses why it has to be recorded here."

"Do you think that will work?" Gabe asked.

Lawrence didn't look convinced. "I don't know. I need to find a song or a project that is irresistible to her so she can't say no."

"Any ideas?" Gabe asked.

Lawrence let out a breath. "Not yet."

"Kayla, just wear the pink and black sundress. Come on, you are stalling and we both know it." Devin was shouting over his shoulder from the living room of her hotel suite. He was right, she knew she was, but she couldn't help it. The butterflies flowing through her were making her feel like she should just get in the car and head to the airport instead. But she promised Lawrence…and Gabe; that was the problem…Gabe. Her heart fluttered again at the thought of him; the never ending thoughts of him. She was completely nervous to see him again…her feelings for him were thundering through her, and her inability to quash them was unnerving. She had not been able to get him out of her head since…well, since she looked up and saw his face in the cafeteria.

She sat on the edge of the bed unsure how to handle any of it. She still had her teeshirt and sweatpants on, and was having a hard time finding the strength to get herself together. All she wanted to do was hide under the covers.

"Kayla? That's it, I'm coming in." Devin walked in and Kayla looked up at him. He crossed his arms and stared at her. "You're pathetic, you know that, right?" he said to her.

She looked at him. "Devin, I can't do this. Go without me and just say I was too tired. That's not a lie, I didn't really sleep today."

Devin was not having it, as he crossed over to her. "Of course you didn't sleep. You were up all night with a gorgeous, incredible, fabulous man, who is clearly head over heels for you, and you couldn't sleep when you had the chance today because you are obviously head over heels for him too; but you can't admit it to yourself, so you are wearing yourself out trying to fight it." He plopped down next to her. "You know, for someone who is so smart, you are an absolute idiot."

Kayla laughed. "Kill me now," she said.

Devin picked up the dress that was laying on the bed. "Let's go. Put it on and face it. We are late already. Those of us who are not yet on Lawrence's favorite list still have to prove ourselves to him; and you making me late doesn't look good!" When she didn't move, he continued. "Kayla, you are making this way too hard for yourself. This is not a high pressure one on one date. It's a big, casual evening grill with Lawrence, Betty, me, Diane, and you know, the man of your dreams. No big deal." Kayla slapped him on the arm as he laughed. "Seriously, this man adores you! You have nothing to be nervous about."

Kayla got up, took the dress and went into the bathroom to change. "I didn't say I was nervous…just tired." She could hear Devin laughing.

"Who do you think you are fooling. Between you and me, I've never seen a man get to you like this. That tells me one thing; you really feel for him. I think you are wasting your time worrying about it my dear. Something tells me, you are in very good hands."

Kayla let out a breath and tried again to push down the rising tide of emotion inside her.

As they turned into Gabe's driveway and headed up the steep

incline, Kayla felt another bolt of nerves shoot through her, but before she could even think about putting the car in reverse and leaving, his front door opened and she saw Gabe come out to greet them. He looked amazing, again, in casual black pants and a white button down shirt.

"I'm sorry, but that man gets finer and finer every time I see him. No wonder you're all fucked up about him," Devin said with a laugh as he opened his door and got out. Kayla heard Gabe greeting Devin as she fidgeted with her purse; stalling for time to catch her breath before she had to face him. She heard a click and looked up to see Gabe opening her door for her and standing there with his hand out to help her out of the car.

"Hi," he said in that sexy voice of his.

She put on her best 'I'm totally fine' smile and reached her hand out to his. When he clasped it she felt that spark ignite in her stomach from his touch and hoped with everything she had that he couldn't tell how much his touch effected her.

"Hi. Sorry we're late," she said with a smile as she stepped out of the car.

"I'm just glad you're here," he said as he looked in her eyes and, once again, took her breath away. "Come on," he said as he led her into his home.

As soon as she walked in, she was amazed at how comfortable she felt. The house was huge, but inviting, with marble floors, high ceilings and large, open rooms. It was warm and cozy, which was surprising considering its vast size and perfectly polished appearance.

Lawrence and Betty crossed over to greet her when she reached the living room, and they hugged her sweetly.

"Hello my dear," Betty said. "Congratulations on last night. You were wonderful." Betty released her as Lawrence hugged her as well.

"Thank you for agreeing to do this one. You were fantastic, as we knew you would be," Lawrence said to her.

"Well, I do love that song." Kayla broke the hug and smiled at Lawrence. Then her eyes found Diane and two men, as well as another woman that she had not met yet. She smiled warmly at Diane, and reached out her hand. "Hello Diane. Nice to see you again. I heard Devin drank you under the table last night." She laughed.

"We did end up calling for rides after that, but it was so much fun. Devin feels like an old friend already," Diane said with a laugh.

"Who you calling old?" Devin added in his humors way.

Lawrence smiled at Devin and shook his hand. "Very good to see you again Devin," he said.

"You too Mr. Rodgers," Devin said politely.

Diane gestured to the man standing by her side who also had a huge smile on his face, and Kayla knew right away was the brother of Gabe.

"Kayla, this is my husband Nick. Nick, this is Kayla." Nick reached his hand out and shook Kayla's sweetly.

"It's so nice to meet you. I've heard so much about you." Kayla instantly liked him. Even though he was a very tall man who could come across intimidating, he had the same kindness Gabe had, not in the same way, but she felt comfortable with him.

Gabe came over and introduced the last man and woman next to him that she had yet to meet. "This is my other brother Andy and his wife Jen."

Andy's smile was equally warm and friendly, as was Jen's. Andy had a very strong but purposefully calm handshake.

"Hello Kayla. So nice to meet you," Andy said.

Jen shook her hand as well. "Hi. You were wonderful last night. We were watching from home," Jen said with a warm smile.

Kayla instantly liked this group she found herself in. They felt like…well, like family; like old friends, just as Diane had said about Devin.

"It's lovely to meet you both. I'm sorry we are late. It took a while to figure out how to avoid the press who were staked out in the lobby. We ended up having to sneak out the back."

"Oh, I know how much you hate the swarm of the press. It's a shame that they so quickly find out where you are staying," Betty said as she sipped her martini.

"Anyone give you any trouble?" Gabe asked.

Kayla laughed it off. "They always give me trouble. They are the main reason I hate doing these things." She tried to keep it light and breezy, but she saw a concerned look in Gabe's eyes. He always seemed to take note of the things that make her uncomfortable so he can find ways to fix them. It was very endearing, but she quickly tried to convince herself otherwise.

Gabe smiled at her. "Drink?" he asked.

"Yes, gin & tonic with -" Gabe cut her off before she could finish her sentence.

"- extra lime. I know." He smiled warmly at her.

"You don't miss a thing, do you?" she asked him with a grin.

He looked confidently at her, "No. I don't," he said.

She averted her gaze before the smile on her face got out of her control, and she saw Lawrence swirl the ice in his drink as he was watching them. When her eyes found his, Lawrence changed the subject, as if, he too, did not want to give away his thoughts.

"So Devin, tell me what's going on with you career wise at the moment," Lawrence said as he gestured to the seating area in the living room.

The evening progressed and time seemed to fly by. The dinner was

wonderful; filled with great conversation and a joyous energy. Kayla
was stunned at how incredibly comfortable she was here. She found
herself laughing and enjoying the discussions (and the company) so
much that there were times when she completely forgot she was in LA.
There was such a feeling of home here…a very distant part of her mind
found it a little unsettling that she could not separate herself and
analyze her enjoyment like she normally would; but she couldn't. She
felt Gabe's strong energy by her side all night long, and she could not
deny how amazing it felt to have him next to her. Being here with
him…it was such a profound feeling…she had never felt this way
before. She found herself not even wanting to try to deny it…which
should have also been unsettling, but the warmth of the energy Gabe
was surrounding her in…it felt like a Heaven on an Earth that used to
be Hell, and, for the moment, she didn't want to protect herself from
enjoying it.

Gabe was sitting on the arm rest of the sofa next to Kayla, laughing
along with everyone else at yet another one of Devin's hysterical
stories. He was recounting his grand, (and unmistakably incorrect)
stage entrance during one of his shows in Switzerland. Apparently, he
had not been paying attention and made his thundering entrance far too
early, disrupting the intimate love scene that was happening on stage.

Devin spoke through his own laughter. "All the eyes in that entire
theater fell on me like a bomb! There I was, in full view on stage, with
no way to cover my mistake," Devin said.

"What did you do?" Diane asked as her laughter broke out.

"What *could* I do? I plastered a big smile on my face, and did the
moonwalk backwards off stage left!" Devin said.

Andy looked at Kayla as the laughter continued. "Did you see it?"
he asked.

"Yes! I was dying laughing. As soon as I got off stage, I suggested he should try to get a window seat for the flight back to the states that he was sure to be on the next day when they fired him for it!" Kayla was laughing so hard she had tears in her eyes.

The joy that was flowing through the room was overtaking all of them, and Gabe was deeply affected at how wonderful he felt in this moment. His house had never felt more like a home than it did tonight. It was funny that it was such a new feeling and yet was so incredibly familiar. His eyes fell on Kayla again as the conversation continued, and he still found himself blown away by what he felt for her. Having her here, with him, with his family and friends…how could he ever go back to the life he had known before her. He couldn't. He knew he couldn't.

He brought his brandy up to his lips and saw that even Lawrence seemed to be enjoying this evening more than anything he had seen in him in a long time. Lawrence met his gaze, and the two exchanged a look that seemed to acknowledge the profound feelings coursing in him about Kayla.

"Can I get you another drink Lawrence?" Gabe asked. Lawrence stood up as he answered.

"Yes, Thank you Gabe," Lawrence said.

"I could use one too," Andy said as he and Lawrence walked with Gabe to the kitchen and the others continued their conversations.

When they got to the kitchen, and were out of earshot from everyone else, Lawrence spoke.

"You know Gabe, I've known you for a long time…I've also known Kayla for a long time…I have never seen either of you quite like I'm seeing you both tonight." There was a look in Lawrence's eyes that was new…he almost looked…bewildered.

Gabe smiled as he poured more whisky into Lawrence's glass.

"The mystified look in your eyes tells me you might just be at the beginning of understanding my own…astonishment about her." Gabe handed Lawrence his glass, and Andy spoke as he poured his own glass of scotch.

"Lawrence, did you ever hear about our great uncle Joe?" Andy asked.

Lawrence smiled brightly, "Your mother talked about him (and your grandfather) all the time. Her twin brother; your uncle Joe, was named after him; and then, when they discovered your mother was in there too, they named her after him as well. Joline always said they both were very intuitive men. I never got the chance to meet either of them, but even I know the stories that have been passed down about your family," Lawrence answered as he sipped his whisky.

Andy put the cap back on the scotch bottle and lifted his own glass. "Dad told me that it was Great Uncle Joe who was the one who coined the phrase 'the boom.' It was his way of describing the unexplainable force that hits a man when his eyes meet the love of his life for the first time. If there was ever undeniable proof that he was right about that, it happened when Kayla looked up at Gabe. Nick and I saw it. Good Lord, we practically *felt* it from across the cafeteria that night in Vail."

Lawrence smiled. "I can still see it," he said.

Andy looked at is brother. "She is amazing, and there is no way any of us will let anything happen to her." Andy lowered his voice slightly as he looked to Lawrence. "Have you figured out how to get her to stay yet?"

Lawrence took another sip and shook his head slightly. "I have a few songs…but I'm not convinced yet. I need something that has that extra special pull on her…I don't think I have it yet."

Gabe filled his own glass with brandy and lifted it to his lips as Devin came in the kitchen with some of the dirty dishes from the living room.

Devin was singing softly out loud as he walked to the sink to place the dishes in it. When Gabe heard him, he lowered his glass back down on the counter in disbelief; as Lawrence and Andy both stared at Devin with the same confused looks on their faces. When Devin turned around, he stopped singing and went quiet trying to ascertain what the looks were about.

Devin had concern on his voice as he spoke. "I'm sorry…did I interrupt something? I was just trying to help clean up."

Gabe was still speechless as were Andy and Lawrence, and the three of them just stared at Devin in bewilderment.

Devin was confused. "OK, umm…I happen to know that the three of you carry guns, and I don't, so it would be great if one of you would start speaking right about now. You are all looking at me like you are about to accuse me of stealing the china or something! What's wrong?"

Gabe found his voice. "How do you know that song?" he asked.

"What song?" Devin asked.

"That song you were just singing. How do you know that?" Lawrence asked him.

Devin finally realized what they were asking him. "Oh that?" Devin laughed in relief, and grabbed his heart. "Sweet Mary and Joseph; you guys had me thinking I was about to be taken out! The way you were all staring at me; my life was flashing before my eyes!"

"Devin, where do you know that song from?" Gabe asked again.

"Kayla. She listens to that song all the time! From the first day I met her, up through the car ride over here tonight! I must have had that thing memorized in the first thirty minutes of our friendship. I swear, it must be the only song that is on her iPod."

"What?" Gabe asked in shock.

Devin looked just as confused as Gabe felt. "That song is her

116

favorite. She loves it. She used to listen to it every night; she said it was the only thing that could help her sleep. She adores it." Devin looked at Lawrence. "I'm surprised you don't know that. You've known her longer than I have."

"I didn't know she still listens to it," Lawrence said.

"*Still?* As sure as the sun will rise, that song is never far from her. She doesn't even know who is singing it, but that voice always makes her feel better. I tried to find out who it was so I could get her the man's album and try to give her some other choices to listen to, but I couldn't find any information about it at all. I don't even know where she got it."

Lawrence looked at Gabe. "I gave it to her, years ago," he said.

Gabe was speechless. Andy looked just as stunned as Gabe felt. Devin politely excused himself and went back into the living room. At long last, Andy broke the silence.

"Wow...I wonder what great uncle Joe would call that?" Andy said before he chugged his scotch.

Gabe saw the smile replace the bewildered look on Lawrence's face. Lawrence took a loaded breath and then spoke.

"I just figured out what to do." He took a chug of his drink and when he lowered his glass, Gabe could still see the wheels turning behind Lawrence's eyes. Lawrence looked at Gabe with a challenge. "...and you're not going to like it, but I think I know how to get her to stay here."

Gabe had a sinking suspicion he knew exactly where Lawrence was going with this, but he didn't hesitate. "If it will get her to stay, I'm all in," Gabe said.

Chapter Nine

Somewhere You

When they walked back in the living room, Kayla noticed a shift in energy. Lawrence was walking with purpose and had that look he gets when his mind is in sharpened focus about something.

Kayla was standing by the big glass doors that led out to the beautifully lit pool and back patio, and her conversation with Jen and Diane seemed to be magically put on hold by the three men who had just entered the room. Gabe had an interesting look on his face as well, and Kayla had a hard time reading it. He almost looked…baffled, which she found odd for a man who always seemed to know everything before it happened. She took a sip of her gin & tonic and looked back to Lawrence.

"You OK Lawrence? You have that…determined look on your face," Kayla said.

Lawrence crossed over to Betty, but directed his attention to Kayla.

"As a matter of fact, there is something I need to speak to you about. There is a project in the works that I would really like your voice on. It's perfect for you and I have a feeling you will love it." Lawrence took a sip of his whisky, but kept his eyes on her.

"What is it?" Kayla asked.

She saw Lawrence reach for his wife's hand as he answered her. "It's a song I gave you a long time ago. It's called 'Somewhere You.' Do you remember it?" he asked her.

Kayla almost had to laugh; *remember it?* That song was practically a part of her very soul. It had been the one constant in a life that had been rocked with turmoil and uphill battles. Of course she remembered it.

"Yes. I know that song well. It's my favorite, actually," she said.

"I want your voice on that," Lawrence said as he waited for her reaction.

Kayla felt a mix of emotions, and she took a moment to phrase what she was thinking.

"Lawrence…that's a very tempting suggestion…and I'm thrilled that you are finally going to use that song for something. It's an extraordinary piece of work, but I have to be honest; that song is so good because of the man's voice who is singing it. Whoever that is… you need *him* to record it, not me. Personally, I can't imagine that song without that voice."

She saw Lawrence smile and look at Gabe, which confused her completely. Gabe had his eyes on her and she was finding it very difficult to understand the look on his face. Lawrence looked back at Kayla.

"I agree, but I want yours on it too. I'm talking about making it a duet," Lawrence said.

A very deep seeded emotion started to rise up in her stomach. She did not understand it, but for some reason her eyes locked on Gabe as she asked her next question. Even before she spoke, she had the very distinct feeling something profound was about to be revealed to her… and it was.

"Who's voice is that?" she asked, almost scared to hear the response.

Gabe took a breath and then he answered her. "Mine," he said.

Kayla felt all the air escape her lungs, and she felt the impossibility of getting any more air back in them to keep breathing. She almost dropped her glass on the floor. Somehow she found her voice after a few moments of silence.

"What?" she asked.

Everyone else in the room seemed to fade away and all she could see was Gabe standing across the room from her. *How could that be possible? How in the world could that be possible?*

Gabe took a deep breath, as if giving her time to brace herself again before he spoke.

"That was me. I recorded that. We never released it, but Lawrence had a copy of it," Gabe said as he kept his eyes softly on hers in an attempt to read what was going on inside her, which she desperately did not want him to see.

All Kayla could do was look at Lawrence, as if he could undo the shock that was racing through her.

Lawrence smiled at her. "He not only sang it, my dear. Gabe wrote it," he said.

Kayla could feel a few tears welling up in her eyes from the surge of feelings thundering through her and she did not like being that vulnerable. She tried to push them back down, but she knew she was losing that battle. Somehow she found what little of her voice was available to her.

"Would you excuse me for a minute? I just need a little air." Kayla turned around and opened the glass door she was in front of and slipped outside to separate herself from everyone. It was not the smoothest exit and she wished she could have covered herself better than that, but sometimes just getting away is the most important thing and it doesn't matter how it looks. She walked quickly to the far side of the patio, behind the pool and grabbed the railing for support. She tried to take a deep breath of night air, but it felt as if her lungs were not even there anymore. She looked up to the stars, hoping the tears would dry up before they fell from her eyes. She heard the door open and softly close and a moment later could hear Gabe's shoes on the sandstone as he crossed over to her.

He leaned against the railing next to her and just stood there with her in silence for several moments before he said anything.

"Years before I was born, my grandfather started that song. He began writing it after his wife passed away. He died not much longer after that, before he finished it. He only wrote the first verse. There's was quite an amazing love story from what I've been told, and it always made a big impression on me. As I grew up, and discovered the song, I wondered why my mother never picked it up. Andy told me she didn't feel like it was hers to finish. For some reason, I did." Gabe let the silence fill the air again as if he knew she needed another moment before she could find her voice; which she still couldn't, so Gabe continued. "I wrote the rest of it and recorded it in the studio I still have downstairs. Lawrence loved it. He wanted to release it."

Kayla finally found her breath and was fighting to keep the emotion out of her voice as much as possible.

"Why didn't you? You're amazing. That song is…" her voice left her again.

"I felt the same way about it; but I had a choice to make. I chose the Marines, and took on an array of missions that were extremely important to me. I made the right choice…*then,*" he said. She could feel him looking at her, waiting for her to turn her eyes to him. "Kayla…," he said softly. Finally she turned to look in his eyes. "What is it?" he asked her.

"I just…I can't believe that song is you. You have been singing to me my entire life…" she hated that the tears were spilling over her eyes. She didn't even know why there was so much emotion invested in this, and she desperately did not want him to see it, but she could do nothing to hide it from him.

His energy was so soft and so warm. His eyes were almost breathing life back into her even as she felt her strength fading.

She tried to wipe away the tears on her cheeks and divert any attention from the emotions running through her.

"I'm sorry. I'm just really tired," she said as she tried to laugh it off, but it didn't quite work.

"Yeah…it's exhausting trying not to feel," he said softly. She lowered her head trying one last time to hide herself from him, but he did not take his eyes off of her. He gave it a moment and then he very gently reached out to her, and drew her into him, wrapping his arms around her protectively. She felt her body fold into him, almost instinctively, and she lost herself in his embrace.

God, it felt so good to hold her again; to have her in his arms. If he had the power to stop the world and freeze this moment he would have done so in a heartbeat. These few moments when she allowed herself to be comforted by him, to need him…it filled him with such a sense of life and purpose that he was overcome with the power of it. This woman meant everything to him, that was undeniable, and even if he didn't understand why his feelings for her were so incredibly strong so quickly, it didn't matter. He had her here, in his home, in his life, and he would not let go of her. He couldn't. There was something here that was beyond them both; and he was thankful to his core for it.

She had been discreetly wiping away her tears as he held her, still doing everything she could to hide her emotions from him, though he was very aware of them. After several moments, he felt her stir and knew her defenses were regaining themselves. She lifted her head off his shoulder and straightened up. He released her, though he did not move his body away from her; that was too much to ask.

She smiled and let out a little laugh. "I'm sorry. I'm being so stupid. I'm just really tired. I still haven't gone to bed. Someone kept me up all night with coffee and chocolate." She smiled at him and he couldn't help but smile back.

"Well, I'm sorry you're tired, but I have to admit, I have no regrets about that," he said softly. He let the air around her settle before he continued. "Do this with me. Record this song with me," he pleaded.

She took a deep breath, as if getting the air back in her lungs had been a problem until that moment. He knew what her hesitation was. He didn't know how he new, but he felt it. He was understanding now, that she backs away when she can't control her emotional reaction to something. Vulnerability was not easy for her and her knee-jerk response is to block it until she feels in control again. He had to admit to himself, he understood that completely. Being in control was a huge part of his makeup as well.

What was even more intriguing to him was how much he wanted to do this with her. This had become much more than simply a tool to get her to stay…there was a magic around the idea of recording this song…with her. Once he made the choice all those years ago to be a Raider, it never occurred to him that this side of him would ever show itself again. He never wanted it to…until tonight. It wasn't the spotlight of it; not at all. He actually hated the idea of the attention it would bring to himself; but that was a significantly small price to pay for being with this woman. He needed her, and he knew that. For whatever reason, this fork in the road where he now found himself; it was not an accident. Somehow, he knew that too.

"You know, I truly believe that everything happens for a reason. How unlikely was all of this?" he said to her. He leaned in, "Let's do this. Do this with me," he said again.

He saw her smile a little. "I thought you hated Hollywood. You know doing this will put you right in the middle of it. You really want that?" she asked him with clear warning in her tone.

Gabe didn't flinch. "I would put myself smack dab in the middle of

Hell itself to be with you; without question and without hesitation." He surprised himself that he actually admitted that out loud to her, but he was glad he did. It got through, and he saw her breathe that in. It took every ounce of strength he had not to kiss her right then and there, but he somehow found the will to hold himself back (just barely.) He wasn't sure how much longer he would have the strength to do so.

She smiled warmly at him. "You sure about that?" she asked him.

"Absolutely," he said. He allowed a few more moments of silence between them; waiting for her last defenses to settle. "Say yes...do this with me."

She took a long moment, and then he saw her relinquish her last bit of resistance. "OK, Hell it is then. Good thing I've been there before," she chuckled a little as she said that.

"Well, this time, you are going to have me by your side. It might even be fun," Gabe said. He gestured out to the city below them. "We'll set the place on fire. We will ignite a shitstorm, and then walk away and leave Hollywood burning." He laughed.

"Oh, that part does sound like fun," she laughed as well.

Gabe heard the glass door open and looked over and saw Lawrence hesitating by the door. Gabe nodded his head and gestured for Lawrence to wait, then Gabe looked back at Kayla. He scanned her and felt like she had gotten her strength back. He reached for her hand and she folded hers into his; God, he loved how that felt.

"Come on," he said as he led her back into his home.

By the time they got back into the living room, Lawrence had crossed back to join his wife by the sofa, and Devin was standing by the glass door talking with Diane. Lawrence looked up to Kayla.

"Well? What do you say?" he asked her.

She took a breath and answered him. "OK. Let's do it."

Lawrence smiled, and behind that, Gabe saw clearly the look of relief that swept over his face. When his eyes found Gabe, he understood the subtle nod from him that demonstrated his overwhelming gratitude.

"That's great," Lawrence said. "This is just…perfect."

Betty was equally thrilled with the whole idea. "I am so excited about this. Kayla, I have a feeling this is going to be the best thing you have ever done!"

Lawrence took a final swig of his whisky, then looked up to both of them. "May I suggest; and knowing Kayla's taste the way I do, I think she will agree, that you record it here; in your studio downstairs, Gabe." Lawrence looked to Kayla. "Gabe has the only analog studio left in the city. One of the benefits of having not used it for years and therefore not upgrading to digital like everyone else did. The deep warm quality of the analog would be the perfect touch for this song," he said.

Gabe looked at Kayla and instantly knew Lawrence had struck a bit of brilliance with that. It pulled her; he saw it, and heard it in her voice as she spoke.

"Oh, I *love* the sound of analog," she said, and then looked at Gabe. "You really have an analog studio downstairs?" She asked him.

He smiled. "Yes I do. I haven't used it in years, so I will need your help with it, but it's sitting there, ready to go."

Lawrence stood with an even deeper look of accomplishment on his face.

"Then it's settled. Kayla, I will ask Tommy to produce this one, and Gary to engineer. You have worked with both of them before, they are good guys, and those projects you guys have done together in the past have always turned out great." Lawrence reached for his wife as she stood. Then he crossed over to Kayla. "I'm so glad you said yes to this, my dear. Thank you." He hugged her sweetly, as did Betty.

Lawrence reached out to shake Gabe's hand. "Thank you Gabe. After twenty years, you finally agreed to dip your toe in the music world." He laughed as he shook his hand. "It's about time."

Gabe laughed. "Come on. I'll walk you guys out," he said with a smile.

As he walked away with Lawrence and Betty, he heard Devin whisper to Kayla.

"Didn't I tell you? God works in mysterious ways," Devin said.

Yes, he certainly does, Gabe thought.

When Gabe came back in, Devin and Nick were clearing dishes, Diane, Andy and Jen were talking softly in the living room, and Kayla had fallen asleep on the big sofa. Gabe couldn't help but smile at the sight of her sleeping in his home. He picked up a big blanket and gently draped it over her. He lingered over her longer than necessary, breathing in the sight of her sleeping, then he reluctantly pulled his gaze off of her and picked up a few of the dirty dishes. He headed into the kitchen to join Devin and Nick.

Gabe crossed to the sink where Devin was washing some plates, and set the glasses down he had brought in.

"You don't have to do that Devin," he said.

Devin shrugged his shoulders, "I don't mind at all. Least I can do. Besides, Kayla finally fell asleep, so I'm trying to kill as much time as I can so we don't have to wake her up," he said.

"You both can stay here tonight. No need to wake her. I have plenty of bedrooms and a pool house," Gabe suggested.

Devin smirked. "Oh, a Beverly Hills pool house? Don't tempt me!" He laughed as he handed the cleaned plate to Nick.

Nick took the plate and began drying it. "Devin, Diane and I have a pool house as well. Since Lawrence wants you recording something on this soundtrack too, why don't you ditch the hotel and stay with us?" Nick said.

"Are you serious?" Devin asked. "I would love that. But I don't feel right about leaving Kayla at the hotel by herself. Especially with the press hounding her like they did tonight."

"Kayla can stay in *my* pool house," Gabe said. "I was going to suggest that anyway. The studio is here, the press is not. Plus, I have this brand new espresso machine that I have no idea how to use; it's perfect," Gabe said with a smile.

Nick laughed. "Espresso machine? You hate coffee. Why would you buy that?" he asked.

Devin laughed and looked at Nick. "Kayla loves coffee," Devin said, and Nick laughed with the now obvious understanding. Devin turned his eyes to Gabe and studied him for a moment. "I'm wondering…do you know you are in love with her, or have you not admitted that to yourself yet?" he asked him.

Gabe's smile expanded beyond his ability to stop it. "Well, what man wouldn't be?"

Devin laughed, "Me, but then again I'm gay, so my love for her is understandably platonic."

Gabe laughed and picked up a dish towel to help Nick with the drying, as Devin continued washing the dishes in the sink. Gabe was well aware he was standing with someone who had known Kayla longer than he, and he really wanted to learn as much as he could from Devin about the secrets buried in her past. He wasn't sure what Devin might know, but now was a good time to dance around the subject and see.

"Devin, you said earlier that 'Somewhere You' helped her sleep back in high school. Any idea why she had trouble sleeping?" He asked it as casually as he could. He caught Nick's eye, and saw his quiet interest in the answer to that as well.

Devin kind of shrugged his shoulders. "Not really," he said as he ran another plate under the stream of water from the faucet.

"What about her parents? Do you know anything about them?" Gabe asked.

Devin handed the next clean plate to him as he answered. "I honestly don't know much about them at all. All I know is that her mother left her when she was five, and her father was, apparently a piss poor drunk. She said something once about finally being free of him when she was young, but I never understood how or what happened. She never talks about it. She doesn't share much about herself."

"Yeah, I've noticed that." Gabe said as he placed the dry plate down on the stack. "Well, who was her guardian in all that time in school?"

Devin shrugged his shoulders again as he picked up the next dirty dish. "I don't know. The few times anyone came to pick her up for anything, they were drivers or nannies," he said.

Nick took the next plate from Devin to begin drying it. "What about summer breaks? Where did she stay?" Nick asked.

Devin laughed. "Kayla never took summer breaks. Interlochen had summer camps as well as the school year programs. When the school year would end, she would just stay and do the summer camps. Then she would go right into the next school year again."

"So in all the time you've known her, you never met anyone from her family?" Gabe asked.

Devin shook his head. "No. The only "family" that came to her shows during the school year were Lawrence and Betty. It never seemed to bother her."

Gabe and Nick exchanged a look of silent confusion.

Diane, Jen and Andy quietly came in the kitchen. Nick hugged

Diane sweetly as she rested her head into his chest.

"You look exhausted," Nick said to her.

"I am. You ready to go?" she asked him. Nick lowered his head and kissed her sweetly.

"Yes. I told Devin he could stay in our pool house while everyone is working on the recordings. OK with you?" Nick asked her.

Diane's face beamed brightly. "Oh, that's a great idea." Diane looked to Gabe. "And Kayla?" she asked him.

"I want her to stay here…in my pool house. Is she still sleeping?" Gabe asked Diane.

"Yes. She is out like a light," Diane said.

Gabe looked to Devin. "Just stay here tonight. I don't want to wake her, and like I said, I have plenty of rooms."

Devin nodded. "That would be great. Thank you."

"Perfect. Then tomorrow you both ditch the hotel. We'll have the pool house ready for you tomorrow afternoon," Nick said.

Devin and Gabe quietly said their goodnights to the rest at the front door, then Gabe closed the front door and engaged his high tech security system.

"Be sure not to open any doors or windows, otherwise alarms will fly, and before you can blink, the house will be surrounded by a swarm of armed guards, ex SEAL's and Marines," Gabe laughed.

"Damn. Saxton boys don't mess around, huh?" Devin said in amazement.

"Not when it comes to protection; no, we do not," Gabe said. "If you need anything, just come get me," Gabe added.

After Gabe led Devin to one of the upstairs bedrooms and made sure he had what he needed, he came back down to find Kayla still fast asleep on his sofa. He quietly sat down on the arm rest and relished in seeing her sleeping so soundly in his home and under his protection.

He lost his breath again at how beautiful she looked with her long hair cascading down the pillow, and he fought every fiber in his being that wanted so badly to get under the blanket with her and feel her wrapped in his arms. He thought about lifting her gently and placing her in his bed so she would be more comfortable, but he did not want to risk waking her. She was here, and he wanted to keep it that way, so he quietly took the big loveseat next to the sofa and stayed awake for as long as he could. Eventually, he leaned his head back and allowed his eyes to close; reminding himself as he did to remain alert so that if she woke, he would know it.

He was dreaming…he knew it, but it felt so real. She was underneath him, pulling him onto her as he slipped deeper and deeper inside of her. The sensations were overwhelming. It was as if he could feel her all around him even in this dream state. He could feel her lips on his and her body pressed into him. She fit underneath him like an intrinsic part of his very soul. He didn't know where they were, but he could almost feel the crisp cold air outside the window. There was a glimpse of a snow covered mountain in the distance, and the crackling of a fireplace from inside the room. Feeling himself making love to her was extraordinary, and he was distantly aware that all his nerves were overloaded with the sensations she stimulated in him. As he fell further and further under the power of his love for her, he could hear his inner voice trying to get his attention. He was in a battle with himself… feeling her the way he was, he did not want to let go of it and did not want to pull himself away from the vision he was immersed in…but his voice was getting louder and louder in his head. Then, like an explosion, it would no longer be ignored.

Gabe…someone is standing right behind you…

* * *

In an instantly alert flash, Gabe was up on his feet, gun drawn and fiercely facing the man standing behind his chair. It was Devin. Gabe took a breath and lowered his gun.

"Devin," Gabe said quietly. "I'm sorry. You ok?" he asked him.

The flash of terror that was on Devin's face began to fade. "Shit. Is my skin white now? Has a black man ever gone that pale before? Damn, you scared the crap out of me," Devin said.

Gabe laughed quietly and looked over his shoulder. Kayla was still sleeping on the sofa. Then he looked back to Devin.

"I'm sorry Devin. I was asleep and heard you behind me. I didn't mean to scare you, I apologize," Gabe said as he put his gun back under his shirt behind his back.

Devin kind of laughed. "No, it's ok. That was pretty hot actually! You did that so fast and with such control! Damn...now I know Kayla is in good hands," he said.

Gabe smiled and then looked at his watch. It was 8:00am. The sun was shining beautifully out the window, and streaming across the room gracing its glow softly across Kayla's face. It was amazing how his heart warmed every time he looked at her. She started to stir and her eyes opened.

"Good morning," Gabe said sweetly.

She sat up, and as the blanket fell from her shoulders, her hair showered down across her skin. Even with the faded remnants of make up, she was so beautiful.

"Good morning," Kayla replied in a sleepy (and very sexy) voice. "I don't even remember falling asleep..."

Devin chuckled. "You were out. We didn't want to wake you, so Gabe let us stay here last night." Devin looked to Gabe, "That bed upstairs is the most comfortable bed I have ever slept in."

Gabe smiled. "Good. I'm glad you got some sleep." Gabe looked back at Kayla. He wanted to jump in before her mind started to kick in again, attempting to make her rethink her comfort here. "Coffee?" he asked her.

She smirked. "How? Are we going to bust into Lawrence and Betty's house to use their machine?"

A sarcastic look of insult flashed across his face. "Have you still not learned yet?" Gabe asked with a sly smile.

Devin laughed. "He has a brand new espresso machine in the kitchen; but he is clueless on how to work it, and so am I. So please, get up and help us!" Devin said.

She laughed as Gabe reached for her hand to help her up; and he was, once again, amazed at how good the feel of her hand in his was.

Kayla made coffee for all three of them and they sat outside on the pool patio, drinking their coffees in the peace of the warm morning sun. Gabe and Devin seemed to have clearly teamed up in the arguments they were making about ditching the hotel and staying at the two pool houses. Of course she wanted to; she did not want to admit that to Gabe, or to herself for that matter, but the feeling of being near him was…incredible. She felt that confrontation inside her between the part of her that was undeniably pulled to Gabe, and the part of her that was desperately trying to keep her from him. Gabe was looking in her eyes, like he knew exactly what was taking place in her mind; and being the soldier that she knew he was, she was very aware that he was not going to let her fight a battle he did not want her to win.

"Please stay here. I could list a thousand reasons why it would be so much easier for you, but the truth is, I would really like you to be here. But if you need other reasons to justify it, here is the list; the studio is right downstairs, the press will not be able to get to you here, you will have an entire pool house to yourself, plus 24/7 access to the main house. And do I need to remind you again of the fabulous espresso machine that is at your full disposal here? You won't get coffee like that at the hotel?" She had to smile, he was so good at persuasion.

Devin chimed in. "Kayla, throw in sushi and a car!" he laughed.

Gabe laughed as well. "Hey, if that would work, done."

Kayla laughed at them both, then Devin broke in again.

"Kayla, come on. It will be so much more comfortable. Besides, I want to be able to tell everyone I'm staying in a Beverly Hills pool house! How often will I have the chance to say that?" Devin smiled.

"Nick and Diane live right down the street. Ten minute walk from here. It's perfect," Gabe added.

Kayla had to admit it, it did sound fantastic. She took a breath. "OK. Thank you Gabe. That is very nice of you," she said.

Gabe's face beamed. "Good. Then it's settled. I'll come with you to get your stuff, this way I can be a buffer for you if the press start hounding you."

"You don't have to do that, Gabe. These might be your last few days of freedom from the press, you might want to take advantage of that. Once the song comes out, they will be after you too." She took another sip of her coffee.

Gabe didn't look flustered in the least. "That doesn't bother me at all. I'm happy to come with you. Besides, I have a few things I need to do at Saxton Security this morning anyway." He took another gulp of his coffee. "Shall we face them now and go get your stuff?" he asked.

She looked at him with her humorously stunned expression. "Oh no. Not yet. I am right in the middle of doing something crucially important," she said.

Gabe smirked. "Oh yeah?" He leaned back. "What exactly is it that you are doing?" he asked her curiously.

"I'm procaffeinating," she said as if he should know exactly what that meant. Devin laughed as Gabe chuckled and looked at her in confusion.

"Procaffeinating?" he asked.

"Yes," Kayla said. ""It's the art of using coffee time as a way of masterfully avoiding any and all things that one does not want to deal with. Facing the press at the hotel is definitely at the top of that list. This could take a while," she said as she took another long, drawn out sip. Gabe laughed.

"Got it," he said as he chuckled. "OK, while you procaffeinate, I will jump in the shower and change my clothes. Then, when you are ready, we will go get your stuff, come back here…and begin this next chapter. Together," he smiled and pushed back from the table to head inside.

Kayla felt her heart flutter again.

"That man is so in love with you, Kayla; and he is amazing. You need to cut the crap and stop trying to keep him at a distance," Devin said to her. "I'm going to speak from my heart, because you know I always do. I love you dearly…but you can't go through life letting me be the only one who does. You need to let him in. I think that man would die a thousand deaths for you," he added.

Kayla took a deep breath.

Maybe that was exactly what she was afraid of…

Chapter Ten
Clinging To Safety

The day passed by so fast, Kayla could hardly believe it. Having Gabe with her even made the swarm of the press bearable; kind of enjoyable actually, because the hesitant reaction from the press at the site of Gabe standing next to her was fun to experience. Gabe was a big, strong man and clearly could be intimidating, which was something she never thought she would see reflected in the press, but somehow, Gabe invoked that without even trying. She and Devin had gotten their things from the hotel with ease while Gabe did what he needed to do at Saxton Security, then Gabe was back to escort them out of the hotel when all their stuff was together and they were ready to check out. Kayla fibbed a little when one rather eccentric, dark haired reporter asked her if she was headed back to Switzerland. She said yes in the hopes that misleading him (and the other reporters standing around them) might give her some peace by causing their focus to shift to someone else.

They had spent the rest of the afternoon meeting with Tommy and Gary in the Paramount Recording Studios off of Santa Monica, going over the arrangements and instrumentation plans for the song. They agreed that Tommy and Gary would take care of all the instrumental tracks there, and then come to Gabe's studio with the tracks to record the vocals on the analog system.

After finishing up what needed to be done at the studio, they dropped Devin off at Nick and Diane's, and even enjoyed a nice dinner with them in their home. The sun had set hours ago, and Kayla now found herself alone with Gabe, back in the comfort of his home.

He was closing the front door as she pushed her suitcase against the wall at the end of the hallway. He was engaging the security system as he called her over. When she reached him, he lifted her finger to the pad and after a few seconds it beeped.

"What's that for?" she asked.

"I registered your fingerprint to the security system. Now, whenever it is activated, if you want to come or go, all you have to do is put your finger on the pad and when it beeps, type in *217. This way, anytime, day or night, you can come and go between the pool house and the main house without setting off the alarms."

She chuckled. "Ahh, high tech security. Is that your way of making sure I don't sneak out without you knowing?"

He laughed as he typed in the last few keys on the pad. "You think I need a security system for that?" He turned and faced her. "Your window for being able to sneak out on me without me noticing has long passed. I'm onto you now," he smiled. "Besides, if my goal was to trap you here, I never would have told you the escape code. My strategy is not to trap you; it's to get you to want to be here."

She could feel that heat between them again and her instinct to buffer herself from it kicked in, causing her to reach for a light hearted redirection of the energy.

"So you have now given me the power to break into your house," she joked.

He smiled at her. "I trust you." He paused for a few moments then continued. "I'm hoping I can encourage you to trust me too."

It was amazing to her; the ease with which he generated such waves of fierce emotional reactions to course through her. She found herself unable to do anything except lower her gaze so he could not see it. She could feel him smiling as he spoke.

"You know, lowering your eyes from me does not prevent me from sensing your reactions to the things I say." He let that comment sit for moment before he spoke again. "Do you think we might be abel to find a way for you to stop hiding yourself from me?"

"I'm not hiding." There was no way for her to stop her words; it was an ingrained defense mechanism that had a voice of it's own. His eyes told her that he knew her response was an outright lie, and part of her felt badly about that.

"OK. If that's true (which we both know it isn't,) then come over to the sofa with me and tell me something about yourself." His voice was so soothing and serene, it was hard not to be pulled in when he spoke to her in that tone. He smiled at her silence and took her hand softly. "Come on. I'll make us each a gin & tonic, and you can prove to me you're not hiding."

She managed to pull him into a conversation about the song as he made the drinks and brought them over to the sofa, and she was hoping the new talking points would erase from his memory the discussion he wanted to have. She thought it was working.

He sat down next to her as he handed one of the drinks to her. He finished his response to her question about the piano arrangements, and then smiled at her in a moment of silence.

"I know you thought that change of focus would make me forget what I really wanted to talk about here. It didn't." He took a sip of his drink as he gauged her reaction to her failure at controlling the conversation. He put down his glass. "Before I begin trying to get you to share something of yourself with me, I have something for you," he said.

"I don't need any presents. Bribes won't work with me," she said.

He laughed. "I know that. I would never even attempt it; well, except for chocolate and coffee, but that's not what this is." He reached in his pocket and pulled out her ankle bracelet.

She was stunned. "I thought I had lost that. How in the world did you find it?" she asked.

"It was on top of the bedsheets in my hotel room in Vail. I saw it that morning when I came back to the room after trying to find you."

His eyes were an even mix of tenderness and regret, and she couldn't help but feel a slap of pain at the thought that it was her actions that caused the sadness she saw in his eyes as he continued. He took another moment before he spoke again, but when he did, he did not shy away from looking her right in the eyes as he did so. "I really hated that moment when I woke and you were gone."

Kayla was both sorry and surprised that her leaving affected him so much. She wasn't sure what to say.

"I'm sorry. It was not my intention to…" She shook her head unsure of how to finish her sentence. "I didn't think that would matter that much to you," she said.

"It did." She could see in his eyes that he meant it. "It's probably to much to ask for you to promise me you will never run like that from me again, but I would like to ask you not to anyway. You don't have to run, not from me. You can always talk to me," he said sweetly.

She lowered her gaze unsure of how to respond to that.

He lightened the energy a little. "Come here." He gestured to her left foot. "Let me put this back on. I fixed the clasp today so it should not fall off again."

She lifted her feet and he gently put them on his lap, removing her heels and putting them to the side. He fastened her bracelet above her left ankle, and then softly rested his hands on her legs, keeping his contact with her as he brought his eyes back to her.

"Thank you. That was very sweet of you," she said.

"You are welcome," he replied in a soft tone.

He sat quietly with his eyes on her, and she knew he was waiting for her to speak, which sent a panic through her that she was desperately trying to hide. She wondered if there was any chance she could divert the discussion away from that topic without him noticing.

"How did you fix the clasp?" she asked him.

His smile eased into a small laugh as he called her on her maneuver.

"Kayla, I know your tactics; probably even better than you do. That's not going to work. The more you try and hide from me, the more I see you." His voice was sweet and strong at the same time. She could feel herself hopelessly searching in her bag of tricks for ways to handle this conversation, but his ability to see through her was a new experience for her, and she wasn't sure how to manipulate her defenses with him.

She took a breath. "What is it you want to know?" she asked him.

"Everything," he said with a smile. "But lets start with something simple. Tell me about your parents."

She couldn't help but laugh. "That's not simple. Couldn't we just start with my favorite colors?" She smirked at him.

"I already know that. Pink and black," he said confidently.

She was surprised. "How did you know that?"

He chuckled. "Observation skills my dear. I see everything, remember? Pink toe nail polish, black shoes. Pink purse, black sunglasses. Pink and black sundress…"

"Ok," she laughed. "Hiding things from you is going to be a challenge isn't it?" she joked.

He didn't take the bait of humor, and instead answered her very frankly with his own question. "Why do you feel such a need to hide things from me?" he asked her.

She shrugged her shoulders in an attempt to soften her response. "It's not you Gabe. It's just how I am. It's a natural habit for me."

"Why?" he asked her.

She didn't know how to respond to him and she ended up just shrugging her shoulders again.

"I don't know," she lied.

"Well, let's work on that. Tell me about your parents," he said again.

"Why are you so interested in that?" she asked.

Gabe did not deflect his answer in any way, and kept his eyes on her as he spoke. "Because I know that is a big key in understanding who you are." He softly reached his hand over to brush away some of her hair from her eyes; removing the last little barrier she felt comfortable hiding behind. Damn, he saw that too. "You are... important to me, and I really would like to know you. Please talk to me. Tell me about your mom. Let's start with that."

She could feel no way out of this conversation, so she decided to take the tact of emotional separation as she spoke. Maybe if she said what needed to be said without showing anything, she could just spit it out there and skip over the entire mess her parents left her in.

She took a big chug of her drink; looking for any boost that could help get her through this discussion.

"There is not much to tell. I never knew her, really. She left when I was young and never came back." It amazed her that saying the words out lout caused a pain in her that she convinced herself was no longer there.

Gabe's voice was soft and his eyes on her empathetic. "I'm sorry. How old were you?" he asked her.

"Five," she answered.

"Why did she leave?" he asked her softly.

Kayla was surprised at the quickness with which she answered him, as well as the negative feeling that question kicked up in her.

"My father was an asshole. He was an alcoholic with no job, no purpose and a temper that always landed on her." She took a deep breath and another swig of her drink trying to separate herself again. "She had enough and left."

Gabe allowed a few moments of silence, which she was both thankful for and extremely uncomfortable with. She so badly wanted to get off this subject, but she could feel he was not ready to let her do that yet.

"She left you with him?" Gabe asked with a voice that was both caring and upset. Kayla just shrugged her shoulders in another attempt to keep herself from looking like a victim.

"Yeah," was all she said.

"Did he hurt you, Kayla?" Gabe asked very carefully.

"Not in the way you might think," she didn't mean to say that out loud, but the words just fell from her mouth.

"What do you mean?"

"Gabe, it doesn't matter. My parents don't matter. They haven't been in my life for years, and I'm fine. You do not need to worry about any of that." She was a little shorter with him than she wanted to be, but treading on this subject was a direct line into an area that she did not want him poking around in, and she needed to end that risk.

He felt her need to close that door, and he understood it. In just those few words she spoke, he gathered a huge understanding of what her defenses were rooted in. He knew there was a great deal more to that story; and he was sure he would eventually be able to gain her trust enough to know those aspects at some point, but for now, he wanted to ease her back.

"Ok. Thank you for sharing that with me," he said sweetly. "You are amazing, you know that?"

She brushed it off. "You don't have to say that Gabe," she said.

"I'm not 'just saying' it; I mean it. You are probably the strongest person I know. I can't imagine how a five year old holds themself together in a situation like that."

"Well, I got very good at protecting myself," she replied.

And there was the key to her. It all came down to safety, and her lack of experience with finding that anywhere but inside herself. His heart broke at the thought of her as a child trying to keep herself safe. It enraged him actually. He wanted to find her parents and smack the crap out of both of them. How could anyone do anything but love this woman? He couldn't fathom it. He wanted to lighten the energy a little.

"Your parents both sound like dip shits. No wonder you don't like talking about them," he said.

She laughed, and he was glad to see it.

"Yeah. That's putting it mildly."

He wanted so badly to dive into this further; to get her to understand she could share anything with him, but he knew it had to be done in stages. She spent her life not trusting anyone, he couldn't ask her to just give that up and trust him because he wanted her to.

"You know…you are not alone in this anymore," he said as she looked up and met his gaze. He held her eyes, and then continued. "I'm not going anywhere, and there is nothing you could tell me about your past that could ever change that. I told you once, and I'll tell you again; I'm all in."

He saw her heart rate increase and heard the breath she took in at his words. He knew she didn't believe him, but he also knew he had many ways of communicating with her, even when words were too much for her. He felt her, and he was pretty sure, underneath all her defenses, she felt him too.

He knew there was more than one way to talk to her; to get her to trust him. Safety was what she needed, and he knew, without question, that safety was something he could give her in spades. Protecting her was not only his greatest strength, it was his deepest need. And he knew, even if she could not admit it yet, that she needed him.

His eyes were locked into hers and that unavoidable spark between them caught fire. It erupted through him entirely, and it took all his strength to hold himself back, and allow her to be the one to move to him; if she chose to. He desperately needed to kiss her, to touch her, to feel her, and, make sure she felt him; but he knew, allowing that fire to consume them had to be her choice. He stayed still, holding her gaze. He felt like he was hanging over the edge of a steep cliff; suspended in mid air…waiting before he was allowed to free them both from the lifetime of distance they had suffered up until this point. She was fighting it; he felt it, and he would not interfere with her internal battle over it. It had to be her decision; if she wanted the safety of the pool house, she would have it, but, if she dared to choose him…he knew he could surround her in more safety than she ever had in her life; without question. He forced himself not to move into her; which was admittedly one of the hardest moments of his life. But then…he saw her give in to the part of her that trusted him…he almost couldn't even breathe…waiting for her to lean over to him…and then, like an answered prayer, she did.

When he saw her move towards him, he did not want her having to complete the initiative on her own; now that she made the choice, he was there to help her, to give her the strength she needed…and because he could no longer hold himself away from her. He moved slowly, and reached his hand out softly to caress her face as he did so; to guide her into him with as much comfort as he could give her. Then, in a moment that felt as though the world itself imploded, his lips met hers. He was overcome with it. Her lips on his suddenly became the supernatural wand that magically revamped his black and white world into a mix of a myriad of brilliant colors. This moment, this woman, was what he had been searching for his whole life, and he knew, without question, that he was deeply and permanently, in love with her. He was suddenly aware of a million things all at once; of which, the most important was the necessity to filter how much of that to release…and when. His passion for her was unlike anything he had felt before, but he knew, he could not just allow it to come barreling out…she was still too unsure of him; he knew that. He felt her needing him and he felt her fear about that. He had to gauge every moment, every touch…there would be a time when he could ravish her (and she him) but that time was not now. Not yet. A very purposeful, and careful foundation had to be built with these first few steps, and he was just fine with that. He would take his time…and an extraordinary amount of pleasure seeped into him at the thought of going slowly with her. Making love to her all night long inspired a feeling of Heaven on Earth to him and he welcomed it with everything he had.

He lightly kissed her lips…feeling her response to him growing with each passing moment. He was slow and deliberate; allowing her the time she needed to adjust to the fact that she was falling into him. He deepened the kiss a little at a time, as he welcomed her in… drawing his arms softly around her, and gently pulling her into his body more and more. The feel of her was unlike anything he had ever experienced, and he pulled her even closer to him like his world depended on it. She melted into his body, and placed her hands on his face, almost as if needing to make sure he was really there. He could feel every touch, every breath, every movement, and each one proved more intense than the last. He needed her. He had needed her his whole life; and even though she could not admit it yet, he knew she needed him, and he would show her tonight that she had him. Every part of him was hers, and with every touch, every kiss and every wave of passion, he would make sure she felt his love for her.

He gently scooped her up in his arms, and brought her into his bedroom. He very gently placed her in his bed, never allowing his lips to part from hers or his body to separate from her. He needed the feel of her and he refused to let go. He settled over her, careful not to crush her while at the same time ensuring his body was on hers; keeping a consistent physical connection to her was important to him. As she reached her arms around him, her kiss deepened and her breathing increased. He caressed her face softly and then he allowed his hands to very slowly glide down her neck. He ran his fingers softly on her skin, and could feel the shivers he created on her. His fingers continued down to the top of her chest, then down the outside of her dress. He wanted the feel of her skin again, so he moved his hand to her arms and relished in the feel of her body again. Every fiber of the animal side of him wanted to tear her clothes off and take her in one swoop. He could feel his body pleading with him to drive inside of her and release the build up that already felt out of his control; but he would not. He would not do so until he knew she was ready for him; and he knew just how to make sure that happened.

His hands came up the sides of her stomach, glazing the outside of her dress, up to the top where her chest was exposed. He teased his fingers lightly on her skin, then just under where the dress restricted his access to her. He flirted back and forth between her skin and the clothing blocking his touch from her, until he succeeded in bringing her to the point where she needed her clothes off just as much as he did. He could read her. He could feel her. Everything he needed to know about her was in her touch, in her breath and in her movements. The silent agreement was there; her dress needed to come off.

He slowly moved his hand around and underneath her, to the back zipper. His fingers found the clasp, and slid it down, ever so slowly. He could feel the dress loosen it's protective grip on her, and fall helpless under his command over it's removal. He slid it off of her with ease and it fell softly to the floor. The desperate need to feel her skin on his surged through him like a tsunami, that was calmed only by the feel of her fingers brushing over him, and slowly releasing him from his own clothing. He only pulled his hands from her body for the needed few seconds to rid himself of his shirt, then his hands were back on her skin, reflecting his inability to tolerate the brief disruption of feeling her underneath him.

Her hands were dancing on his back and a wave of shivers swept across him. The extraordinary feel of her touch on him was almost impossible to believe and he reminded himself of the need to remain in control so he did not overwhelm her; but even the simple touch of her hands on his back demonstrated to him how difficult that would be.

As the passion in the kiss between them intensified, he desperately wanted to be free of his pants so he could feel her even more, but he wanted that to be in her control, so he did not make a move to undo them. Instead, he concentrated on her; lowering his body on her and feeling her response to him as he explored her with his fingers; sliding them across her skin…and near her panties. Every inch of her felt amazing, and he knew, when he did finally enter her tonight, he would be overcome with the intensity of it. He felt himself get even harder than he already was and he was sure he was on the brink of exploding with his need for her.

As he gently teased and glided his hands on her, he felt her move towards his pants and begin the process of freeing him from them. She undid the button, and slid the zipper down. That was all he was waiting for, and he gladly took over and did the rest. He lifted himself just enough to slide his pants and underwear off, and was hovering over her, in awe at how amazing she looked underneath him. Never in his life had he been filled with such an urgency to be inside a woman as he was in this moment. It took all the Raider skills in him to remain in control and continue the slow move towards the euphoria that was about to overtake them both.

He lowered himself back down onto her warm skin; slowly, but with complete purpose. He ran his hands up her thighs, across her hips and up to her chest. His fingers slid over her bra and magically landed on the front clasp. He flirted with it just long enough to gauge her response, and then he flicked his fingers softly, as the clasp bent to his will, and the bra fell open. He gently slipped the bra down her arms and released it to the floor. His hands slowly roamed over her skin and back to her chest, now free to glide across her breasts and relish in the feel of her in his large hands. God, she felt amazing.

He moved his lips from hers, across her neck and down to where his hands were holding her. His lips found her nipple and kissed it sweetly. Shivers shot across her skin and he repeated the soft touch of his lips on her breasts until the need to have her in his mouth overrode him and he masterfully played with her, gently sucking her into him with his lips and tongue. Her back arched and he felt her push her hot center up to his.

In an instant, his lips were back on hers, kissing her with more intensity than he had so far and he relished in feeling the thundering desire in her matching the passion beating just as heavy in him. He slid his fingers back down her sides, across her stomach and down to the panties that were the last obstacle between them.

He teased her skin just under the panties, and the sound that escaped her at his touch was almost too much to bear. He needed her; desperately. In one smooth movement he had her panties off and on the floor. His breathing at the sight of her complete nakedness underneath him was only outdone by the rate of his heartbeat. She was, without question, the most beautiful woman he had ever seen in his life and he was so filled with his love, and passion, for her that he truly felt like he would die without the feel of her. He lowered himself back down on her, and as his rod rested on her center, the pleasure of the heat that shot through him forced a moan out of him that he could not control. The enigmatic energy between them was almost excruciating and he knew it was only a matter of minutes before he would have to release them both.

He moved himself off of her in an attempt to cool his fire slightly; he didn't know if she was ready for him yet, and he did not want to give in to his own pleasure before making sure she was on the brink of her own as well.

He lowered his lips to her stomach, kissing her skin as he did so. Then he moved lower…and lower. He brushed his lips softly over her center and relished in the sigh that escaped her mouth. He slowed his movements even more, and he felt her fall helplessly under his control. He held the moment, as his heart pounded in his chest from the absolute stillness she fell into…waiting for him to release the pleasure that was desperate to be set free. He slid his tongue across her and almost came right then and there from the sound that escaped her mouth as he did so. Her body shivered and she fell more and more under the control of the spell he was weaving with every stroke of his tongue on her. He continued her build until he was sure neither of them could stand the wait any longer. He moved his lips back up to hers and she kissed him with a fierce passion she had not allowed from herself so far. He was mesmerized at how powerfully she pulled the same degree of passion out of him. As he kissed her with all the force in him, he slid his fingers inside of her, causing a cry of passion from her while she kissed him intensely; holding onto him with desperate need. He pushed his fingers in even further. She was so wet he could hardly handle it.

Her arms were pulling him down on her and her hips were pushing up to him in a need that seemed to tell him she could no longer breathe without the feel of him. That was all he could stand. No man could wait any longer, he had pushed himself passed what he even thought he could take. He had to have her, now.

He slid his fingers from her and moved his hand up her body, across her arm, and clasped her hand in his, folding it protectively inside his strong grip. His rod had found its way to her entrance and he was using whatever strength he had left to resist the temptation to just drive right in and fuck her brains out. He waited until his lips were back on hers, and he could feel her yearning for him at it's highest point. No force on earth or in Heaven could prevent him now. He released them both, and he entered her.

The mind blowing feel of her all around him was absolutely unexplainable and he let out a sound he had never made before in his life. She moaned under him as he moved in further. He felt as though every single nerve in his body was in overdrive, and the intensity of the pleasure overtook his entire being. He lost track of time. All his senses were overloaded, and the excruciating pleasure was firing off throughout his entire body. With every movement in and out of her, he was more and more overtaken by the searing ecstasy of her. Being inside of her…being on top of her…having her underneath him, needing him the way she was…it was extraordinary. He could feel her pulsing all around him as he drove faster and faster, deeper and deeper. The surge of pleasure was coming to its breaking point; he could even feel his size increasing inside of her as the explosion neared it's release. He squeezed her hand even tighter. Another scream of pleasure escaped his mouth just as the explosion from deep within him came shooting out. He came deep inside of her, with a flood of white fire that seemed to be never ending. The animalistic side of him that was marking his territory inside of her was overcome and seemed to increase his load even more. He was pulsing, shaking, quivering, and still coming. With his strength almost completely gone, he was amazed to find that, even on the brink of absolute exhaustion, he was still coming.

Her body was throbbing all around him. She was holding on to him with everything she had; and he knew she was clinging to the safety she felt with him. That realization almost made him come again. His lips were back on hers, kissing her deeply as the last throbs pulsed between them. He was still unwilling to pull out of her. He needed the feel of her all around him, and he was a slave to the power of her.

As their breathing came back under control, and the reverberation between them quieted, he was overcome with that sense of calm he only felt with her. He reluctantly lifted his lips from hers so he could look in her eyes. Though he knew she could not say it, or even admit it, he saw it in her eyes…she needed him. She loved him, and he knew it. He could feel it. He was blown away by the incredible sense of complete euphoria, unlike anything he had ever known.

He wanted so badly to tell her he loved her…but he knew she was not ready to face that. Not yet. So instead, he told her without words. He graced his fingers across her cheek, and wiped away the tear he knew she didn't want him to see. He lowered his lips to her softly, and kissed her with all the love for her that he felt. He knew she heard what he was saying. Her vulnerability with him right now was clear to him, and he knew that she had no defense against it; and he refused to let this opportunity slip by. He kissed her deeply and reached for her hand as he did so; softly squeezing her hand with his to emphasize his feelings for her.

At long last, he rolled slightly off of her and pulled her into him as he did so. She folded into his body and he was amazed again at how perfectly she fit into his frame. She pushed herself as close to him as she could, and he relished in welcoming her into his embrace. He covered her with his arms; wrapping his body all around her protectively. He pulled the bedspread over them both and squeezed her into him even further. He kissed her head and lowered his on the pillow right next to her, softly breathing in her ear.

He was overcome with an almost otherworldly sense of calm, and he relished in the warmth of it. His eyes remained open as he listened to her breathing and felt her falling asleep in his arms. Even in her sleep, he could feel her pressing into him, needing the feel of his strength around her; which filled him with such love and purpose, he could hardly believe it.

His gratitude for having her in his life was overwhelming, and was only matched with his absolute vow that anyone who would dare try to harm this woman, would find themselves instantly destroyed, by him.

***

As he opened the car door and got in, the dark haired man tossed his gun to the passenger side, smacking the camera and landing on top of the fake press badge that had been haphazardly thrown on the seat. He slammed the door behind him and let out a breath of enraged defeat. He looked at his watch and held his phone ready in his hand. After a few minutes, it rang and he answered.

"No," he said before the voice spoke. "She didn't show up for the flight. It's possible she could have taken an earlier one."

An extremely unhappy exhale could be heard through the line, then the deep voice spoke to him.

"That is not what I wanted to hear." The man on the other end took a breath and then continued. "Well, if she got a flight back there, I have men ready to move in tomorrow anyway. If she is still in LA, it falls on you," he said in a clearly threatening tone. "I want her brought to me. Get it done," he commanded.

"Yes sir." He hung up and reached his right hand to the key for the ignition. As he twisted it, the snake and devil horn tattoo on his wrist seamed to twitch with a life of it's own. He let out a pissed off breath and kicked the car into drive, determined that he would not pay the price of his boss's anger if he failed.

***

Chapter Eleven
What Lies In-between

She was floating on fluffy clouds. Ivory white comfort all around her, and soft as anything. She knew it was just a dream, but it was still mesmerizing; the incredible sensation of it. There was a word for this, the Germans had it; they called it Geborgenheit. It described an incredible, physically tangible sense of emotional security. She felt that now. As she breathed it in, beautiful pink rose petals began to fall from above, gracefully dropping all around her, and bouncing softly on her skin. It was beautiful...for a moment.

A breeze blew past her that stirred up her inner warnings; bringing her mind back to that familiar, relentless ghost in her head. The pink rose petals looked darker now...they weren't pink anymore, they were blood red. A few of them now seemed to be shiny...she reached out her hand to catch one. When it landed in her hand, it was no longer soft and beautiful. It had thorns, and one of them bit into her hand like the fangs of a snake; causing a drop of thick blood to seep out from her skin. Then she saw little splatters of red falling around her. The shiny red rose petals that were coming down now were wet...with blood. The red splashes were staining the beautiful white clouds. Then she saw a mirror image of herself, standing over herself with that warning she understood before her voice even spoke.

Kayla, you can't do this...

Her eyes opened from the dream. Immediately she felt Gabe's strong, warm body on her skin. God, the sense of relief in feeling him was mind blowing. She closed her eyes to give herself another few moments of serenity before the images of the dream would kick up her internal battle again. She hated the fight. She was tired of it, but she didn't know what else to do.

She stayed wrapped in his arms for several minutes…longing to stay there forever, but those hidden corners of her past had sharp edges…and it wasn't fair to him. Her breathing started to increase and she felt that need to get up and control her fears.

She stirred a little, to test and see if he was awake. He did not move. She slipped out from his bed before, maybe she could do it again. A little at a time, she maneuvered her way out from under his arm and quietly slid off the bed. He stayed where he was, beautiful as ever. It was amazing to her; that he was so muscular, so masculinely strong and yet had the most gentle touch she had ever experienced. He was the most incredible man she had ever met, and she admitted sadly to herself that he deserved to be with an equally incredible woman who did not come with the baggage that she did. Her past was not fair to anyone; not even herself, but these were the cards she had been given and she could do nothing to change that. But bringing any of that into his life…she did not have to do that, and she could protect him from all of it.

The sadness started creeping in again and she needed a little air. She slipped into the bathroom and splashed some cold water on her face. It helped, a little. After a few minutes, she put on the robe that was hanging on the back of the bathroom door. It was his, and she was swimming in it, but she wrapped it around herself anyway. It smelled like him…and that filled her, again, with the geborgenheit that she so badly wanted to cling to.

She softly walked out of the bathroom. He was still sleeping on the bed, breathing softly. Of course a huge part of her wanted so badly to get back under the covers with him and wrap herself in his arms. His touch, his feel…even the thought of it caused a mass of shivers to run across her body. She took a deep breath trying to settle her desire for him; an impossibility when he was right in front of her. She needed distance, air…that was the only way to pull herself back.

She quietly walked through the bedroom door. She pulled it behind her almost all the way, but she did not close it out of fear the sound would wake him. She needed time before he woke up to convince herself last night was not as unbelievable as it actually was. She had to get a grip on her feelings for him. Being this…lost under him was unsettling.

She took several more steps into the living room, and placed her hand on the back of the big loveseat to give her some extra strength to hold herself up. She stood there for a long time as she attempted to rebuild that fortress around herself that had so easily been destroyed by him last night. It was extraordinary; a lifetime of fortification… impenetrable to everyone else, and yet, all her defenses just crumbled under the slightest touch from him. His touch…*my God*…what he did to her body…she had never experienced anything like that in her life. The power this man wielded…it was absolutely unexplainable, and completely indomitable. She could still feel him inside of her…all over her actually, and the feel of it was so comforting…so invigorating… and so completely spellbinding; but she knew, she could not allow herself to give in to any of that. She fought with herself internally as she understood that an overwhelming part of her needed him. Needed his touch, his caress, his enveloping energy…how the hell was she going to pull herself back from him now?

"Good morning," his voice was soft, but it scared the shit out of her when he spoke.

She whipped around to see Gabe leaning casually against the door frame of the bedroom. She had no idea how long he had been standing there, but it was her gut feeling that he had been there pretty much ever since she walked into the living room. He had on sweatpants and nothing else, and, of course, looked incredible with his chiseled muscles, five-o-clock shadow, and those eyes that looked right into her very soul.

"Gabe," she said as she lost her breath. "My God, you scared the crap out of me!"

He smiled calmly and gave her a moment to regain her composure. "Yeah, I wish I knew how to stop that from happening," he said with that tone he uses when he means more than one thing. "Are you ok?" he asked her.

She tried to slow her heart rate and catch the breath that had just been yanked from her lungs.

She put on her 'everything is fine' smile and looked at him. "Yeah. I was just heading to the kitchen to make some coffee," she said hoping that he hadn't been standing behind her long enough to know that was untrue, but she could tell from the look on his face that he was not convinced she was ok. She wanted to lighten the direction and keep him from asking the question that was forming in his eyes. "How long have you been awake?"

He softly pushed himself off the wall and crossed over to her.

"I woke up about two minutes before you did. I heard your breathing change, so I knew you were waking up. I was hoping you would come back into bed when you came out of the bathroom, but you didn't." When he reached her, she could feel herself wanting so badly to flush into his body and allow herself to be hidden in him. Falling under the shelter of this man's embrace was such an irresistible temptation.

He moved his body a breath away from hers and held her gaze softly. She did not want to speak, or allow him time to ask her again if she was ok, so she gave in to her need to feel him again, and leaned herself into his chest, relishing in the feel of his strong arms folding around her and pulling her into him even more.

The feel of him was igniting that spark in her again, and before she knew it, a fire seemed to be coursing through every nerve in her body. She was instantly filled with the memory of the pleasure he pulled out of her last night, and she felt herself desperate for those feelings again. She suddenly didn't care how weak she was, she didn't care about the part of her that was trying to keep him safe from the past she did not want touching his world…she needed him…again. She would figure out how to resist him another time. Right now, she knew enough to know she had no power over this at the moment, and the way he made her feel…she didn't care.

His lips found hers, and she felt him shoot through her with his kiss. The searing hot pulse that was throbbing inside her overpowered her and she felt herself clinging to him in a way she never had with any other man in her life. She couldn't get enough of him. It was unfathomable to her that she had even been thinking about trying to keep herself from him. It couldn't be done. It was like asking her small body to withstand the overwhelming gravitational pull of a black hole on a planet…it was simply impossible.

She could feel the sexiness of his strong cheekbones as she held his face. Feeling him kissing her was causing such a burn through her body she was sure the heat would be too much to bear. Her arms found their way around his broad shoulders to his back, and she felt herself clawing into him, trying to get closer.

His heartbeat was just as fast as hers and she could feel it through the pulsing muscles in his chest. His arms were pulling her into him with just as much need as she felt thundering through her. He picked her up with ease and laid her down on the big sofa, covering her body with his. The way he moved with her…it was amazing. She could feel the animal side of him…hovering over her; dominating her with his size and passion, and yet equal to that was his ability to control himself…to keep her safe while taking her at the same time. It was the most thrilling experience she had ever known.

She slid her hands down his rock hard abs, across his stomach, and she felt this strong man shiver at her touch. She slipped her fingers inside his sweatpants, and went lower.

She slowed her hands as she got closer to his manhood, and she felt him fall still with the anticipation of her touch on him. It was a remarkable feeling…that this huge man fell quiet under the movement of her small hands. She kissed him deeply as she allowed her fingers closer to where he was begging for the feel of her. Then she ever so softly brushed her fingers along the length of him. Sound escaped his mouth and shivers overtook his body. She kept her touch light, teasing him, playing with him, enjoying how much control over his body he gave her. It was igniting a fire in her that was even hotter than last night; which should be impossible, but clearly was not. She could feel him begging her with his kiss…pleading with her to wrap her hands around him and stroke him further. So she did.

Her fingers gripped him tighter, and she felt him quiver in her hands. He was so hard and so big, she needed both her hands to be able to completely wrap around him, and it felt amazing to be touching him the way she was. She could feel his heartbeat even faster than before, and he was so hard it felt like he could explode at any second. He let out another sound of pleasure, and his hand was caressing her face as if he was trying to regain some level of control over himself, but she refused to slow her hands or let go of him. She couldn't. Making him feel this burn was a need in her and she couldn't stop it. She needed him. She needed him inside of her; all over her.

His hands fell down her sides, touching every inch of her along the way. He untied the belt of the robe and it fell open, exposing her complete nakedness underneath him. His hands glided back on her skin, on her stomach and then swept lovingly lower, and lower. Then his hands found the spot she was begging for him to touch; and he did. Softly, teasingly, he swept his fingers over the spot that forced her under his control, and a cry of unbridled pleasure escaped her mouth. He kissed her even deeper at the sound she made, and his fingers found their way to her entrance, then slid inside of her. Another sound of absolute ecstasy escaped her at the feel of him deep within her. She could hardly stand the intensity of the pleasure he invoked in her. He suddenly had such control over her body, that it caused her to release her grip on his rod and reach around him; grabbing a hold of him for dear life. Her arms were pulling him down on her as the fire flared up inside of her, consuming them both.

She couldn't control anything anymore, and her voice broke out without her knowledge.

"Gabe, fuck me, please." she begged him. Him driving inside of her was the only thing that could save her from the incredible, and almost unbearable, build of intensity that he was causing inside of her. She needed him desperately; and he answered her need with his own.

He slid his fingers from her and grabbed her hand. Then, with his lips still ravishing hers, he drove himself inside of her; deeply. They both released sounds of uncontrollable pleasure, and he pressed his body down on her as he drove himself deeper inside of her. The passion was unlike anything she had ever even imagined and he continued his rhythmic push and pull in and out of her; throbbing with every glide. The orgasm he created in her was impossible to believe and it overtook her entire being. She screamed in his mouth as her explosion rocked through her lower core and shot up through her chest. Silver pulses of lightening were shocking through every nerve ending in her body and firing out through her very skin. Her body was shaking as his explosion chased her own. She felt his size expand just before the shooting release of his hot liquid inside of her, and the feeling was so euphoric she couldn't even think straight.

He continued to push deeper in as he came in her and she found herself pulling him as tightly as she could; unable to even allow air to be in-between them. She could feel him pulsing inside of her; quivering with wild throbs and it felt amazing.

She could feel him trying to regain his control over the eruption of passion that had overtaken them both. With his kiss deep, and his body strong, he used every inch of himself to bring them both back down to earth. He slowed his body in her, he slowed his kiss on her lips and his hands were lovingly brushing against her cheeks, caressing her face as he kept his mouth on hers. He was still inside of her, and was making no move whatsoever to change that, which she was grateful for. Feeling him inside her was a comfort like nothing she had ever known, and she wanted him to stay there for as long as possible. She knew the time would come when she would have to force herself away from him, and the realization broke her heart. But she had to push those feelings down for now, or he would see it in her eyes. It would be hard enough to make herself walk away from him; if he joined in the fight to keep her near him too, she would not win; and she couldn't do that to him. So she made the decision; she would not allow herself to think about it until the moment when she had to go. Then she would force herself to leave before he knew what she was doing. She pushed the painful thought away by clinging to him even more.

She was holding onto him again so tightly, and he loved it. Having her back underneath him after feeling her slip from his bed this morning…there were no words to describe it. He knew she was trying to pull herself away from him again, though he was still unsure why.

But he sent a prayer up to God, asking that he always be granted the power to bring her back in to his arms, and demolish that part of her that was still trying to keep herself from him. He didn't know what the real reason behind that was, but he could feel it. Even in his sleep, he knew. His awareness of her every sound, every breath and every movement, woke him before her internal struggle woke her. He had been alert and in tune with her, and he had a feeling she would try to move away from him; but he let her think he was sleeping so he could gauge just how drastic that need to run from him was. He didn't know at that moment if she would actually try to leave, or if she had just needed to create space between them to try and rebuild her defenses. But when she had slipped out of the bedroom, he had gotten instantly on his feet, quietly pulling on his sweatpants just in case she had been intending to head to the front door.

He had watched her standing in the living room, and could practically see the struggle she was putting herself through. Why did she feel such a need to pull herself back from him? He had to admit, even for him, the power in what happened between them last night, and just now, was incredibly intense and overwhelming…but her fear…it was something more than that. He needed to start getting the truth of that out of her, so he could know how to dismantle that as well.

He kissed her softly, and pulled her into him as he lowered himself behind her and wrapped her into his body. He softly placed the blanket over them that was hanging on the back of the sofa and just held her as their breathing settled back down to a normal rhythm.

He wasn't sure how much time went by, but his eyes opened to the sound of his landline ringing. Without loosening his grip on Kayla, he reached over with one arm to pull the phone from it's holder on the end table, and he answered it.

"Hello," Gabe said as he squeezed Kayla into his arms while

listening for the response.

"Good morning Gabe," Lawrence's voice came across the line. "Are you guys up?" he asked.

"Good morning Lawrence," Gabe answered in a cheerful tone. "Yes. We are just about to have coffee," he hugged Kayla again as she turned over and pressed herself into him further. *God, she felt amazing.*

"Well, make it to go, and come over to Nick's. He and Diane are throwing together a breakfast spread for everyone...and...I need to talk with you and your brothers." Lawrence's voice was casual enough, but Gabe knew him well, and was instantly aware that a private, secure discussion was being asked for with the layer of not wanting Kayla to know about it. Which he was in agreement on.

He put on an even more cheerful voice. "Well, Diane does make a great breakfast spread, so count us in. We will be there in twenty."

Gabe hung up the phone and whispered in Kaya's ear, kissing her and talking to her at the same time.

"Nick and Diane want us all over for breakfast. She makes great eggs and hash browns," he said as his hot breath caused shivers on her neck.

"That sounds great actually," Kayla said.

"We can procaffeinate on the way. I have to go cups above the sink. You can make us coffee, and we can drink it on the way over. Sound good?" he asked.

She lifted her eyes up to face him and her beautiful smile almost stopped his heart.

She slid her fingers gracefully across his cheek.

"Anything with you right now sounds good," she said.

He leaned down and kissed her with a passion that could very easily have gotten them both worked up again. Had he not understood that a discussion of importance had just been requested by Lawrence, he might have ignored everything and taken her again right there, but, if this had anything to do with Kayla's safety, he would not be distracted. Not even by this. Her safety was too important to him, so he would make sure he was part of the upcoming discussion.

With the coffees in their hands, and the sun shining brightly, they walked over to Nick's instead of driving. He had her hand in his and felt her keeping herself as close to his side as she could, which filled him with such joy he could hardly believe it. . He wrapped his arm around her and pulled her into him as they walked to his brother's house. Behind his thoughts around how good Kayla felt, he was wondering what was hidden in Lawrence's voice this morning. He knew him well, and was aware that the topic he wanted to discuss was important, and also, private. He was anxious to dive into it and figure out what was bothering him so he could take the appropriate steps to ensure everyone's safety; especially Kayla's.

As they walked in, two young teenagers ran up to Gabe with excitement.

"Hi Uncle Gabe!" they said as they hugged him.

Gabe smiled brightly and hugged them both. "Hey there!" Then he turned to Kayla. "These are Jen and Andy's kids, Jessica and Connor." The two smiled warmly at Kayla and said hello. As they did, two more kids, slightly younger, came bounding down the front hallway to greet them as well. "Hey guys!" Gabe said to them and then introduced them too. "…and these two are Nick and Diane's kids, Mahria and Daniel," he said.

Kayla greeted them all warmly, and Gabe could tell the girls were enamored with Kayla, which didn't surprise him.

Nick came around the corner with a kind smile. "Hi. Good timing, Diane just pulled the cinnamon rolls from the oven," Nick said as he hugged Kayla sweetly. "How are you Kayla?" he asked as he released her.

"Fine, thank you. I can smell the cinnamon rolls from here. They smell great," she said.

"Come on in. Everyone is in the kitchen." Nick led them down the hall and into the kitchen where everyone was casually gathered around, with coffee, orange juice and even mimosas. Devin was over by the counter helping Diane with the glaze for the fresh made cinnamon rolls, while Betty, Lawrence, Jen and Andy were talking at the counter.

After the good morning greetings fell through the group, the kids found their way back to the living room to continue with their video game on the big screen tv, and Diane handed Kayla and Gabe each a fresh made coffee.

"I never thought I'd see the day that Gabe would enjoy coffee. Thank God for you Kayla!" she laughed. "It's unnatural to not drink coffee; I always worried about him!"

Gabe took his coffee with a laugh while at the same time attempting to size up the energy around Lawrence. He had known him his whole life, and he was very good at picking up on his state of mind. Lawrence was bothered, and Gabe knew something was not right, even though they were all smiles and others might not see it. His eyes met Lawrence, and then his brothers…the look on Andy's face had his attention too…something was definitely under the surface here and he was anxious to find a smooth way to separate them from the rest so they could get into what was going on; but Gabe was very aware that not allowing Kayla to know something might be off was extremely important, so this had to be done discretely.

After all the drinks were handed out, Diane suggested everyone get a plate and take what they wanted from the spread she had in the dining room, and then head out to the covered eating area by their pool.

Gabe stayed close to Kayla as they crossed outside with their breakfast plates, and they sat on the far end of the big table. He still found himself not wanting to let go of her, but he did so, just long enough to pull her chair out, and then had his hand on her again when he sat down next to her.

They dove into chit chat on various topics as they ate and enjoyed the morning sun. The conversation was now drifting into discussions on the soundtrack, and Devin was really excited about the one Lawrence had given him to record.

Devin reached for his iPod and head phones. "Kayla, you have to hear this one. It's so beautiful," he said to her.

As much as he didn't want to leave her side, this was creating the perfect opportunity to step away with his brothers and Lawrence while Kayla was involved in something else. Andy must have had the same realization, because he jumped in.

"Gabe, while they listen to the song, Lawrence was having an issue with one of his remote cameras. I think the glitch is on our end. You mind popping into Nick's office downstairs with us to take a quick look?" he asked.

"Yeah, that's fine. Let's go." As Lawrence, Andy and Nick stood up, Gabe looked at Kayla. "I'll be right back, ok?"

She smiled sweetly at him, "Sure," she said to him.

It was funny; he didn't even think about it, but he leaned over and kissed her softly on the lips, as if that was already an ingrained habit for him. He saw Betty smile after his lips parted from Kayla's and he brushed his hand softly across her cheek.

They made their way past Nick's front office, to the back where his hidden office was located. After closing the door and moving into the room, Gabe turned to face Lawrence.

"What's going on?" Gabe asked.

Lawrence took a breath.

"Jacob Sykes is out," Lawrence said.

"What?" Nick's shocked voice reflected the stunned feeling that shot through Gabe. "How? When?" he asked.

Andy spoke. "Two nights ago. I've had Jasper on every movement surrounding the prison, and he was able to hack even deeper into their system yesterday after he noticed several of their surveillance cameras going off line and malfunctioning." Andy handed Nick a small thumb drive that was in his pocket, and continued. "He downloaded the files he got his hands on, and I went through them last night. It looked organized as hell to me, and the crickets from the media coverage about it, has my nerves up that this was clearly a high level inside job. He had a shit load of help with the escape." Andy looked at Lawrence. "My opinion? This couldn't have been done without Matthew."

Lawrence punched his hand on the big desk in frustration.

Nick took the drive and plugged it into the computer. A few moments later, several files appeared on the screens; including a few video files that looked like they had come from surveillance cameras.

"What are the video clips?" Nick asked as he flipped through the information they had in front of them.

"Unfortunately, not much. It was all Jasper could upload. It shows a little footage before the camera's each spontaneously clicked off." Andy said as he came around the desk and pointed to the one he wanted Nick to play. "This one is the entrance to the prison. Jasper tried to run some photo recognition software on these two guards, but they came up unknown."

Gabe studied the movements of the men. "Those are not security guards," Gabe said with certainty. He knew from the undisciplined way they moved and the fact that their guns were not holstered correctly;

nor were they the standard issue guns for prison guards. Gabe felt a cold sweep through his bones. "They are spending an awful lot of time looking over their shoulders instead if right in-front of them. Nick, can you zoom in?" Gabe asked. Nick did so and they watched one of the men passing his fake ID through the window for clearance. Gabe saw a mark on the wrist of one of the men. "Freeze that," he said. "Can you zoom in any more on his wrist?" Nick did so, and they all recognized the mark immediately. "Snake and devil horn tattoo," Nick said. "Shit."

"Sykes's men. How the hell did he get them in there?" Gabe asked.

Lawrence spoke through an obviously angered voice. "Andy is right. It has to be Matthew." He took another moment and Gabe could see his layered thoughts. "The question is, how far is Matthew in? And why?"

Gabe looked to Andy. "Do we have any idea where Sykes is?" he asked.

Andy shook his head. "No. Jasper couldn't get anything from the outside cameras. They had been tampered with long before any vehicles drove up, so we have nothing to trace. He is in the wind."

"Shit," Gabe leaned against the chair that was in front of him and took a breath. "Do we know where Matthew is?" he asked.

"Sacramento, I think. Last I checked a few days ago anyway. But he is still not taking any of our calls," Nick said.

"We need to figure out if Matthew is willingly or unwillingly working with Sykes," Gabe said.

Lawrence jumped in, "Either way, Matthew is a threat. I'm not sure the why matters much anymore."

Gabe had to concede that Lawrence was right about that, but he couldn't help notice the anger in Lawrence's voice about it. "Lawrence, don't fault yourself that Matthew knows it was us behind the Sykes takedown. We will get to Jacob before he can do any harm to you…or Kayla, or any of us." There was still a look in Lawrence's eyes that Gabe could not quite read, but there were more pressing issues to deal with at the moment. "OK, here is what we need to do. Andy, keep Jasper on the prison. Have him hack anything and everything to see if we can figure out any clue as to where Sykes went and how we might be able to trace him. Nick, get on Matthew Edson. Find out where he has been, where he is now and where he might be going. If Sykes is communicating with Matthew, we need eyes and ears on all of it. My guess is, Matthew knows exactly where Sykes is, because he needed Matthew to get there." Gabe pulled out his phone. "I will contact Braidon. He is the captain of the current alpha Raider Team. We will need their assistance on this once we figure out where Sykes is hiding."

Nick spoke up. "In the meantime, I suggest we put extra security on your house Lawrence, 24/7. Yours as well Gabe."

Lawrence shook his head. "I don't want Kayla to see anything that could concern her. She hates LA as it is and she spooks easily. If she gets the feeling something is wrong, she could very easily just get up and leave. That would make her extremely vulnerable and we can't take that chance."

Gabe swallowed his pain at the thought of that. Whatever the demons were that were causing Kayla to feel she had to pull away from him, adding this to the mix would only make that worse. Lawrence was right.

"Just have security on 24/7; close by, but not at the houses. I don't think Sykes's men can get in here anyway. Our security is far too good. But outside those gates it could be an issue," Gabe said.

Andy added his thoughts. "Lawrence is right. No one upstairs can know something is going on. We need to be on this quietly; it's the best way to keep everyone safe."

They all agreed on that.

When the men came back upstairs, they found everyone scattered throughout the living room. Devin, Connor and Daniel were standing in front of the big screen TV, doing their best dance moves to the video game they were playing. When they finished, their score flashed on the screen and the three of them cheered triumphantly.

"Ha! Beat that suckers!" Devin said proudly as he turned to the girls who were waiting their turn. Jessica was ready to take them on, but Mahria was hesitating. As Gabe entered the room, he stood in the back next to Diane and watched Kayla get up and cross over to Mahria.

"Don't you let them intimidate you. Come on. We got this," she said to her.

Mahria looked up at her, clearly not convinced. "Their score is so high. I'm not that good, and I don't want to lower our score," she said to her.

Kayla brushed off her fear sweetly and spoke. "Don't you even think that. Here is the secret, my dear…it's not the moves that have to be good. It's the attitude behind the moves that matters. It's you that matters. Dance like you are the best thing on the planet, and I guarantee you…that score on the screen won't matter. You will win. Come on." Kayla grabbed her hand and pulled her up to the front of the room with Jessica. The three of them took their turn and Gabe couldn't keep the smile from his lips if he wanted to. He had never seen little Mahria so bold and so happy. The girls were ripping it and everyone cheered as their score went higher and higher on the screen. Then their turn was over and the winning team flashed on the tv. The girls won. Everyone cheered and laughed.

Diane turned to Gabe. "You better marry her. She is the best thing that ever happened to you."

Gabe was still smiling. "Diane, I would marry her today," he answered. "The question on that isn't me. It's her."

Diane tilted her head at him. "Why is that?" she asked him.

Gabe directed his eyes back to Kayla, and watched her hugging the girls and laughing with Devin as he answered Diane.

"There is still a part of her that doesn't trust me. I'm not sure how to fix that yet," he said.

"Just make sure she knows you see her. The real her, and not just the sparkling persona that everyone else sees," Diane said.

"That's part of the problem. She keeps trying to block that side of herself with me. I feel like every time I start to see the real her, she backs away from me," Gabe replied.

"That's probably because no one else has ever done that with her before. Trust me Gabe; the hardest thing for a man to understand is the absolute loneliness that often surrounds a beautiful woman. Once you understand that, the rest will fall into place."

Mahria ran up to Diane and interrupted them.

"Mom did you see? Did you see me? We won!" She was so happy it was precious. As Diane hugged Mahria to celebrate her win, Gabe's eyes found Kayla's, and warmth swept through him at her smile. Every time he thought he couldn't possibly love her more...he did. He made his way through everyone, across the room to her.

"Thank you for doing that for her. Mahria has always been a little insecure, but somehow, you magically changed that," he smiled at her.

"She did it herself. I just gave her a nudge." Kayla smiled back at him.

Gabe's eyes deepened on her. "Yeah, sometimes you just need to be reminded that its ok to show who you really are, Right?' he asked her.

Kayla dropped her eyes to take a moment, and then looked back up at him. "Sometimes," she said.

Gabe kept his eyes on her as he drew in a deep breath. What was it that she was still allowing in-between them? He had to find a way to discover what it was; either he had to get her to trust him, and reveal it herself, or he had to discover the answer regardless of her help. But something stirred in him, telling him the clock was ticking and his time to solve it was running out.

Chapter Twelve
Destiny's Circle

They were weeks into the recordings now and Kayla was still being nit picky about a few notes here and there. Devin was lounging on the sofa along the back wall of the studio, as Kayla made Tommy and Gary play the last line back again.

"Kayla, how many different versions of perfect do you think there are?" he asked her.

She kept her eyes on the mixing board as she answered him.

"I don't know, let's find out." She listened to the playback again, and turned to Tommy. "I have to punch that. I know I can do it better."

Devin let out an exasperated exhale as Gary laughed.

"Kayla, it sounds fantastic," Gary said. When Kayla shook her head, he turned to Devin. "Her OCD about her vocals has gotten worse, hasn't it?" he asked.

Devin chuckled. "You have no idea." He straightened up as Kayla stood. "The sad thing about it is, I've seen her do this a thousand times...find a note that she couldn't possibly make better, and then, somehow...she does," he said.

"Yeah? How long does that usually take?" Gary asked with a smile.

Devin looked at his watch as he stood and stretched. "Gary, you know that Star Trek episode where Picard encounters that probe that sucks him in, and he lives an entire lifetime...years and years go by... and then at the end, just before he is about to die of old age, he opens his eyes and it's actually only been a few minutes?" Devin slapped him sympathetically on the shoulder. "That's how long. Good luck Captain." Devin turned to Kayla as she headed for the vocal booth again. "I'll be upstairs with Gabe and the rest. It sounds great. I don't know how you are going to make it any better."

"Where there's a will, there's a way." Kayla smiled. "Tell Gabe they don't have to wait up. I know it's late."

"I don't think Lawrence is going anywhere until he hears this tonight, and I'd bet my life that Gabe won't go to bed without you. Just come get us when you're ready to play them the rough mix," Devin answered her.

Gabe took a sip of his brandy and looked back at the plans on the table in front of them, as Braidon made note of a few things they had discussed. It was a good move for Gabe to bring him in tonight to meet with them while Kayla was involved in the studio downstairs. Braidon had done a good job as Gabe's replacement on the Raider team, and he wanted Braidon's team ready in an instant as soon as they got a location on Sykes. Moving in on Sykes quickly would be the key, and the help of the Marine's equipment for that would be essential. Not to mention that military intervention was going to be needed in order to deal properly with Matthew.

Braidon had been a little surprised at the involvement of Matthew, but considering the high level officials they had previously taken down since these missions started (which went even further up the pole than a governor,) it wasn't a shock to a man like Braidon.

Gabe liked Braidon; he was tough, strong and got things done, and most importantly, he deferred to Gabe's knowledge about Sykes and the men they were up against; and he knew Braidon had no ego as far as Gabe's leadership on this one. Gabe's reputation was stellar with the Marines, and everyone knew who Gabe was; along with the details of what he had done. It went without saying that they had his back. Gabe knew that, and was grateful, because Sykes needed to be taken down as quickly as they could do it. If they could take him down before the media ran with the story, it would be better for everyone. So Gabe wanted Braidon in on this from the ground up, ensuring that no time would be lost when the opportunity presented itself to end Sykes…in whatever form that took.

Nick dimmed the lighting slightly and came back over to his chair. They had been going over the security details for the upcoming movie premier for hours, and were just now beginning to relax.

Nick lowered his glass of Woodford, leaned back in his chair and stretched his long legs out.

"I don't think it's going to be much different than what we normally do at an event like this, even with our…heightened concerns. We've done premiers at the Grauman's before. This time, we have the added benefit of actually being in the VIP crowd as guests. There is a certain advantage to that," Nick said as he lifted his glass for another sip of his drink.

"I don't think Sykes or his men would have the balls to even attempt something at a big movie premiere, but if they are that stupid, we will be ready for them," Andy said as he lowered his glass back to the table, and looked at Gabe. "You will be right by Kayla all night, and Nick and I will cover Lawrence."

"I'm happy to be there if you want, Gabe," Braidon offered.

Gabe shook his head. "I would rather you stay quietly informed and be ready with your team as soon as we know where Sykes is," he said.

"We will have our security team sprinkled all over the premiere. Plus, there will be cameras everywhere, with Jasper and his team on remote surveillance all night. I don't think we've over looked anything," Nick said as he took another swig of his Woodford, and then placed his glass on the end table near his chair.

"I would almost like to see them try…it would be so much fun to watch Gabe demolish them again!" Nick was almost laughing as he thought about it.

Braidon laughed as well. "Everyone still talks about that. I wish I could have seen it. Rumor has it he was like the Terminator, Ironman and Rambo combined!" " Braidon added as he laughed. "Gabe is a fucking legend with the Raiders."

Gabe chuckled but said nothing, choosing instead to simply reach for his brandy and have another swig.

"Oh, you have no idea," Andy said. "It was amazing."

Nick laughed a little and looked at Gabe. "Yeah, he was insanely impressive. But how come the Raiders walked away with all the fame for that one and not the SEAL's? I mean, we did clear the way for you," Nick said with a smirk.

Gabe laughed, as Andy chimed back in. "Yeah, but it was the big bad Raider that stormed right into the heart of it, knocked out everyone of Sykes's personal guards, and hog tied him in record time." Andy laughed again. "It was fucking great!"

Braidon lifted his glass to Andy and they cheered. After a swig of his whisky, Braidon looked to Gabe.

"Please tell me you beat the shit out of him before you tied him up and handed him over," he asked.

Gabe laughed a little, but said nothing, so Nick did. "Before, during and even a little after. Gabe was…extremely motivated to see some justice brought down on that son of a bitch. We all were. Probably should have just killed the bastard right there."

"Well, considering what that man had done, it must have been extremely hard not to. But don't worry. We will get him. Raiders always do…and SEAL's, of course," Braidon said.

Lawrence leaned back. "Any new info on Matthew?" Lawrence

asked Nick.

Nick shook his head. "No. His official schedule keeps changing, he has not returned any phone calls and his people are very hush hush about his whereabouts. I still think he is in the mansion in Sacramento, but to be honest, I'm not entirely sure. I have some of our guys running point on trying to locate him, but so far, they have not gotten confirmation on his whereabouts."

Braidon looked at Lawrence. "He is being very careful," he said with clear suspicion in his voice.

"Yeah. Especially with us, which I find…confusing," Gabe added.

Lawrence had that look on his face again, but said nothing. Gabe was just a bout to prod him further about what his thoughts were regarding Matthew's behavior, but they were interrupted by Devin coming up the stairs from the studio.

Gabe looked at his watch; it was almost 2am. "And? Is she satisfied with the last note yet?" Gabe asked, laughing at the exasperated look on Devin's face.

Devin collapsed in the chair between Nick and Braidon. "That girl…I love her dearly, but I am about ready to clock her over the head with something heavy. She is in the booth again."

Lawrence laughed. "That's Kayla. She is an absolute pain in the ass with it, but, this is also why every song she records makes a hit soundtrack. I want to hear this thing."

"We may have to drag her out of there to get the song done by the time the premier happens," Andy said with a laugh.

"Well, it's a good thing you're here Braidon because it may just take two Marine Raiders *and* two Navy SEAL's to do it!" Devin added. "Then again, I caught a very quick glimpse of Gabe in action several weeks ago…I bet he could drag her out all on his own. No offense to the two SEAL's and additional Raider in the room," Devin added with a laugh.

Lawrence chuckled. "What happened?"

"It was that first night we all gathered here. Gabe let Kayla and I stay here because she had fallen asleep on the sofa. Well, the next morning, I made the mistake of quietly coming down the stairs." That statement already had Braidon laughing. Devin acknowledged it with his own laugh, and then continued. "Gabe had fallen asleep in the loveseat next to where Kayla was sleeping. I wasn't even close to his chair yet, but before I could even blink, Gabe jumped up, whipped around and had his gun pointed right at me! Oh, Lord, I about met my maker right there and then!" Devin laughed.

Andy and Nick couldn't help but laugh as well.

"That must have scared the shit out of you," Braidon said as his laughter grew. "Sneaking up on a Raider is never a good idea!"

"Well, I know that now! Ooh, scared doesn't even cut it. I think I am still a few shades too lite, I went so pale! I couldn't believe how fast he moved," Devin said in astonishment. "In one flash, he was wide awake, gun drawn and looking at me with the fiercest look I have ever seen in my life!" Devin was laughing again.

"Well, Raiders are a tough bunch," Braidon said with a nod to Gabe.

"I believe it. I didn't know much about Raiders...I only really knew the name from that famous take down years ago of that asshole Jacob Sykes."

Everyone got a little quiet at the mention of Sykes, but Andy didn't stay quiet for long. "Yeah, that was the famous take down. That put the name of the Raiders on the map."

"It was all over the news. That little girl, Livy Ann (God rest her soul,) and the Raiders that took Sykes down," Devin said.

Lawrence lifted his glass to his lips and took a sip of his whisky.

"I'm surprised you remember that, Devin? You were young when that happened."

"Yeah, but everyone knew about that. My mom followed that story closely. There were teenage girls from our neighborhood that were abducted by Sykes and forced into that ring. Believe me, young or not, everyone cared about that man getting busted for what he had been doing." Devin looked at Gabe. "It was the first time I ever heard my mother refuse to say a prayer for another human being. But she hated that man," Devin admitted.

"I would assume most women feel that way, considering what he spent his life doing to women and young girls," Andy added.

"Amen. My mom is a God fearing, little old Christian lady, but even she wanted to tear his junk off and feed it to the wolves," Devin said.

Nick couldn't help but laugh. "Yeah. A lot of men wanted to do the same thing too. Me included."

Devin looked at Lawrence who had been quietly listening to the conversation. "My mother and I were always hoping that someone would make a movie about Livy Ann. We still say a prayer for her every time we go to church. Her story should be out there."

Lawrence was still, and very quiet. Gabe could see that depth in his eyes again before he spoke.

"There is a big part of me that agrees with that, Devin. But doing a movie like that would be…tricky. It would shine a big spotlight on a great number of very powerful, famous people who were involved with it; Hollywood is certainly no exception. It would both be a huge success and also the match that burns down the entire establishment. Even I don't have the power to make that happen without many forces trying to stop me from doing so…at any cost," Lawrence said. He took a final gulp of the remaining whisky in his drink. "But, that doesn't mean I won't. And it certainly doesn't mean that action hasn't been taken since Sykes's bust," Lawrence glanced at Gabe and his brothers as he leaned forward, then looked back to Devin. "A quieter road has been walked in taking down a great number of individuals who were involved with the whole mess." He looked back at Devin. "Have you noticed over the years how many actors, producers and entertainers have been arrested, or fled?"

Devin thought in silence for a moment and then nodded his head. "As a matter of fact, I have noticed that. But I didn't know it was connected to Sykes. Was it?"

Lawrence nodded. "Almost all of them were."

Gabe swirled his drink. "Sometimes, stopping the crime is more important than exposing it. Ever since the night that Livy Ann handed over that small bag of video tapes…there has been a steadfast…under the radar move to end the trafficking, and get rid of those involved. It's a big part of what the Raiders have been doing."

Devin had a look of awe on his face. "That's amazing. I was already completely impressed with you, but now, even more so." Devin looked at everyone else. "All of you actually. That is…exceptional. Are you guys ever worried about your safety because of it?" he asked them.

Gabe smiled. "Well, fortunately, we are extremely good when it comes to protection. It would be really hard for anyone to catch us off guard."

Devin laughed. "Yeah, I learned that in one second when I came down the stairs that morning you were sleeping in the chair!"

Gabe picked up his drink with a chuckle, and Andy caught his eye.

"Well, that will teach you. Don't sneak up on Gabe when he is watching over the woman he loves," Andy said.

Gabe felt Lawrence look in his direction, assessing Andy's comments, and weighing it against what he saw on Gabe's face. Gabe felt no need to hide the truth of it, so he met his eyes.

"Is that true?" Lawrence asked him.

Gabe swallowed his brandy and answered him very frankly. "I think everyone in this room knows that's true. Yes, I do love her, very much." Gabe had to admit he felt a slight wave of nerves course through him at saying it out loud, but he was not going to run from it. He saw Lawrence smile and lift his drink to his lips.

Devin sat up. "Have you told her that yet?" he asked.

He took a moment before he answered Devin's question. "No. I have not said it out loud," he said.

"Why not?" Andy was confused.

Gabe took a breath and swirled his drink. "I don't think she is ready to hear that yet," he said simply.

Devin laughed. "Yeah, you have to walk a very careful line with her, Gabe is right."

Gabe found that interesting coming from Devin, and he was curious what insight Devin might be able to offer into it.

"Do you know why that is, Devin?" Gabe asked.

Devin leaned back in his chair. "I don't know the why, I only know how she tends to react; but the answers that you need…I don't have those. I have been her best friend since she was thirteen years old, and even I know there are huge chunks of her life I know nothing about." Devin shrugged his shoulders acceptingly. "I don't need to." Devin looked at Gabe. "But you do. It's a much harder line for you to walk," he added.

"Any suggestions?" Gabe asked him.

Devin thought for a moment. "Walk the line…but don't be afraid to cross it when you need to, and don't be afraid to make her cross it too. My personal opinion is, she needs to share whatever that side of her is that she hates…she needs to know that someone can love her through whatever that darkness is."

Lawrence let Devin's words sit for a moment and then spoke. "Good advice, Devin." When Gabe met Lawrence's gaze, Lawrence only allowed a brief moment to hold before he changed the energy and stood up. "OK, times up. I want to hear the song now. Let's go."

Devin stood as well with a grin. "The boss has spoken."

Braidon stood and reached his hand out to Gabe. "I will head out before you go down. Tell Kayla it was nice meeting her. I'll call if anything comes up on my end. You do the same." Braidon turned to shake Devin's hand as well. "Very nice meeting you as well Devin," he said before Gabe walked him to the door.

After Braidon left, they headed down to the studio. When they got to the control room, Gary and Tommy were at the board laughing, and Kayla was sound asleep on the sofa along the back wall. As they walked in, Gabe saw Gary handing a twenty dollar bill over. Tommy looked up triumphantly at them.

"Gentlemen, never underestimate the wisdom of Devin Wilkons. Thank you Devin; I bet that you were right and I won," Tommy said.

"She did it? She made it better?" Devin asked.

"Better? My God…she just made the song with it. You aren't going to believe what she did," Gary said.

Lawrence smiled at Gabe. "Told you."

Lawrence crossed over as Tommy stood to give him the preferred center seat to hear the mix he had been waiting all night for.

Gabe went to the sofa to sit next to Kayla, softly lifting her head and placing it in his lap as he settled right next to her. She stirred slightly, but nestled into his lap and fell still again. He knew how exhausted she must be; she had been working on the recording non stop for weeks. He softly slid his hands along her arms and gently pulled her closer to him.

Tommy dimmed the lights in the studio slightly as Gary stood over the controls, ready to hit play.

"Lawrence, this is just the rough mix, but I do believe you are about to hear your next number one hit. This is even better than I was expecting," Gary said, and then he hit play.

When the song started, Gabe felt his heart flutter. The piano was beautiful, with a simple, but sweeping string arrangement behind it. His voice came in first, and he saw Devin smile at the sound and give him a thumbs up as he listened. Everyone seemed to be swept up immediately in the feel of the song and Gabe had to admit, he was really impressed with it. Then Kayla's voice came in and shivers shot across his skin. He instinctively held her closer to him as the song continued. When their voices hit the chorus together, he saw Lawrence shift, as if the power of their blended voices actually physically moved him. *Man, it sounded fantastic.*

When the song was almost done and they were at the last line, Gabe saw Gary and Tommy exchange an eager look of excitement before the final note was about to come out…and then he understood why. Their voices belted out the last note together, but then Kayla pushed her voice to a much higher note and held it out with his, with such strength and power, it invoked such an overwhelming emotional reaction he could hardly breathe when he heard it.

When the playback finished, Devin was the first to speak.

"My God! Amazing. That is amazing!" Devin said.

Lawrence took a long moment before he turned his chair around to face Gabe. When he did, Gabe saw immediately the look on his face that he gets when he knows he is on the verge of something big.

"Brilliant." He looked at Tommy. "I need a copy of this tonight. I have to get it to the director," then he focused back on Gabe. "This song has just gone from title song on the soundtrack to a featured part of the movie itself. This is going to be record breaking, I know it," Lawrence smiled. "I find it so fascinating that this song you wrote all those years ago, is now about to be a world wide hit...with you and Kayla." Lawrence held his gaze as the wonder in his eyes sparkled. Then he stood and shook Gary's hand. "Fantastic as always."

Tommy and Gary were thrilled to hear it. "Thank you. We knew you would want a copy tonight; already made it for you. Made one for you and Kayla too." Tommy handed the drives to Lawrence and Gabe.

"Thank you. You guys did a great job. The song sounds fantastic," Gabe said.

After Gary shut down the studio, Gabe walked everyone to the side door. Lawrence was the last to say goodnight and he shook Gabe's hand one more time.

"This song is going to be a hit. You ready for this?" he asked him.

"Absolutely," Gabe said.

Lawrence had a smile on his face that Gabe couldn't quite read.

"What is it Lawrence?" Gabe asked.

Lawrence kind of shook his head. "Nothing. It's just...fascinating to me..."

Gabe was unsure what he meant. "What is?"

Lawrence just smiled again and let out a breath. "How life works," he said simply as he walked out the door and up the patio steps. "Good night Gabe," he called over his shoulder.

Gabe knew there was something more underneath that, but he didn't know what it was, and he was too tired to try and figure it out.

He engaged the security system, and then walked back in the studio to see Kayla still fast asleep. He gently scooped her up in his arms and carried her upstairs, to his bedroom.

She didn't wake as he slipped under the covers next to her, but she did instinctively push herself into his body. He pulled her close to him and covered them both with the comforter. He kissed her sweetly and lowered his head on the pillow right next to her, relishing in the feel of her body wrapped tightly in his.

He closed his eyes and fell asleep to the mesmerizing sound of their voices blended together in the song he had written so many years ago…about a woman he had not met yet…but who he now knew, beyond a shadow of a doubt, was Kayla.

Chapter Thirteen
Revelations

Kayla had her coffee in her hands as she took in the view of the late morning sky through the kitchen window. It was overcast, gray and ominous. It was always somehow a welcome feeling; rain in LA. Maybe because it so rarely happened. Whatever the reason, it somehow seemed to ease the pressure of the boil stirring inside of her; balancing the scale of the darkness she felt creeping in, with the bright spotlight that now enveloped her, and the man she loved.

She knew she did. As much as she had been trying to convince herself otherwise, every moment in the studio with him…singing with him…making love with him…just being near him…she wasn't sure there was a force on Earth or in Heaven that could have prevented it. She stopped trying to lie to herself about it, and switched her focus to what her life could do to his. She had to keep reminding herself how unfair all of this was to him and that her best move, for everyone involved here, was to find a way to slip from him…if she could. The thought of it filled her with such pain and heartbreak, it was unbearable; but she knew she had to. She promised herself she would not let any of this touch him, and the only way to prevent that was to leave. But the sudden burst of fame around them both now would make that even more difficult.

It was amazing, and even Kayla was surprised by the response. Lawrence had made the decision to release their song before the movie premier, and had kept them busy with promotions and interviews. The song shot to number one in what seemed like a heartbeat, and was playing on all the major radio stations. The build up of anticipation it caused for the movie was palpable, and she knew the premiere was going to be a huge success.

Trying to describe the contradicting feelings that swept through her every time she heard the song…it always left her at a loss for words. It conjured a simultaneous feeling of euphoric comfort, and an unimaginably overbearing feeling of sadness. How can something manage, in one moment, to heal her heart, and break it, both at the same time?

She knew her time here in LA had to come to an end, and that moment when she would have to pull away from Gabe was nearing. It brought tears to her eyes and ineffable waves of torment to her very soul. Every time it overcame her, she had to use everything inside herself to force a shut down of it from her mind so he would not see it in her, but hiding her feelings from him had been getting harder and harder. He knew her so well, and it was a constant struggle to keep him thinking she was doing ok. She had the fantastic excuse of exhaustion from working herself so hard in the studio. Her relentless work ethic was the perfect cover for her inability to eat or sleep. The stress and heartbreaking pain at the thought of leaving him was constantly making her nauseous as well. She knew he didn't miss a thing. He tried, unsuccessfully to get her to eat last night when they got back from their press junket, but she just couldn't do it. It didn't surprise her that he got up extra early this morning to make her breakfast before he went with his brothers to do a final security sweep of the Grauman's Theater before the big premiere tonight.

She wanted to eat, but she couldn't. She felt sick.

Devin, however, was happily digging into the bacon and pancakes. "Kayla, why aren't you eating? This is fabulous. You must be the luckiest woman in the world. You have the most amazing man ever; being a living superhero and all, *but* he can also cook! Damn, it doesn't get much better than that!"

"He isn't mine, Devin," she said defensively.

Devin just looked at her like she was trying to convince him that two plus two equaled seventeen. "Please. You need to cut it out already. You know damn well that man is in love with you," he said.

She lifted her gaze and looked out the window from the kitchen table, and watched the raindrops hit the glass.

"Kayla, why are you trying to convince yourself that's not true?" Devin asked as he lifted his coffee. "Everyone knows it. You can't step into the room without his eyes lighting up, and try as you might, yours light up too. What's going on with you?"

Kayla didn't know what to say. Her emotions were just under the surface, threatening to beat their way out of her and she didn't even want Devin to see her in such a weakened state.

"I guess I just worry…there's a lot of chaos with all of this…just not sure its fair to bring all this into his world," she said as impassively as she could.

Devin was looking at her with that expression he uses when he unapologetically calls her on her crap.

"Please. You are so full of shit, I'm amazed you don't own a farm," Devin said with a laugh.

Kayla couldn't help but chuckle a little as she lifted her coffee mug to her lips. God, even the coffee didn't taste good this morning. She lowered her mug back down and looked for a way to change the subject.

"So now that you have a fabulous song on a major soundtrack, what are you going to do next?" she asked him.

Devin leaned back in his chair and held his coffee cup in his hands.

"I don't know. LA has grown on me…maybe I will spend more time out here. What about you?" he asked with an inquisitive smile as he lifted his coffee cup to his lips.

Kayla shrugged her shoulders and looked out the window at the rain. It was coming down harder now and the sky in the distance was heavy with dark clouds. She couldn't help but feel like it was a warning somehow...she shivered at the unease slinking under her skin.

Devin leaned forward. "Kayla, what ever it is...you have to talk to Gabe. Let him in. You can't keep holding whatever this is."

Tears formed in her eyes and she was powerless to hold them back. Her voice was tired and whisper quiet as she spoke. "I can't Devin. It's too much," she said.

Devin took a breath. "No, the only thing that is too much for that man, is anything that keeps you from him. He can handle anything, I'm sure of it. Gabe is stronger than Superman, and you can trust him," he said.

"It's not a matter of trust," she said, but Devin jumped on it.

"Bullshit. It is completely about trust. And let's face it, you suck at that," Devin said frankly.

Kayla couldn't help but laugh again.

A deep rumble of thunder crept through the air as the sky got even darker.

"Damn. Thunder in LA...that doesn't happen often," Devin said.

"No, it doesn't. Kind of creepy, isn't it?" Kayla said as she stood to look out the window. She glanced over at the patio table that was getting drenched by the falling rain, and saw her iPod and earphones. "Oh crap. My iPod is out there. Damn...well that's ruined."

Devin reached in his pocket and pulled out his iPod and headphones. "Here, you can use mine. Just give it back to me later."

"Thank you. I'll give it back to you tonight. My dress has a hidden pocket on the inside of it. I'll slip it in there so I don't forget to bring it." She picked up the headphones. "Nice. Are these the new bluetooth airphones? I hear these are amazing," she said.

"Yeah. Fantastic sound and the added benefit of the 'find my airphones' app. Seriously, how many times did I have to lose my earphones before I learned?!" he said with a laugh. Devin threw back the last swallow of his coffee and stood up. "I better go before it really gets bad out there. Have to pick up my tux for tonight." He gave her a hug and a kiss on the cheek. "You need anything?" he asked as he reached for his car keys.

"No thank you. I'm just going to lounge in a hot bath, and take all the time in the world to get ready for tonight. I'll see you later." Kayla walked him to the door. Gabe had insisted on keeping the alarm system on while he was gone today, so she lifted her finger to the pad, and punched in the code to open the door.

With a wave over his shoulder, Devin ran to his car trying to dodge the rain drops falling on him. Kayla closed the door and heard the alarm system click back into secure mode. She took a breath and headed for a long hot bath.

The day had past very quickly, and Gabe was now standing in the kitchen in his tuxedo, leaning against his marble countertop and adjusting his gold cufflinks. He was going over all the security aspects in his head, and he found it kind of funny that he was focusing his attention on the security side when at the same time, he knew full well he was now also about to be a VIP celebrity at the premiere too. What a strange turn for him, and yet he had to admit, it felt perfectly right to him. Everything with Kayla felt right to him. Each time he heard the song…that song…being sung by both of them…it was such a powerful thing; so cosmically perfect.

Perfect and yet he was fully aware that he still needed to break down that final barrier with her…and he was at a loss of how to do it. He knew, there was more behind her exhaustion from the blitz around recording the song and doing the promotional events Lawrence asked for. He could feel her unease…her sleep was only deep at those moments when she was absolutely wiped out, but he knew it wasn't restful. She wasn't eating and her nerves today seemed especially up.

When he had come back from the security walkthrough this afternoon, he had wanted some time to talk and try to find out what was going on with her, but Lawrence had interrupted them with a visit, to request they all get to the premiere a little earlier than planned for some extra camera time on the red carpet. Apparently there had been several requests for it and Lawrence felt like it was important to honor that.

Gabe looked at his watch, it was 4:30pm. He was just about to call across the livingroom towards the bedroom to see if Kayla was ready yet, but the door bell rang before he could. He crossed to the door, adjusting his sleeve and tuxedo jacket as he did so.

Gabe opened the door, and everyone was all smiles, and looking fabulous in their tuxedos and designer dresses.

Gabe smiled at them. "Good thing it's not raining anymore. Come on in, Kayla is still getting ready," he said.

"Of course she is. Women always take longer," Andy said as Jen laughed.

"I do believe you took longer than I did tonight, Andy," Jen corrected.

"Kayla can take all the time she needs, that is a woman's prerogative," Diane added.

Lawrence looked at his watch. "Don't encourage that Diane. We need to get her and Gabe on that red carpet or the press will have my hide. I promised them," he said.

Gabe laughed and hugged Betty. "You look fabulous my dear. I love the silver in your dress. It brings out your eyes," Gabe kissed her sweetly on the cheek as she smiled.

"Thank you darling. You look dashing! I love a man in a tux," Betty replied.

"Well, tonight you will be surrounded by five men in tuxedos," Nick added.

"But only one of us has Gucci shoes," Devin added with pride.

They all made their way to the living room and their chatter of compliments to each other on their evening wear was promptly interrupted when Kayla opened the door, and walked out of the bedroom to join them.

When Gabe looked up and saw her, his heart just about stopped. She looked incredible. Even more than he expected. She was wearing a long dark gray dress, with lines of black and hot pink accents; interspersed with little diamond sparkles throughout. The front of the dress was shorter than the rest, and the back of the dress swept around her waist like a cape, falling open off to the left side, exposing her long leg and that sparkling ankle bracelet he had loved since the first moment he saw her. She absolutely took his breath away.

Lawrence spoke first when Gabe was still trying to find his voice.

"You look stunning my dear," he said as he kissed her on the cheek sweetly.

Kayla smiled. "Thank you Lawrence. And may I say, this is an exceptionally good looking group! You all look amazing!" Kayla said as she redirected the attention back to everyone else.

After all the greetings and compliments went through the group, Kayla's eyes finally found Gabe's, and all he could do was smile at her. Then he hugged her close and whispered in her ear.

"Jesus…you look amazing," he said, and then he pulled her even closer to him, wrapping his arms around her tightly and finding himself not wanting to let go. He finally allowed himself to pull back to look at her again, and then he kissed her.

"Come on. We need to get a move on. I made promises to certain magazines and reporters that you guys would be there early, so let's not make a liar out of me, shall we?" Lawrence said with a smile.

As everyone moved towards the door, Gabe held Kayla back for a moment of privacy before the night was to begin. She looked up at him.

"You ok?" she asked.

He couldn't help but laugh that *she* was the one who spoke those words.

"That's *my* question. Are you ok?" he asked her.

"Yes." Gabe was not buying it. Something was on her mind and it was stirring an apprehension in him that she was not sharing it with him.

"Kayla…"

She smiled sweetly. "Gabe, I'm fine. Just tired. Think it's just the stress of everything. We've been on a whirlwind here," she said.

"Yes we have…but I know you….and I know there is more than that going on inside your head. I would very much like to have a serious talk with you tonight when we get back about…everything." Gabe said as he looked in her eyes. She lowered her gaze and did not respond. He gave her a final moment to hide from him, but that was the last one that he could allow. He softly lifted her chin and brought her eyes back to his. "Kayla…whatever it is…it's time to talk to me. I need you to let me in now." He saw the fear flash in her eyes, but he kept talking. "You should know by now that you can't say anything to me that would make me walk away from this. I'm all in, remember? I don't want this in-between us anymore," he said sweetly.

Lawrence called from the front door.

"You guys coming?" he called to them.

Gabe held Kayla's gaze another moment and then looked up and called back to Lawrence.

"Yes. We're on our way," he said. He kissed her one more time, feeling the apprehension that was swirling around her now, but he needed this to be addressed. He took her hand tightly in his and made note to himself to stay close to her tonight; to give her as much strength as he could so she didn't pull herself away from him. He couldn't let that happen.

As their caravan of limos pulled up to the VIP drop off section at the start of the red carpet, Gabe and Kayla were in the last one.

Lawrence and Betty were the first to pull up and step out to the flashing of photos and calls from the press. The next to join them was Devin, followed by Nick, Jen, Andy and Diane, who enjoyed a few moments of the carpet, but then they walked to the side to allow for Lawrence and Devin to pose for pictures.

As their limo pulled up, Kayla smiled at Gabe before their driver opened the car door. "I told you you didn't know what you were getting into," she said.

Gabe laughed. "Kayla, somehow I knew…the first moment I looked up and saw you outside the airport…my world changed in that moment. I didn't know how, I didn't know why…but I knew. And I'm so very grateful for it; for you." He held her gaze and kissed her deeply. He heard the click of the car door, and pulled his lips away from hers. He smiled at her as he took her hand in his. "Let's do this," he said.

Gabe stepped out and the flurry of clicks and flashes filled the air immediately; only to be drastically increased as Kayla stepped out to join him.

The eruption of media activity was mind boggling. It was like being suddenly caught inside a tornado of flashing lights and voices calling out and blinding them in an explosion of chaos. Kayla and Gabe found themselves the center of attention on the red carpet, and the sudden intensity of it enveloped them completely. Gabe felt Kayla pull her body close to his and he wrapped his arm around her waist, standing strongly next to her as they posed for the photos. A gust of wind swept up Kayla's dress and blew it gracefully behind them, exposing the full length of her leg; to which an even greater burst of snaps, clicks and flashes went off. Gabe was pretty sure they had just made the cover of every magazine here, in that one moment.

After indulging the press for what felt like a lifetime, they waved and smiled as they turned to begin the walk down the carpet into the theater to join the rest.

On the outside, Gabe was playing the part of the celebrity well, but internally, he was very much the Raider; keeping his eye on everyone and everything around them. So far, nothing looked out of the norm.

***

Inside the theater, holding a tray of champagne, the dark haired man glanced at his wrist quickly, double checking that his snake and devil horn tattoo was still covered. He pulled on the cuff of his white shirt, and then adjusted his red waiter's uniform jacket ensuring that he looked the part.

He caught the eye of his colleagues, some of whom were also dressed as waiters, and one of whom was not. They were strategically placed through out the theater, in constant eye contact, and would be waiting for his go when the moment presented itself to get the girl and bring her to his boss. It wouldn't be easy, but the plan they came up with was a good one. An unexpected distraction had been arranged, and was always the best course of action when trying to pull eyes off the target just long enough to make their move.

***

After mingling with the A-list celebrities who starred in the film, everyone moved to take their seats for the premiere. Andy, Nick and Gabe did a quick exchange with each other before they sat, double checking that all was good on the security front, which it seemed to be. Andy was in communication with Jasper who had eyes on the cameras. Nothing seemed out of the ordinary so far.

Gabe sat next to Kayla and as the lights went dark, he took her hand. She met his eyes and he lifted her hand softly to his lips and kissed it, then lowered her hand back down, resting it on his leg and protectively inside his grip.

As the movie played, Gabe was doing his normal balance of observation on the screen as well as Kayla. She was holding onto his hand tightly and he was glad for that. The feel of her holding onto him was everything to him. It was strange…as much as he was honored to be part of the magical swirl of this evening, to be in this position that many would kill for, he really just wanted to get her back to his home and dismantle the barricade that was blocking this hidden part of her. Something in her was stirring now more than ever. With their work on the project done, he had to admit, he was…concerned; about her…and about her pulling away from him.

His attention was brought back to the screen as that familiar piano introduction of their song started, and then he heard his own voice sweep through the grand theater. He felt everyone fall under the spell of the music, and even more so when Kayla's voice came in; and just like it had with Lawrence; when their voices joined together for the chorus, he saw a physical shift in the audience as the emotional response of their blended vibrations actually moved them. It was an extraordinary moment to experience. The power of the feelings in music on the human soul…and that power was coming, in this moment, from Kayla and him. It was almost otherworldly; as Gabe listened to the words of the song he had written so many years ago… that his grandfather had started even years before that…and understanding it was now a deep part of the love story on the screen… as it was for the love story of his grandfather…and even his own love story with Kayla. It was remarkable…the hands of fate. It brought tears to his eyes, and he was exceptionally moved by it. It was a remarkable glimpse into the cosmic power of love; it's endless life, and it's ability to connect itself through the timeless vibrations of limitless forces. He had never felt his place in that quite like he did in this moment. His hand squeezed Kayla's tighter as she did the same with his, and their eyes met; tears falling from both of them. He held her gaze, and then that force between them pulled them together again. He leaned in, as did she. The timing was serendipitous; his lips took hers just as their voices ignited the audience with the power of their last note, and he kissed her deeply. He felt the power burst through him, and felt it all around him, as his lips held hers. My God; he loved this woman, and he would tell her tonight, whether she was ready to hear it or not.

She found a great deal of comfort in the fact that Gabe kept himself close to her all night. He was steadfast in keeping his connection to her as the swarms of people continued to come up to them with rave reviews of their song and performance. As always, Gabe was exceptional at holding his own, and he morphed into this role of celebrity artist with such ease, it was almost amazing to her that he had never done this before.

Gabe had managed to maneuver them over to the buffet; she knew he was concerned about her lack of appetite and she was certain he was going to try and get her to eat something; which she had no desire for, but would do it anyway to keep him from worrying about her.

He was gathering a small plate of shrimp and finger sandwiches as they continued their conversation with Rick, the director of the film. As she suspected, Gabe sweetly handed her the plate as Rick commented on the answer Gabe had just given as to the origins of the song.

"That's amazing. That's a movie right there, isn't it?" he said with a smile.

"Well, we are very glad you like it. You worked it into the movie beautifully. It's an honor to be part of it," Gabe said as his arm was back around her waist.

Kayla ate the shrimp and saw Gabe's relief that she was eating something. She knew he was waiting for that. She still didn't want to eat anything, but she did it anyway to ease the concern she knew was floating through him about her.

Someone across the room called to Rick, and after he acknowledged him, he turned back to Gabe and Kayla.

"Gabe, might I steal her for a moment. I Would very much like to introduce Kayla to Michael Freeman. He is one of our biggest financial investors and asked if I would be so kind as to do so."

Gabe did a quick scan of Kayla to make sure she was ok with it, and then he smiled and released her.

"Of course." He gave her a reassuring look, and she knew it was his way of letting her know he was there.

Kayla handed him back the plate of food and crossed the room with Rick.

Rick introduced her to Michael, and she shook his hand politely. He seemed nice enough…at first…but Kayla couldn't help but feel a slight cold start to course through her as her conversation with him continued. Something in the way he looked at her…she didn't like it, but she was doing her best to cover her unease as they discussed the movie. To her delight, Diane came over to join in their conversation.

"Diane, this is Michael Freeman. Michael, this is Diane Saxton. She is a fabulous actress," Kayla said, grateful for the distraction and the comfort of having someone she knew standing with her.

Michael politely reached out his hand to shake Diane's and Kayla caught sight of a mark on his wrist just under his cuff. At first, she thought it must have been a mistake of her eyes, but it became even clearer as his hand moved, and the mark revealed a little more of itself. Kayla froze. Her heart rate increased and she backed up instinctively, accidentally bumping into the waiter that was standing right behind her, and spilling a glass of champagne on his hand.

Kayla was flustered as she tried to apologize; but when she looked up and saw the waiter, she had an instant feeling that she recognized him. He had an eccentric look behind his dark eyes and dark hair. Wasn't he the reporter that asked her if she was on her way back to Switzerland? Why was he dressed as a waiter? For some reason, her eyes got pulled to where he was wiping away the champagne that she had spilled on his wrist, and she saw the mark…again. Her eyes lifted as the absolute shock and fear exploded in her, sucking out what little air she had left in her lungs.

"Kayla, are you ok?" Diane asked.

Kayla struggled, but found a small part of her voice, shaky as it was, and spoke as she moved herself backwards towards the hallway. "I feel a little sick actually. I think it was the shrimp. Would you excuse me for a minute?"

As she stepped back even further, the crooked smile on the waiters face stripped her of any need she had to cover her exit smoothly. Terror filled her entire being. She felt as though the pressure under her entire world was thundering to an uncontrollable breaking point, and she almost felt like she was on the brink of either passing out or throwing up all over the place. The waiter had his cold eyes on her, as did Michael. Lawrence was heading over to her, with a look of concern on his face. She thought she heard him calling for Gabe, but the horror rushing through her overpowered everything else, and she couldn't think straight. *Run!* It was the only thought that screamed out of the chaos erupting inside her. *Kayla, run! Now!*

Kayla whipped around the corner and made a break for one of the many doors towards the back of the theater. She chose one at random and had no idea where it led to, but she didn't care. She had to get the hell out of here.

Just as she was slipping through the door, she heard a sudden commotion from the main room, and without warning, all the lights in the theater instantly shut off. After the door behind her closed, she could hear a few screams of panic, glass breaking and what sounded like a stampede. She could hear men yelling, and heavy footsteps running down the hall, past the door she had just escaped through.

Fuck. She was terrified. She had to go now. Her eyes found their way through the complete darkness to an emergency exit sign just down the stairs. Kayla flew like the wind towards it.

As she came out the door, her ankle bracelet caught on something and snapped off, spilling the diamonds on the street around her. When she made it through the exit, and the door closed with a hard smack behind her, she found herself outside on the sidewalk behind the theater.

As she was trying to gather her bearings, she looked up and saw a very unexpected sight.

Matthew Edson.

He looked just as surprised to see her.

"Kayla," he said. "What are you doing out here. I thought you were inside celebrating your big hit."

Matthew was smoking a cigarette, standing with his security team infront of their SUV's.

Her breathing was panicked and she had a hard time catching her breath enough to speak. "Matthew. What are you doing here?" she asked him.

He thought for a moment before he answered her. "Smoke break. Can't smoke inside anymore." He put his cigarette out and moved closer to her. "Are you ok? You don't look so good?" he asked.

Kayla's fear was flooding through her still and she didn't know what else to say. "Matthew, I need to get out of here."

A smile came across his face as he gestured to his cars behind him. "Then let's go," he said.

One of Matthews security men opened the car door for her. It wasn't her first choice, but she had to get away from here fast, so she got in.

Matthew grinned at his security man as he followed her into the car. The man closed the car door…and the snake and devil horn tattoo on his wrist twitched as he pulled his hand from the handle, and moved to the drivers seat. They had her now.

Gabe was furious! He was livid, and in complete shock that Kayla was missing.

"How the fuck did this happen?" he yelled as they entered the Saxton Security building.

After casing the theater trying to find her, he made the call to leave half the team at the theater to continue the search, and pull the top team back to the Saxton building so he could push them to the brink to find out where she was and get her back.

As Nick and Andy were ferociously barking orders to the various department heads, Gabe stormed into the main room and snapped harshly at Jasper.

"Damn it Jasper, tell me you have something now on the outside cameras!" Gabe yelled. "I need to know every single car that was around the building. I want traces on every fucking one of them!"

Jasper was working feverishly at his computer and tried to answer Gabe as calmly as he could. "Every camera in the theater was knocked out by the outage. I'm trying to pull from the independent cameras across the street behind the theater. I need a few minutes," Jasper said as he continued to work at hyper speed.

"We don't have a few minutes! I need the footage from those cameras now. Where the fuck is she?" Gabe yelled.

Lawrence spoke through a fear filled voice. "Don't you have a tracker on her, Gabe?" he asked.

"I did have one on her. I put one on her ankle bracelet, but it broke off on the street by the back exit of the theater." Gabe turned to Jasper again. "Jasper, I need footage of that exit. Now!" he ordered. "Nick, get Braidon on the phone. We need the Raiders ASAP." Nick did so as Jen, Diane and Devin stood motionless in the back of the room, unsure about anything.

Andy looked up from his phone to Gabe. "We have all of Sykes's men from the theater (including the waiter and Michael) in the holding room downstairs," he said. Gabe nodded. He was about ready to punch holes in all the walls of this place.

He was so angry…with himself as well as his team. "Fuck!" He yelled as he punched the desk.

Andy stepped up. "Gabe, we will find her," he said.

Gabe thought out loud. "What the Hell happened? Why did she run?" He looked to Diane. "Diane, tell me everything you remember about those few moments before the lights went out. You were standing right next to her. Tell me everything you recall," Gabe instructed as calmly as he could.

Diane was clearly shaken but did her best to gather her thoughts.

"She…umm…she went really pale and said she didn't feel well. I think she was sick to her stomach and wanted to clear the room and head for the bathroom," Diane said.

Lawrence was losing his temper. "What about her cell phone. Can we trace her with that?" Lawrence asked in a panic.

Gabe let out a frustrated breath. "I have her phone. She asked me to hold it for her during the movie, and I didn't think to give it back to her," he said. Before Gabe had a chance for another burst of anger to fly out of him, Jasper called out.

"I have it," he said.

Gabe leaped over the table to see what he had, and the rest quickly gathered around as well.

Gabe felt his heart stop when he saw the image from the camera footage of the governor's caravan parked out back of the theater.

"Matthew Edson? What the fuck was *he* doing there?" Gabe said in shock.

"Our team had him tracked in Sacramento. I just checked in with them. They reported that he was still at the mansion with his SUV's out front. They said it looked like he was getting ready to go somewhere, but he still hadn't come out yet," Nick exclaimed.

"The SUV show at the mansion was a decoy. Damn it!" Gabe said.

"There she is," Jasper announced as they watched the camera footage showing Kayla come out of the theater and land right infront of Matthew.

Lawrence and Gabe both had a look of horror cross their faces as they watched Kayla get into Matthew's car.

Gabe was completely astonished. "What the Hell? Why would she do that? She would never get in a car with someone she didn't know…" his fear for her was all over his voice.

Lawrence was quiet for a moment, then spoke. "She *does* know him. At least…she thinks she does," he said.

Gabe was shocked. "What? How does she know Matthew?" When Lawrence hesitated with his answer, Gabe lost it and he threw a coffee cup across the room in anger. "Kayla's life is on the line Lawrence! I need to know everything so I can figure out how to get her back. What the fuck is going on?" he yelled.

In the silence that filled the space after Gabe's outburst, Betty stood.

"Lawrence, tell him," she said in a very calm voice from across the room. "You need to tell him."

Lawrence looked up at his wife, and then turned to Gabe. "Secure room, now," Lawrence said.

Gabe kept his eyes locked on Lawrence for a moment longer, then snapped another order to Jasper as he turned to follow his brothers to a secure room.

"Track those cars. Now," he said.

Andy opened the door to the closest secure room they had. Gabe stormed in, followed by Lawrence, Nick and then Andy. Seconds after the door shut tightly, Gabe's voice was harsh and stern.

"Out with it right now Lawrence."

Lawrence was clearly struggling with what to say and Gabe could not fathom what could possibly be causing his hesitation, but he was getting angrier by the second. "Lawrence, you were right there! Right by two of Sykes's men when the lights went out. They could have easily gotten you and swept you out through the back exit, but they didn't. They went after Kayla. Why on earth would they do that if Kayla was the tool to target you?" When Lawrence looked at him but still could not find his voice, Gabe slammed his hand down on the table in frustration. "Lawrence, answer me!"

Lawrence finally spit it out. "Because *I* was never the target!" he yelled. There was fear and pain in the anger in Lawrence's voice, and the outburst caused the room to fall deathly quiet. An immeasurable weight filled the absolutely stunned silence; no one spoke…or even seemed to breathe. Lawrence settled his emotions as best he could and finished his sentence in a voice heavy with anguish. "*Kayla* is the target."

Gabe lost his breath. "What?"

Lawrence met Gabe's eyes. He gave it a long moment and then continued. "I spent my life trying to protect her. Sykes was always after Kayla," he said with a terrified surrender.

Gabe felt a piercing cold ice through his entire being. On a deeper level, his mind was piecing it together…but he couldn't quite bring himself to see it yet. He felt it in his bones, a shocking revelation was about to make itself known. He heard his voice ask the question. "Why?"

Lawrence took a very deep breath. He locked his eyes on Gabe, and then, in the needed surrender, he spoke the truth he had hidden all these years.

"Because Kayla is Livy Ann."

Chapter Fourteen

Hell Hath No Fury

Gabe was stunned. Speechless. Even for a man who had taken his share of sucker punches in the gut, this felt like the knock out punch he had never quite experienced. Until now.

"What?" was all he could get out as he tried to regain some semblance of control over the flood of emotions and memories that had exploded throughout his body.

Lawrence repeated the chilling words again. "Kayla is Livy Ann," he said.

Gabe could hardly breathe. It was such a cosmic shock to him; throwing him so off balance he was struggling to keep all the thoughts in his head from crashing into each other and causing his brain to overload.

Andy was the first to break the silence. "Jesus." He couldn't get out any more than that. Andy leaned on the chair in front of him for support.

Nick finally found his voice. "Why didn't you tell us that Lawrence?" he asked.

Lawrence still hadn't pulled his gaze from Gabe, but reluctantly did so to address Nick.

"I couldn't. I couldn't tell you back then because I needed your teams to keep looking for her after she disappeared." Lawrence looked back at Gabe. "Sykes's men were watching every movement. If you had given up, even a little, they would have known we had her hidden. The only way to throw them off our trail was for them to think we had no idea where she was. The media had to keep reporting your efforts in trying to find her. And the simple fact; the less people who knew, the safer she was."

Gabe's control was coming back to him and he was able to get his inner Raider to separate from the man inside him that was terrified for Kayla. The revelation that she is in fact Livy Ann…her life was in more danger than he realized, and the clock was ticking. These men would kill her tonight if he couldn't find her first. He pushed that unbearable thought away, and allowed his anger to replace his fear.

Now he had to use his head; quickly, efficiently and put all the pieces in place to destroy these men once and for all. The tactical side of him was stepping back up, and his training was kicking in again. It had to. Saving her was the only option. He needed to gather all the facts, and quickly put them together.

"Who knows?" Gabe asked.

"Betty and I…and Matthew Edson. "

Gabe shoved the chair that was in front of him at hearing that; but his mind rapidly explained it to him just as Nick was asking the question.

"Why on Earth does Matthew Edson know?" Nick asked.

Gabe didn't even need to look at Lawrence for confirmation. His mind zeroed in on what Lawrence had told him when they first had the conversation about Kayla's protection.

"Because, at the time, Matthew was working for the FBI. Witness protection." He looked up at Lawrence. "You didn't call him in to help you *find* Livy Ann; you called him in to help you *hide* her."

Lawrence nodded. "Yes. I did."

"How did Livy Ann end up with you that night, Lawrence?" Nick asked.

"T-bone," Lawrence answered. "T-bone's partner was the officer who was patrolling that night when Kayla escaped, and he was the one who found her. As soon as he did, he called T-bone."

"Terry Bonen," Nick said with fondness. "He was one of the best boots on the ground we had with the local police. He was with us from day one when we wanted eyes on Sykes's house. I can't believe he never told me."

"He never told me either," Andy said, then looked to Lawrence. "He kept that secret to save her life. And his."

"Yes," Lawrence said. "He knew immediately the danger she was in, especially when they discovered the evidence in the bag she had with her. He did some very clever footwork to keep her out of sight, then he called me. It was T-bone's actions that saved her."

"We all knew T-bone. If he didn't even tell us, than he certainly didn't tell anyone else that she survived," Andy said.

"No, he did not. Up through the day he died, he never told a soul. Once he handed her off to me that night, he slipped out of the picture completely so he could never be traced to her disappearance. He knew she lived, but he did not know Livy's new identity. Matthew is the only other person, besides Betty and I, who knew that."

Gabe spoke through the turning wheels in his mind. "So that's why Matthew was able to climb up the political ladder so fast." He looked up. "He had the info Sykes needed, and he used it." Gabe was livid.

Andy let out a breath. "It's no secret that Sykes still had tremendous influence, even from behind bars."

"Yeah. He still had plenty of men and hidden evidence on the outside to hold serious pressure over a lot of people. The one thing he didn't have, was Livy Ann," Nick added.

"Her actions ended everything for him. Stripped him of his power, his lifestyle and his freedom," Lawrence said. "I had eyes on him while he was inside. I was told he spent all his time combing through every detail of every person known to be involved that night. He knew his men never found her, so he knew she was out there somewhere."

Lawrence looked at Gabe. "My sources told me he was paying very close attention to the take downs of his celebrity clients, and it didn't take him long to figure out I had a big hand in all of that; it triggered him, and I knew he was looking into me because of that. When he started down that road, I knew it was only a matter of time before he stumbled onto Matthew Edson because of my friendship with him. His position with the Witness Protection Program and his proximity to me would never have slipped Sykes's attention." Lawrence looked at Gabe. "His anger at Livy Ann never faded; it got worse. She destroyed his delusion of invincibility; and that destruction, ironically, not only came from a woman, it came from a little girl. It enraged him. I was told that his need to…punish her for that, was his daily focus. Once I saw Matthew's career projection suddenly going up, and his communication with me going down…I knew. Then when he won the election as Governor…I knew she was in trouble."

Gabe looked up at his brothers after another moment of contemplation. "OK, so we have to assume everyone of Sykes's men knows who she is." Gabe turned to Andy. "We got all of Sykes's men who were at the theater?"

"Yes," Andy affirmed.

Gabe checked his watch as his mind registered the pressure of the ticking clock. He gathered his control and spoke.

"First; this info about Kayla does not leave this room," Gabe instructed.

"Without question," Andy agreed as Nick and Lawrence affirmed that as well.

"We have to find Matthew. He is the key to finding Kayla and Sykes." Gabe centered his mind and slowed his breathing. He needed to use all his strength to separate his emotions around the danger Kayla was in, and focus everything he had on getting the information he needed; but one thing was crystal clear to him, and he needed to make sure his brothers understood it. Gabe had never felt a stronger pull from his inner Raider as he did with the next words about to leave his mouth. He looked at his brothers and spoke in a calm, but very cold voice. "This time…we're doing things differently…" Both his brothers nodded, and he had no doubt that they knew exactly what he meant.

When they walked out of the secure room and back to the main control center of Saxton Security, everyone was bustling at their stations, working with a fever pitch.

Jasper waved them over when they came into view, and Gabe made a beeline over to him, with his brothers and Lawrence close behind him.

"We can't track the Governors cars. The plates were fake, and we lost a connected camera trail when they made it on the 101 heading North."

Andy spoke. "If they are headed North, that might take a water escape off the map. But I will have the SEAL teams standing by just in case." Andy was already on the phone with the Navy Commander.

Gabe thought for a moment, then looked to Nick. "They could be heading to Van Nuys. Private airfield." Gabe looked at his watch. "Damn it. If that's where they were headed, they would be there by now."

Nick pulled out his phone. "I'll make a call. Have them shut down any take offs from there. Just in case."

"No need," Braidon's voice interrupted as he crossed into the room to Gabe, with his Raider team behind him. Everyone cleared the way for them as they appeared.

"Braidon. Why? What do you know?" Gabe asked as he reached him.

"The FAA reported a few minutes ago to NORAD. Private plane took off from Van Nuys fifteen minutes ago, and switched their transponder off ten minutes into the flight. Private Charter reported confirmation of Governor Edson's presence on the plane, along with four other passengers, including a woman."

Gabe slammed his fist on the desk, causing another coffee cup to smash on the ground. "Damn it. Do we have any idea where they are taking her?"

"No," Braidon admitted.

Rita, who had been quietly trying to do what she could to help, bent down to pick up the pieces of the broken cup and throw them away.

"Think! I need everyone in here to think! We have to find a way to track them," Gabe yelled.

Rita backed away and went to sit down next to Devin and Diane.

Gabe turned to Andy, "Can we track Matthews phone?" he asked.

Andy went to his station and began punching in his commands on the keyboard in front of his huge computer. A few minutes later, he looked up in disappointment. "He ditched it at the Airport. It's tracking at Van Nuys." Andy slammed his fist on the desk.

"Damn it!" Gabe's anger was escaping him again. "I should have put a fucking tracking chip *in* her! How many times do I have to lose this woman before I learn?!" He knew the outburst was unworthy of a Marine Raider, but Kayla was in so much danger...every minute he wasn't moving closer to her was a minute closer to him never seeing her again, and he could not accept that.

But his outburst triggered something in Devin and he shot up from his seat. "Gabe! Find my headphones! Find my Headphones!" Gabe had no idea what Devin was saying, but the look on his face had his attention, as Devin quickly crossed over to him. When Devin reached him he spat it out. "Kayla has my headphones! I have that 'find my headphones' app. Will that work? Can we use that?"

Gabe was confused. "What do you mean Devin? She didn't have a purse with her. That's why she needed me to hold her phone. I didn't see her with your headphones tonight," he said.

Devin shook his head. "She told me she had a hidden pocket inside her dress. She borrowed my Ipod and headphones and she promised me she would bring them tonight. She had a pocket…if it was empty, she would have put her phone in there, but she needed you to take it. I think she has my iPod and headphones in there. Can we track that?"

Gabe was instantly filled with a surge of hope. "Andy! Get his info and pull it up."

Devin ran over to Andy's station with Gabe, Nick and Braidon close behind. A few minutes later, a blinking dot appeared on the big screen in front of them. They had her.

A cheer swept through the room at the sight, and Gabe felt an amazing sense of relief, but only for a second. Then his tactical side kicked in hard. Now that they could track her, they needed to gain an advantage. They needed to get ahead of her,

"We have to figure out where they are headed," Gabe said.

"This is exactly why he ditched Saxton Security. He knew you would be able to see all of his information if you guys still ran things," Lawrence said.

"Yeah, would have been as easy as opening the front door," Nick replied.

Gabe looked up at that. "What about the backdoor?" Gabe looked to Andy. "You always put in a backdoor…did you do that when we re-did all his security protocols?" he asked him.

Andy nodded, but didn't look convinced. "Yeah, of course I did. But any good security team would have wiped that when they took over. I can't imagine that would still work."

Jasper chimed in. "Yeah…any *good* security team; but from everything we've seen so far, this new security team that took over for Edson is Sykes's men. They aren't tech savvy…they might not have thought about a backdoor. Hell, they might not even know what a backdoor is."

Gabe looked back to Andy. "Try it Andy," he said.

A few minutes later, a surprised relief swept Andy's face. "Jesus. I got in!"

Gabe felt his heart rate kick into high gear, and Nick barked a general order. "All heads, plug into Andy's station and start sweeping." As he gave specific areas for each department to focus on, Gabe chimed in.

"Look for any large sums of money being transferred. Any expensive properties or big purchases," Gabe instructed.

After a few moments, Jasper spoke up. "How about forty five million? Sound like what we're looking for?" he asked.

Gabe spun around and made a dash over to his desk. "What is it?"

Jasper pointed to the map on his screen. "Looks like a small island in the Caribbean. Virgin Islands, Little Pikos. Matthew's records show he purchased it quietly a few months ago with a money transfer from off shore banks."

"That's Sykes. Matthew doesn't have that kind of money," Nick said.

"Virgin Islands," Gabe checked the trajectory of the tracer they had on Kayla. "That's in their direct path, That's got to be it."

"We can beat them there. I'll call the VI Air National Guard and fill them in and get assistance. The base there will have everything we need," Braidon said as he lifted his phone.

* * *

By the time they entered St. Croix airspace, Gabe felt like a lifetime had gone by. He was counting down each second in his head and the time it took to get there, though faster than anyone else could have done it, it was far too slow for Gabe. His only reassuring thought was that he believed Kayla was still alive. He knew the kind of man Sykes was; ego driven, vengeful and believing himself omnipotent. Men like that thrive on taking their own revenge; especially when the target of their anger had landed their own punishing blow first. A snake that bites back is always harsher than the one that bites first. He knew Sykes would have given orders that Kayla was not to be killed by anyone but him. And he was pretty sure Sykes had a long, punishing plan for that. Which meant he had time; but that didn't make his impatience or his anger any lighter. Gabe's inner rage was breathing ferociously just under the surface; like a dragon poised to strike, and he knew, when he saw Sykes, it was going to come out whether he wanted it to or not. The truth was…he couldn't wait to get his livid hands on Sykes, and pull him apart limb by limb before grabbing his neck and twisting it slowly. Every time he thought about what he might have done to Kayla…he felt his hands clench even tighter. Sykes was a dead man.

The command center at the Air base had been in constant contact with Gabe and his team during the flight, and they had managed, with the use of high-tech drones and other equipment to surveil Sykes's compound on the island. There was no sign of any women or civilians other than Sykes and his men, so the only rescue needed would be Kayla's. They had the confirmation they needed. Sykes was indeed there, along with fifty of his men, ten of whom always seemed to be close to Sykes.

They were given the layout of the compound and had spent much of the flight going over their plan of attack. Now it was just a matter of time until the private plane with Kayla and Matthew showed up, and Gabe could save her, then take the rest out. Gabe checked his watch again…Damn, he wanted to charge in right now.

After the wheels hit the runway, and the doors opened, Gabe's pace was wicked fast as he exited the plane . He, and the teams with him, made their way for the command center in the Headquarters of the Virgin Islands Air National Guard building in front of them.

Andy, Nick and Braidon's team were right behind him, as were all of Sykes's men they had captured from the theater. They were bound at the hands and being handled by SEAL team Twelve A, several of whom had actually been trained by Andy. There was no question this group of men were not playing games, and even the decorated officers approaching them for the welcome greeting had looks crossing their faces that suggested a very healthy respect for the arrivals.

The younger of the men spoke the introductions as he reached his hand out to Gabe, whom he obviously recognized.

"Captain Saxton, I am Adjutant General Mick Sans." He continued the introductions as Gabe shook his hand. "This is Lieutenant General Scott Killman, Chief Master Sgt. Phillip Keems, and Commander Debrah Hayden." Polite nods and hellos were exchanged as they kept their pace towards the command center.

"Orders from the top are that you have carte blanche. So whatever you need, you got it Captain Saxton," Lieutenant General Killman said.

"Good, because I have a list." Gabe handed him the piece of paper with his requirements. "And we need it now." The general looked over the list. Gabe saw the look of surprise underneath his nod; the fire power he was asking for was extreme, but the general did not hesitate.

"Consider it done. We have all the equipment you will need inside. Follow me." He led the way.

The admiration for Gabe and his men was crystal clear as they walked past the myriad of soldiers all standing at attention with complete respect for them.

On the far end of the room, a full display of various combat weapons were there for their choosing.

"Take what you want," General Killman said. "Adjutant General Sans will provide you with whatever you need. I will get the rest of your requests in order."

As the SEAL team remained on the far end holding Sykes's men, Gabe and the rest followed Sans to the weapons. The choices were impressive.

"We have everything here from your standard bolt action M1903 bayonet rifle, the squad automatic M1918 Browning, the Johnson M1941 machine guns and the M27 if you want the classics. But we also have the M249 which you know has a much greater volume of fire power and tactical benefit; plus throw on a six inch suppressor on the end of the 16-inch IAR, and you've got yourself a pretty killer medieval Pike, which I know some of the boys like." Sans continued to the rest of the equipment. "We have the MK48 with the 7.62 mm caliber and the popular M38 which can hit targets at a distance of 600 yards or more; my personal favorite as it proved very useful in Iraq and Afghanistan. We have the Heckler & Koch K416, the MK 13 & MK48 and the M4 Carbine; some of the best machine guns out there, as well as grenades and explosives. For your CQB, if you want to get that close, we have the colt 45, the Glock 19, the Eotech XPS and your Bowie knives with 9" & 10" blades. As well as all the PEQ's and night vision equipment. For communication we have the Invisio X5's and the RAP 4's. Take what you need."

Gabe did not need the explanation; he knew every piece of equipment backwards and forwards. He allowed the others to take the weapons they wanted; and they did.

Sans turned to Gabe. "If my understanding is accurate, Captain Saxton, you were also a handler, is that correct?"

Gabe nodded. "Yes."

Sans gestured to his right just behind the table and escorted Gabe in that direction.

"This is Private First Class Walter Miggs," Sans said as the Private stood at attention for Gabe. Gabe nodded his hello, but his eyes were drawn to the two with him…at his feet. "He is the handler of two of our best MPC's," Sans said as he gestured to the two fierce looking Belgian Malinois sitting perfectly still at the sides of Miggs. "This is Zeus & Dev," Sans said proudly. "The Dev is short for Devour. She actually holds the K-9 Medal of Courage," Sans said.

"Yes Sir. She outranks me, Sir," Miggs said. "…and Zeus is the best tracker I have ever seen. He can detect a scent anywhere from zero to five hundred yards away. They are at your disposal, sir."

Gabe hadn't thought about that until this moment, but the nose of a K-9 might be the perfect additional tool for him to find Kayla as quickly as possible once they breeched the compound. Gabe knelt down to Zeus and pulled out the remnants of Kayla's ankle bracelet. He held it out to Zeus, who instantly stood on all fours, sniffed feverishly and then sat perfectly still, closed mouth and his eyes directly on Gabe.

"He's got the scent, sir. He's ready to go," Miggs said.

"Thank you. Their help would be much appreciated," Gabe said, then he took control of both dogs with one command. "Fuss!" Both dogs moved from Private Miggs to Gabe in one quick motion, and sat obediently by Gabe's side; eyes on him waiting for their next command. Gabe put the broken bracelet back in his pocket, and addressed Chief Master Sgt. Keems, who had crossed back over and rejoined them. "Sgt. Keems, how many of your soldiers here want a piece of this tonight?" Gabe asked him.

Keems smiled. "All of them, Captain. Sykes's arrival here is… unwelcome."

"Fine. I could use all of them you can spare to create a complete perimeter around the compound. No one runs. No one walks away. Not this time. But make sure they keep a very solid distance," Gabe said.

Keems tilted his head in a bit of confusion. "You don't need any of our men entering with you?" Sgt. Keems asked.

Gabe just shook his head as he turned back to the display of weapons . "No need," he said simply, as he looked over the remaining weapons in front of him.

Gabe had his own Colt 45 under his shirt, but didn't see the harm in grabbing another one, so he did. He grabbed the 10" Bowie knife as well, then turned to walk towards his men.

Sans was perplexed. "Captain Saxton, is that all you want? That knife and gun is for close quarter combat only," Sans said.

Gabe spoke without hesitation. "I know." His answer was simple, but it swept a physical chill across Sans's skin that caused him to shift in his boots. Sans looked to Braidon for confirmation. Braidon just grinned slightly and spoke quietly to Sans as Gabe walked a few more steps towards the men.

"Shit is about to fly," Braidon said.

Gabe addressed his men as they all stood ready with their weapons and equipment.

"This is very simple. We have two missions. The first; save Kayla Knight," Gabe instructed.

"And the second?" one of Braidon's men asked.

"Obliterate everything else," Gabe ordered.

Sans shifted at the ice cold that fell through the air, and looked to Braidon, "Is that…correct?"

Gabe heard him, and turned to face Sans. As he held Sans's gaze and stepped towards him, he called over his shoulder to one of the SEAL's holding Sykes's captured men from the theater. "Captain Langley bring over one of the men. Any one of them," he ordered.

"Yes Sir," Langley answered and pulled a random man from the line up and crossed over with him in his custody. When they reached Gabe and Sans, Gabe still had his eyes on Sans as he spoke to Langley.

"Remove that mans sleeve from his left arm." Gabe ordered.

"Yes sir," Captain Langley did so.

"Adjutant General Sans, what do you see on this piece of shits arm?" Gabe asked.

Sans took his eyes from Gabe and looked at the exposed arm. "A bunch of little teardrop tattoos, sir,"

"How many?" Gabe asked.

Sans took a moment to look then answered him, "Twenty four, sir."

"How many of each color do you see Adjutant General Sans?" Gabe asked, his voice getting colder with each question, and Sans getting more and more uncomfortable.

"Seven black, ten gray, seven pink, sir," he replied.

"Do you know what that signifies?" Gabe asked him coldly.

Sans shook his head, clearly concerned about learning the answer to that question. "No sir. I do not,"

"Raping women is a game to these men. They keep score. Each teardrop represents each rape. Black is for adult women. Gray is for underage women. And pink is for children." Gabe was holding back his disgust as best he could to drive his point home to Sans who was going a bit pale. "Adjutant General Sans…how many of those teardrops have a red dot?" he asked him harshly.

Sans looked to the man's arm then back to Gabe. "Five." Sans was losing the strength in his voice.

Gabe's voice got even colder. "Which color teardrops have the red dots Adjutant General Sans," Gabe asked him.

Sans went even paler as he looked at the man's arm, then back to Gabe. "All five red dots are in the pink ones," he replied.

"Do you know what that signifies?" Gabe asked him. When Sans just shook his head, Gabe answered it for him. "A red dot in the mark signifies that the victim was murdered either during or right after the rape, by the man proudly displaying the fucking tattoo." Gabe was not quite able to keep his anger from his voice. Sans looked like he was going to throw up. "You still have a problem with the order I just gave?" he asked.

Sans straightened up and replied strongly. "No sir."

Gabe turned to Langley. "Get these assholes on the chopper," he ordered.

"Yes sir," Langley responded as he moved the man back to the rest and shouted the order to his team to move out. Gabe gave his own orders as well. As he headed out to the choppers with his men, and Zeus & Dev at his sides, Sans turned to Braidon.

"Do you want medevac choppers ready?" he asked him.

Braidon turned his attention from Gabe to Sans. "Just one, in case Kayla is hurt," he said.

"Are you sure you don't need more?" Sans asked.

Braidon had his eyes back in Gabe's direction and answered in an ominous voice as he watched Gabe walk towards the choppers. "We're not going to need it."

Kayla was drifting in and out of consciousness, trying desperately to focus her mind and figure out where she was and what had happened. Her shoulder hurt like hell and moving her right arm was almost impossible from the pain of it. Flashes were shooting through her mind...Matthew Edson...the limo...she had a vague memory of the limo ride...Jesus, Matthew's security man had the mark on his wrist. When she saw it there was an immediate struggle as she tried to escape the car, but she was overpowered by Matthew and his security guard, who had twisted her right arm so hard, she was sure her shoulder was dislocated. She remembered Matthew sticking a needle in her arm...and she went blank. She couldn't remember anything after that; until this moment.

She felt herself being carried roughly through a hallway and up several flights of stairs. She heard a door open and felt herself get thrown on a bed. It sounded like two men arguing with each other as one of them harshly put a metal cuff around her wrist and then she heard the other end of it snap to the bed frame behind her. She pulled at it, but it did not budge. She knew she was trapped.

She heard the door close and the room fell quiet. She was pretty sure she was alone, for the moment, but she still couldn't get her eyes to focus.

Her head was killing her and the incredible weakness was impossible to fight. She couldn't move. Even focusing her mind was an unachievable goal. She couldn't think straight...but she knew one thing for sure. He found her...and it was only a matter of time before Sykes would walk through that door, and she would be finished. The fear was indescribable and the only thought she could muster to help ease herself now, was Gabe. She felt herself longing for him...needing to feel him near her just one more time before she met her end on this planet. God, she prayed he was ok. She was thankful she ran when she did. Because she ran, they would not have wasted time going after Gabe; only her. Gabe should not be in any danger. She could never have forgiven herself if anything had happened to him because of her. As much as she desperately wanted to see him walk through that door and wrap his arms around her, she needed him to be safe; to not know any of this. She tried to ease herself in the belief that Gabe would remember her as the strong woman standing by him on the red carpet…who sang with him on the song that meant so much to both of them…and not the victim of Jacob Sykes; not the girl who had been running from him since she was six years old. She prayed to God that he would never know that, and that he remained far away from all of this, so none of this darkness would ever touch him.

Kayla was not sure how much time passed, but she was shocked back into consciousness again when two men stormed into her room and wrenched her from the bed, unlocking the cuff attached to the bed frame and placing it quickly back on her other hand. She tried again to pull her hands free, but she was tightly bound with no hope of undoing it.

One of the men got right in her face and snarled. "Sykes wants you first…but we're all taking a turn with you tonight." He licked his lips like a slobbering bulldog and she had never been more disgusted and afraid in her entire life.

They whipped her out of the room and down the stairs. When they came to the end of the hallway, the men knocked on the door and she heard that voice…that horrible voice she had prayed she would never hear again. Her gut filled with ice cold terror.

"Come in," Sykes said in a wretchedly giddy tone.

They opened the door and threw Kayla in, following behind her and closing the door again.

Kayla felt all the life fall out of her in one second. Sykes. He was across the room, coming out from behind his big desk. His evil eyes were locked on hers as he moved. She could hardly breathe and she knew she was shaking. It was all she could do to keep her knees from buckling and collapsing to the floor.

He crossed to the middle of the room and stood a breath away from her. Then he spoke.

"Livy Ann…" he almost seemed to be savoring the words. "Livy fucking Ann…" An enormous wave of anger swept over his face and he slapped her so hard across her cheek that she flew to the floor, with searing pain coursing through her entire being. She still couldn't breathe.

She felt him hovering over her, screaming at her with a force she had never heard in another human being.

"Do you know what you did to me?!" He screamed his anger again as he kicked her hard and she caved into herself under the pain of it.

Two of the men in the room picked her up coldly and made her face him. Sykes got as close as he could and grabbed her face with his heartless fingers, squeezing until she screamed again.

"Tonight, you will pay dearly for your…behavior." He shoved her face backwards and stepped back towards his desk. There were at least ten other men in the room, all of whom had vicious, depraved looks in their eyes. The cult atmosphere in the room was chilling, and Kayla found herself praying for a quick death instead of what she knew was coming next.

The UH-60 Blackhawk's were the first to quietly arrive over the private island of Little Pikos. The stealth choppers could not be heard or seen on radar and they had no issues hovering in to drop off the teams going in for the strike.

Gabe gave the order through the X5's to all teams waiting for his go.

"Drop. All teams to positions now," Gabe instructed just before he jumped from the chopper to take his own. Zeus & Dev jumped out with him and stayed by his side as they moved towards the target.

Within minutes, they had the compound surrounded, and confirmation of both the Raiders and the SEAL's all inside the circle. Gabe spoke again through the X5's to everyone awaiting his commands.

"All teams in position?" Gabe asked. Affirmative answers came from Braidon for the Raider team, Langley for the SEAL team, and Andy with the men he was leading. Everyone was in their preplanned locations. Gabe spoke again. "Blackhawks pull back. Ground teams, take out all targets outside the compound. Go." Gabe could hear the sound of several bodies falling, but the guns had remarkable silencers on them so no shots rang out to warn anyone inside.

"All clear. Outside targets down." The response came in from each team leader.

"Viper and Dragon, pull in and hold. Wait for my go. I need Kayla out and away from the target before any firepower engagement. Copy?"

"This is Viper. Copy," the pilot said of the Bell AH-12 Viper as it rose into view with it's missels and rockets ready.

"This is Dragon. Copy. Holding," the pilot of the MH-53E Sea Dragon replied as it too, rose into view on the opposite side; fiercely displaying it's GAU-21 .50 cal ramp-mounted machine gun.

"All ground teams, go for breach," Gabe gave the order to his men, then the order to Zeus & Dev. "Fuss. Pas Auf."

From all sides of the compound, the teams moved in. Nick and Gabe made their way to the front where the main entrance was, towing one of Sykes's captured men with them. Gabe then spoke the next command to Zeus. "Zeus, Suchen." Zeus began feverishly sniffing the ground, the walkway and the grass. Gabe watched him closely and then saw the sign he was looking for. Zeus had found Kayla's scent and was following it towards the front entrance. "Dev, Fuss. Pas Auf." With that, Gabe and Nick strode after Zeus to the front entrance with Dev close by Gabe's side with her ears straight up in heightened alert. Gabe had his colt 45 ready, as Nick had his MK13 aimed and ready. They placed the captured man in front of the door. Nick and Gabe both had their guns pointed right in his face as they released the cuffs from him and backed out of view to each side of the door.

"One wrong move and your death will be slow and painful. I promise," Gabe said.

The man was successfully terrified and, so far, seemed to be following the orders he had been given. He raised his right arm up to the peek hole, displaying his snake and devil horn tattoo, and knocked twice.

When the door opened, their captured man tried to scream to warn them, but Gabe was ready for it. He shot him dead center in the head and wedged his foot inside the door frame just in time to prevent it from closing. In one incredibly quick movement, Gabe was inside the front hall. Three of Sykes's men were standing there, still trying to get their weapons out as Gabe shot each one of them before they succeeded in doing so. Nick's quick reflexes worked to their advantage when he heard another man behind them. Nick turned in a flash and shot him dead as well. It was remarkable…four men dead in seconds and not a sound made. The house was quiet except for the sounds of paws on the marble floor and Zeus's feverish sniffing as he followed the scent of Kayla.

Nick and Gabe followed Zeus's lead, carefully keeping their eyes on all sides of them as they advanced deeper into the house. When they entered the open foyer, bodies of more of Sykes's men dropped as the Raiders were advancing in from the left and the SEAL's from the right. Zeus started up the stairs, but then doubled back as the scent took him down the hall further instead of up. Gabe signaled to three of the

SEAL's to go and search upstairs, and three of the Raiders to go down the opposite hallway. Every time they encountered some of Sykes's men, they were taken out instantly; without a sound or a thought.

Zeus stopped by a door at the end of the hallway, and sat down, mouth closed and eyes on Gabe. Zeus found her. She was in there. He signaled for the remaining team members behind him to stop, then he and Nick took each side of the door; Dev still obediently glued to Gabe's side. Gabe put his ear to the door to listen and gauge how many men were in the room and if he could locate Kayla's position inside. While he did that, Nick was slipping a small camera under the door so they could get a visual on what was happening in the room. Gabe studied the images on the camera, memorizing every detail as he took it in. The first thing he noticed was the open balcony doors on either side of the room. He immediately knew that would be an advantage. He signaled to the remaining SEAL's and Raiders with him; instructing each team to go to the outside entrances of both balconies so they would have cover from three sides once they made their move. All six of the men left to follow his instructions, leaving only he and Nick at the door, with Zeus and Dev as well, ready for action once the command was given.

Gabe listened impatiently to the sounds coming from the room. He knew, if possible, he had to hold his attack off just until his men reached the balconies, because once this door opened, he would have a matter of seconds to shield Kayla from flying bullets while at the same time taking out everyone else in there with her. If they all entered from three sides at once, that would give them the best advantage; but he would not allow Kayla to get hurt, so if he had to enter early to prevent that, he would.

His eyes were back on the camera. Kayla was being led over towards the big desk on the far side of the room. He could hear the conversation taking place, and he tuned into what Sykes was saying as he watched the images on the display. His anger was boiling…he forced the tactical side of himself to concentrate…to wait as he listened and make sure he gauged the correct timing for the go order.

As Sykes rambled on about all he lost because of Kayla, Gabe memorized everyone's location in the room. There were ten men in the room, plus Sykes and Kayla. Each man had a pistol from what he could see. Gabe also took note of anything and everything in the room that could be utilized like a weapon when he advanced on Sykes. He was listening for confirmation from his men that they were in position outside the balconies, but he had not received it yet. His attention was pulled back to Sykes as he saw him move closer to Kayla. Gabe was not going to be able to hold himself back for long.

Sykes's voice was ringing out again. "So now…my dear Livy Ann…you are going to begin paying the price for what you did." Sykes was undoing his pants as he walked towards Kayla, and Gabe's hands clenched with fury on his colt 45. Nick saw it, and did what he could to calm Gabe and remind him to wait. Sykes pulled his pants and underwear off as he assertively displayed himself infront of Kayla. Gabe could feel his blood boiling to a raging breaking point.

"As I recall…that night you jumped from my window…you snuck out on me before I could teach you your submissive place under me." Gabe saw him move even closer to her. "You will now be taught that very important lesson. Harshly and completely; and then, you will learn that lesson from every man in this room. After that…I will take you again…" he moved closer to her, right up in her face, to finish his sentence. "…and…I will kill you while I do it." Sykes ripped the cape of her dress off, spun her around and threw her against the desk as two of his men held her down.

That was it. He could take no more. The dragon in Gabe's blood overtook him and he exploded in an unstoppable rage; bursting through him in an instantaneous detonation. He kicked the door down with one, massive blow of his powerful leg. Commands were shouted to both dogs, who sprang immediately into action, while in the same moment, Gabe's colt 45 began taking men out. He aimed at the men farthest from him first. Two of them were down in seconds, as Nick stepped in and blew away three more. Then Gabe had the man closest to him in a headlock, as he flipped himself over him and kicked the man behind him to the ground. He snapped the neck of the man he had his hands on, and spun around with his bowie to end the other. Then without losing a beat, Gabe used his precision aim and put a bullet dead center in the foreheads of each of the two men who were holding Kayla. Within what felt like a heartbeat, Sykes was the only man still standing. Dev got in-between Kayla and Sykes and was growling at him ferociously as Zeus guarded Kayla from three more men coming in the room on the far end.

Chaos erupted instantly as a swarm of Sykes's men entered through the door behind Gabe and Nick, while simultaneously, Gabe's men came crashing through the balcony windows on each side.

Gabe maneuvered like a tornado and somehow demolished the first four men who came through the door, and then was out of the way enough for Nick to blow away the next three with his weapon, as Gabe's colt got smacked from his hand. He pulled his bowie and regained his advantage over his attacker, and ended him with his blade.

Dev had Sykes pinned to the corner wall as Gabe saw Andy and Braidon enter the room from opposite ends. Gabe saw a man enter from behind Braidon with his gun raised…at Kayla. He heard Sykes call out.

"Shoot her!" Sykes ordered.

"Braidon!" Gabe shouted.

Braidon tackled the man whose gun was pointed at Kayla, but a shot went off just as he was taking him down, and Gabe heard Kayla scream in pain, and saw her fall to the ground.

"No!" he shouted. His heart stopped. She was hit. He was just about to run to her, but the distraction gave the last man coming in the room the needed second to wrap a rope around Gabe's neck and pull. After a struggle, Gabe's incredible strength gave him the advantage again, and he broke free and flipped backwards, throwing his attacker off balance and landing him on top of the man, with his hands around his neck.

Gabe heard Andy call to him. "Gabe, call Zeus. I need to get to Kayla, but he won't let me. Call him off!"

Gabe shouted the command across the room and heard Zeus's growling stop. As Gabe continued his strangle on the man's neck he called back to Andy.

"Is she ok Andy?" his voice was stressed. She *had* to be ok. He couldn't handle it if she wasn't.

"Looks like a shoulder hit. That's all," Andy replied.

"Get her out of here Andy. Now!" Gabe called.

As he finished off the man underneath him, Gabe saw Andy scoop Kayla up and take her out towards the choppers. He called across the room to Gabe as he exited on the far end.

"I've got her Gabe. I promise," Andy said as he carried her out and away from the danger.

The last of the one on one struggles ended, with Sykes's men dropping dead to the ground. Gabe and his men were the only ones left standing...along with Sykes, who was still being pinned up in the corner by Dev; his junk dangling out, dangerously exposed right in front of Dev's snarling fangs. The terror in the vulnerable position Sykes found himself in was plastered all over his face; it was a beautiful sight.

Gabe stood up, and retrieved his colt 45 that had been knocked out of his hand during the fight. "Report," he asked over the X5's.

"All exits successfully blocked from the outside. Every enemy combatant visually seen has been taken out. No one on the outer perimeter," Langley said over the line.

"Andy? Is she safe?" Gabe asked.

A few moments later, Andy's voice came on the line. "Got her on the medevac now. I'm taking her in. Bleeding is under control. I've got her Gabe," he said.

Gabe felt a sense of relief that Kayla was out of here and Andy was with her. He was worried…he didn't know how bad the bullet wound was, but she was in the best hands, and, in order for her to be safe, he had to finish this job. And he would.

Gabe locked eyes with Sykes, who was terrified against the wall as Dev was snarling ferociously at him; a breath away from his most prized body part. Gabe enjoyed the sight. He commanded Zeus to cross over and join her, and he did, displaying the same savage fangs and angry snarls that Dev was, which caused the horror in Sykes's face to increase even more.

Gabe looked to Braidon and Nick. "You guys can go. Everyone fall back. I got this one."

Braidon was clearly not in favor of the idea. "Gabe, the F117 is on it's way…" he said.

Gabe looked at him. "Don't worry. This won't take long," Gabe said.

Braidon nodded and signaled to the men. Then he and his men moved out, leaving Gabe alone with Sykes and the two Malinois.

Gabe moved closer to Sykes, eyeing him like a vicious silverback ready to rip his throat out, as Dev and Zeus both continued their snarling growls at Sykes, perfectly pinning him against the wall in fear.

"We've been in this position before, you and I." Gabe slowly put his Bowie knife down on the desk. "As I recall, I beat the shit out of you, and then hog tied you like a piece of meat." Gabe put down both his colt 45's next to the Bowie knife and cracked the knuckles on his large hands. "Everyone said it was the right thing to do…to hand you over to the authorities and send you to prison, instead of ripping you apart limb from limb and killing you myself." Gabe eyed him coldly. "But after seeing what you were about to do to my woman tonight…I am convinced that was not the right call…and I will not make that mistake again."

Sykes tried to play him. "Wouldn't you rather see me rot in jail. Killing me would be too quick, don't you think?"

Gabe shrugged his shoulders in agreement. "It doesn't have to be quick…or painless," Gabe said, and then called out. "Dev, fass!"

At the command, Dev sank her razor sharp teeth deeply into Sykes…specifically, into Sykes's favorite appendage. Sykes screamed in overbearing agony as Dev clamped down hard around him. "Call him off! Call him off!" Sykes screamed a blood curdling cry. Gabe gave it a very long moment, then spoke.

"Oh, call him off?" Gabe asked. "Ok. Zeus, platz." At that, Zeus laid down right where he was, but kept his extremely alert eyes on Sykes, and his ears on Gabe, listening intently for another command. Dev, however did not let go of her excruciating grip on Sykes.

"I said call him off!" Sykes screamed again.

Gabe was calm as can be. "I did call him off; but it's not *him* that has your privates in his mouth. It's her." Gabe laughed. "I find it so pleasantly ironic that it's a girl who has you by the balls…and more… and poetically, it's a girl who is going to end your ability to use them." Sykes looked terrified. Gabe didn't give a fuck. "And after she does that, I will be the one to end the rest of you." Gabe stood; and then he spoke the minacious words. "Dev. Aufreissen!" It was a quick command, and Dev…well, she certainly lived up to her name. She completed the task in one savage bite, leaving Sykes weeping and crying in a blood curdling scream of agony. Within seconds, Gabe had his large and extremely livid hands around Sykes's neck, lifting him off the ground and squeezing tighter and tighter as he did so, and his eyes stayed searing into Sykes's, as his hands twisted his neck and broke it. All signs of life instantly escaped Sykes's body, and he went absolutely limp in Gabe's grip. There was no pulse anymore. Gabe opened his hands and let the bastard drop.

Sykes's body fell to the floor, dead; and the world was suddenly a better place for it.

Gabe picked up his colt 45, and turned towards the balcony door, calmly calling for Dev & Zeus as he walked away.

When Gabe walked out to the parameter his men were holding , he turned to see the compound. The sun was beautifully up in the sky, casting it's red and orange lights out like the perfect backdrop for the view of the next order about to be given. Braidon crossed to him for the report before the final call.

"Matthew Edson is dead. One of my men found him shot in the basement. Pretty sure it was Sykes's order. He wasn't going to let him be a loose end. Sweep confirmed no civilians. No women or children. Only Sykes's men, and if any of them are still alive, they did not escape. No one breached the line." Braidon looked at Gabe. "Sykes?" he asked.

"Dead. Very, very dead," Gabe said. The news was a welcome relief to all the men within earshot who heard the answer. "All our men are out?" Gabe asked.

"Affirmative. Pilot is waiting your command," Braidon said as he handed the radio to Gabe.

Gabe picked it up, pushed the button and gave the go. "Nighthawk? You're a go. I repeat…you are a go. Blow the fucking thing to kingdom come," Gabe ordered.

It didn't take long for the F117 Nighthawk Stealth Fighter to come into view. The power and impressive fierceness of it was something to behold as it flew it's course towards the compound and then completed the final order. Smart bombs flew from it's holder and shot down into the compound, exploding and blowing the entire building to smithereens. If there was anyone alive in there when Gabe and his teams walked out…they certainly were not anymore. Sykes and his men were finished. He was not the problem of Man any longer. That was in the hands of God…or the Devil…it didn't matter to him which. Kayla was safe and that was the only thing he cared about.

He turned to his men. "Let's go," he said.

The UH-60 Blackhawk's were called in, and as they waited for their evac, Gabe took one more look at the burning fire that was all that remained of Sykes and his trafficking ring. In front of him was the ultimate vision that he had longed to see since the day he started on this path; Sykes and his men were now destroyed.

Within minutes, the choppers came hovering into view to pick up Gabe, his men, and the two dogs, who had, at long last, completed the final take down of the Livy Ann missions.

Chapter Fifteen
From The Flames

As Gabe was escorted into the hospital, his only thought was Kayla. He was led to the private wing, and saw Andy sitting in one of the large chairs outside the empty waiting room. He crossed to Gabe as soon as he saw him.

"Gabe. She is still in surgery. They said they would come right down as soon as there was any information," Andy's voice was calm, but Gabe's worry gained a little traction. Andy saw it. "I've seen my share of GSW's...this one did not look bad, Gabe. I'm sure she will be fine." Andy placed his hand on Gabe's shoulder to help reassure him.

As Gabe and Andy were talking, Nick and Braidon came into the wing as well.

"Any word?" Nick asked.

"Not yet," Gabe replied. "Still waiting."

Andy looked to Gabe. "And? Sykes?" he asked.

"Dead," was all Gabe said, but Andy prodded a little with a very slight smile on his face.

"Just dead? Or Gabriel Saxton dead?" Andy asked.

Gabe allowed only a touch of the grin on his face to show. "Let's just say...his end was an ample serving of poetic justice...which reminds me," he looked to Braidon. "...make sure they feed Zeus tonight."

Braidon laughed, "Dev already ate?"

Gabe shrugged his shoulders, "Well...appetizer."

Braidon laughed. "I'll go get us some coffees," Braidon said before he turned to head down the hall, leaving the Saxton brothers alone in the waiting room.

Gabe looked to Nick and Andy. "Thank you. You both were amazing," he said.

"Of course," Andy replied.

"Goes without saying," Nick added. "We would do anything for each other. Always have, always will."

"Family," Gabe said. The three held the moment, relishing in the ties that ran true between them. Then Andy smiled at Nick.

"You think the SEAL's will get any credit this time? Or will it all go to the big bad Raider again?" Andy asked with humor.

Nick laughed. "He did it again Andy. Fucking tornado! I swear, I don't know how he does it. We are going to get swept under the carpet again, I'm sure of it!"

All three of them laughed as the surgeon entered the waiting room. Gabe addressed him immediately.

"How is she? Is she ok?" he asked.

The surgeon nodded his head. "She is fine. Amazing actually. I think the fact that her shoulder was dislocated may have, ironically, helped her tremendously. The bullet did not hit the brachial artery, the blood loss was significant, but not dangerous, and the bullet went clean through with very minimal damage to anything."

Gabe let out the breath he had been holding since the moment she got hit. "Thank God," he said.

The surgeon continued as he looked over the chart in his hands. "The surgery was very quick and we kept the anesthesia as light as possible; but even so, I don't see any complications or danger to her or the baby from it, so there is no need for concern."

The breath Gabe had just gotten back in his lungs suddenly vanished again, and he felt the world stop as he registered what the surgeon had just said.

Andy and Nick were speechless as well.

Gabe found his voice. "What? She is pregnant?" he asked.

The surgeon smiled. "Yes. According to what we see here, she is seven and a half weeks."

Nick was stunned. "Holy shit. That would mean...late March..."

The surgeon looked at his chart again. "Yes, conception is calculated as...March 22nd."

Andy looked at Gabe. "Holy fuck. Your birthday."

"Vail," Nick added.

Gabe was instantly filled with so many emotions he could hardly keep them coherent in his mind. He was filled with such joy, and amazement...and fear that he could have lost both of them so easily today.

Nick slapped him on the back, "Congratulations my brother. That is incredible."

Gabe was still at a loss for words as he thought about the profound meaning behind...everything. He knew that night in Vail was exceptional...he never forgot the power of it...and now...even more so. He really had found his family when he thought he would...that feeling he had had since he was a boy...it was right. He had managed to stumble perfectly into his own destiny, even when he didn't know he was. Devin's words came into his mind...*God really does work in mysterious ways...*

Andy hugged him,."Congratulations Gabe. This is fantastic news."

Gabe hugged him back and then Nick. "Oh my God." He couldn't hold back the tears that formed in his eyes. He was overwhelmed with the love that filled his heart at the news. He looked back to the surgeon.

"Can I see her?" Gabe asked.

"She is still under, but yes. Room 326, just through those doors on your right. I'll be back to check on her in a little while."

"Go on Gabe. We'll be here," Andy said.

When Gabe entered her room, she was sleeping. He crossed over to her quietly and breathed in his relief that she was ok. She was here; with him, and no one would ever hurt this woman again. Ever. He swore it. No one else would ever put their hands on her. She was his; his wife, his family. She had been since the moment he looked up and saw her by the taxi stand outside of LAX. She made him complete. She filled him with everything he had been missing in this life up to the moment his eyes finally found her.

He brushed his hand softly on her face and leaned down to kiss her head. Then he gently placed his hand on her stomach and relished in the knowledge that his child was in there. His family was right here with him, safe and sound and forever under his protection.

He pulled a chair up to her bed, took the seat and held her hand in his. After watching her sleep and listening to her breathe, he lowered his head on the bed near her and closed his eyes; keeping her small hand held tightly in his, with his other hand resting gently on her stomach. He was filled again with that otherworldly calm he only felt with her. He breathed deeply, and it felt as if the very air itself that was coming into his lungs was somehow…magical. He felt…at one with everything. The peace of the moment, coupled with his complete exhaustion, pulled him into a calming sleep.

He woke to the sound of someone coming in the room. When he looked up, he saw Lawrence walking in.

Lawrence spoke in a quiet voice so as not to wake Kayla.

"Don't get up," Lawrence said as he moved into the room further. "How is she?" he asked.

Gabe sat up but did not let go of Kayla's hand. "Surgeon says all is good. No damage."

"Good." Lawrence smiled at Gabe. "Congratulations," he said warmly.

Gabe couldn't help but chuckle. "Which one of them told you?" he asked.

Lawrence smiled. "They both did. Don't be mad at them that they spilled the beans on it. They are so excited for you; I think they would have had an aneurysm each if they hadn't let it out." Lawrence laughed as he crossed to the other chair next to Gabe. "I remember, when you were seven years old, you talking about the family you were going to have. I've never known a child to be so certain...so focused on something like that at such a young age. Now, you are about to have that family you always saw in your future. And no one deserves it more. I'm so happy for you. For both of you," Lawrence said.

Gabe took in his words; feeling the same astonishment about the cosmic connections that weaved their way into his world. "It's amazing to me...how our lives were connected from the beginning...and I didn't know it until so many years later," Gabe said as he looked at Kayla sleeping.

Lawrence laughed. "Yeah. It's fascinating how life works, isn't it?" Lawrence looked at Gabe. "Your mother would be so proud of you. So incredibly proud of you."

"Thank you." Gabe looked at Lawrence even deeper. "For everything. You saved the woman I love. If it weren't for you..." Gabe couldn't even finish the sentence.

"I would never have done anything but. As soon as T-bone brought her to our door...Betty and I instantly vowed to do everything we could for her. She is remarkable. So are you. You guys are more than a perfect match. In so many ways." Lawrence was almost laughing again. "I remember...that night all those years ago, like it was yesterday. I thought she had fallen asleep, I was thinking about Joline…and you…what you did that night in taking down Sykes…avenging your mother and saving all those girls…I pulled out your recording of "Somewhere you" and was listening to it softly, amazed at the choice you made and how right you were. That's when Kayla walked in and heard your song. Heard you singing." Lawrence shook his head in bewilderment. "I saw it in her eyes…it made her smile. She asked me if she could have it so she could listen to it, so I gave it to her. Little did I know how very significant that was."

Gabe lifted Kayla's hand and kissed it. Then addressed Lawrence again. "I'd like to know what the truth is about her parents."

Lawrence took a breath and then spoke. "I had investigators look into both of them after I got Kayla safely away. Her mother died of a drug overdose not long after she left Kayla."

"…and her father?" Gabe asked.

Lawrence took a moment, then answered that too. "I made sure he found his way to prison. My understanding is he was killed while behind bars. Prisoners have a…strange moral code. Anyone in for crimes against a child…well, that is not something they tolerate. Word got out that he was the one who sold Livy Ann to Sykes…once they knew that…they finished him quickly," Lawrence said.

"Does she know what happened to them?" Gabe asked.

Lawrence was quiet for a moment, then answered him. "No. She never wanted to know. I offered, a few times to share with her what I discovered…but she…she made the decision for herself. When they left her…she left them…and she never looked back."

"I don't blame her for that," Gabe said.

"Neither do I," Lawrence added. After a few moments of silence, he continued. "I hear from your brothers that Sykes and Matthew are dead?"

"All of them are. It's over," Gabe confirmed.

Lawrence took a deep breath. He allowed several moments of relief and gratitude to fill the air between them. The lifetime of work they had ventured into together…the missions they both risked their lives for; to rid as much of that evil from this world as they could…the equanimity in the realization that after all these years, they had achieved their goal and closed that door. It was a remarkable moment to experience. Lawrence took another breath, and then spoke again.

"You have done an exceptional job in this life, Gabe. So has Kayla. Lord knows the two of you deserve to live the rest of your lives in peace…enjoying the family you are building together…far from all of this…and I will always honor any choices the two of you make," Lawrence said.

Gabe looked at him, "But?" he asked.

"No but, just…a thought," Lawrence added. He looked at Gabe. "I think Devin is right. I think her story should be told. Your story should be told. For many reasons. The two of you represent a good in this world…unlike any I have ever experienced. Allowing that goodness to be known…I think it could be a very powerful seed of inspiration to many people. And if the two of you ever decide you agree with that, I want you to know…you have my full support, and help to do so."

Gabe took a deep breath. "Even if that burns the place down?" he asked.

Lawrence answered, "Especially if it burns the place down. Hollywood needs to clear itself of this. It's a stain that should never have been allowed, and anyone still protecting that secret, should face the heat for it."

"It certainly would ignite a shitstorm." Gabe laughed. "Might be fun," he added.

Lawrence chuckled in agreement, "Well, one thing is sure. There is nothing quite as stunning as a Hollywood Fire."

***

Kayla's ankle bracelet caught the light as she stepped out of the limo onto the red carpet. Gabe held her hand in his as he pulled her into him, wrapping his arm around her waist. The explosion of flashing lights and calls from the press were blinding as always, as Kayla and Gabe stood, in this very familiar position on the red carpet posing for the pictures and magazine covers that would be lining the shelves the next morning. Betty and Lawrence joined them for a few more photos, then Devin and Diane added to the group. After several more minutes, they made their way into the theater. They crossed over to Braidon who was laughing by the bar with Andy, Jen, and Nick.

Jen raised a glass as they crossed over to join them.

"Congratulations. My prediction? This will win best picture when the Oscars roll around. It's fantastic," Jen said proudly.

They all cheered as Gabe spoke. "Thank you all for being part of it and doing this with us. It means a lot."

"Family is everything; and all of us, we are family. Forever and always. Through the good and the bad," Andy said.

As the lights started to blink in the theater, indicating that everyone should take their seats, Gabe looked to Nick with a nod.

"All good?" he asked.

"Yes. You guys enjoy yourselves and all of us will see you back home tomorrow night," Nick answered.

Kayla was confused. "What do you mean?"

Gabe smiled at her and took her hand, as he spoke to Nick. "Thank you," he said to him, "Don't let Lorraina and Brennon trick you into two scoops of ice cream. They will try!"

"Don't worry. Their charms don't work on uncle Nick," Nick said as Diane laughed.

Diane looked to Nick, "Oh, please! You are totally going to let them have as much ice cream as they want, as soon as I turn my back," she said.

Nick didn't even try to hide it. "Of course I am. That's why I am the favorite uncle," Nick responded.

"Hey, I let them stay up past their bedtime to watch TV," Andy protested.

Nick laughed, "Ice cream always beats staying up late," Nick replied triumphantly. "Favorite Uncle," he said proudly pointing to himself, then he cheered to Gabe who was laughing. "They are in good hands! Have fun," Nick said.

Gabe pulled Kayla closer to him as he led her through the crowd towards the back hallway. "I have a little surprise for you. Come with me."

She followed him out the door, through the exit to the street behind the theater. She looked up and saw a limo ready and waiting, with the door open and the driver smiling warmly at them. She looked to Gabe. "What's this?" she asked.

Gabe pulled her close to him. He gestured to the theater behind them. "We've seen it. We've lived it. We've worked on it for...well, our whole lives really. We don't need to be here anymore tonight...and I know how much we both dislike the Hollywood BS. I thought I would sweep you away, out of LA, while no one was looking, and take you back home with me." He pulled her lips to his and kissed her.

She smiled. "That sounds fantastic. What about the twins?" she asked.

"Taken care of. Nick and Diane are watching them tonight (with the help of endless ice cream apparently,) and then everyone is

catching flights back home tomorrow. Andy ordered lobsters from
Maine for this weekend, and Nick is taking care of the filet mignons.
Diane wanted a Surf & Turf Saturday to celebrate the release. Devin
promised to bake his three layer chocolate cake, Braidon is bringing
the scotch & brandy, and Lawrence and Betty have stocked up on the
champagne. But first...I wanted some quality alone time with my
wife," he said. Kayla smiled and pulled him into her again. She took
his lips with hers, and relished in the feel of him. After a moment, their
lips parted and Gabe took her hand sweetly in his. "Let's go. Our plane
awaits."

Their home in Vail was beautiful. The luxury mountain estate was
private, and had the most amazing views of the snow covered
mountains outside the windows. Nick and Diane had bought the estate
on the left, and Andy and Jen bought the one on the right. Even Devin
and Braidon moved into the same community. Lawrence and Betty
kept their mansion in Beverly Hills, but added a second home ten
minutes away from their's in Vail as well so that this big family of
theirs could stay close. And they did.

The Holidays were always joyous and celebrated with each other.
The kids were all close and carried on the same strong, loving bond
that always weaved itself into the Saxton lines. Being there for each
other was a permanent spoken and unspoken truth, and the immense
gratitude for this love and connection in their lives was ever present
and powerful.

Kayla loved every second of her life with Gabe. She was ever
thankful that their children would always know what it meant to have
family; unconditional support and friendships that went beyond what
words could describe. The absence of that from her own childhood
made no difference anymore; it was a forgiven past that had no power

over her now; and never would again.

Their twins were beautiful, happy and healthy. The serenity she felt with Gabe made everything in her past fade away like a distant memory. She had an amazing family, incredible friends and an entire forcefield of love around her. Her days of running and being controlled by the fears of her past were long gone.

Gabe crossed into the bedroom and lit the fire in the fireplace, and the warm red glow of the flames filled their room. He took off his tuxedo jacket as he came back over to her, and his chiseled cheekbones held strong against the dancing reflection of the heat from the fireplace. He looked amazing, and he made her heart flutter just as he had that first moment she looked up and saw him.

He swept her up in his arms and carried her to their bed. Passion consumed them both and within minutes he had her dress off and her naked underneath him. He kissed her deeply and she was overcome with that passion that only he ignited in her.

Her hands undid his zipper, and she had his clothes off just as quickly, with her hands sliding over his skin, and feeling the rippling muscles of his strong body on top of her.

His hands traced her body, exploring her curves as if it was the first time he touched her, and he caused shivers to run the course of her body. She felt his heat, his desire for her and she was overcome with her own for him. She pulled him down onto her and found herself begging for his touch.

He made love to her with such passion, such intensity that she was just as overcome by it as she was the first time he touched her. Their climax, so perfectly in tune with each other, exploded through both of them just as strongly as it had that first night they met. This man meant everything to her and her love for him was more than she ever thought possible.

As their breathing slowed and he held her hand, she broke the kiss and looked in his eyes.

"I love you Gabe," she said.

He smiled. "I love you too Kayla." He held her eyes a moment longer, then kissed her, as if his very soul was seeping into hers through their lips.

He slid off of her slightly, and wrapped his arms around her, pulling her body into his; protectively holding her as he had done since the first time she fell into his bed. It was her favorite moment of every day; when he enveloped her in the geborgenheit she only felt with him.

It was inevitable; his place in her life. As if the hands of God had predestined this course for her, and she was eternally grateful. Their place in the cosmic tapestry of fate; their story in this life…it meant everything to her; and now, that story was being shared with the world. Though parts of that story were…ugly…harsh and cold…none of that lasted. It only takes the love of one person to heal everything that hurt before. Just one love can turn the darkness to light, the cold to warmth and Hell to Heaven.

Kayla understood that now. She knew it. She lived it. It breathed in her like a force of life that could never be stripped from her again. The infinite power of love through it's endless circles of astral influence. One glimpse of it changes everything. Forever. She was not the girl she was. The fear and pain that had it's grip on her for so many years had been completely obliterated by the man who saved her life in more ways than one. He dove into the fire with her; unafraid, and ever the hero. Then, they chose to ignite an even deeper fire; together, and allow it to burn all around them, knowing there was life on the other side of it. He freed her from everything that had haunted her and allowed her to be reborn in the love he felt for her.

Their story is now out there…her story that he pulled her through and saved her from.

She was every bit the phoenix rising from the flames…of that stunning…but now powerless…Hollywood Fire.

The End

Lyn Liechty

Lyn Liechty has recorded and performed the hit duet **"Here In My Heart"**
with the world renowned Scorpions off the platinum selling album
"Moment Of Glory." She has also created a big name for herself performing
leading roles in world premiere blockbuster shows such as **"Jekyll & Hyde,"**
"Dance Of The Vampires," "Miss Saigon," and **"Dracula."**
She has worked closely with Lionel Richie, Roman Polanski, Jim Steinman,
Frank Wildhorn and Leslie Bricusse to name a few. Lyn's first single **"CaveMan!"**
off her album "At Last", has gotten over 1.6 million views on YouTube,
and charted at #11 on the Billboard hot Singles Charts.
Lyn is the author of several books including **Winter Mountain**,
A Wynken, Blynken & Nod Adventure (Children's book,)
The Magic Of Poems, The Magic Of Night (Children's poems,) and two cookbooks;
Recipes Of Home (The Main Collection and Sweets Treats and Desserts.)
For more info, please go to:

www.LynLiechtyMusic.com

CPSIA information can be obtained
at www.ICGtesting.com
Printed in the USA
BVHW072051060820
585567BV00005B/360